PRIMORDIAL INTERLUDE

Sue slumped slightly as another wave of nausea passed over her. She couldn't be having a miscarriage, she just couldn't. Pedarius was in the middle of the soft, melodius solo passage. She should ask Jimmy Higgins to help her off the stage. But how could she? How could she totally disrupt . . . the baby, that's why. The baby was much more impor . . .

The excruciating pain forced a loud, agonizing scream from Sue's throat as her head whipped back then forward again. She grabbed the neck of the cello firmly but knew she was slipping into unconsciousness. As Sue slumped forward against the cello, her arm drew the bow across the strings and a distinct six note passage echoed through the silence of the hall, stilled momentarily by shock. The audience and orchestra members alike gasped in unison as Sue Arcomano tumbled heavily to the stage floor, spilling her cello and music stand noisily around her.

Other Avon Books by
David Combs

THE INTRUSION

THE
SURROGATE

DAVID COMBS

AVON
PUBLISHERS OF BARD, CAMELOT, DISCUS AND FLARE BOOKS

THE SURROGATE is an original publication of Avon Books.
This work has never before appeared in book form.

Cover illustration by Wayne D. Barlowe

AVON BOOKS
A division of
The Hearst Corporation
959 Eighth Avenue
New York, New York 10019

Copyright © 1982 by David Combs
Published by arrangement with the author
Library of Congress Catalog Card Number: 82–90463
ISBN: 0–380–81133–2

First Avon Printing, October, 1982

AVON TRADEMARK REG. U. S. PAT. OFF. AND IN
OTHER COUNTRIES, MARCA REGISTRADA, HECHO EN
U.S.A.
Printed in the U. S. A.

WFH 10 9 8 7 6 5 4 3 2 1

For Miss Daisy

I

DECEMBER 1975

Sue Arcomano separated the thin slats of the Levolor blinds and peered down at West Sixty-ninth Street, three floors below. She smiled slightly, mentally patting herself on the back for having devised such a fail-safe barometer. The pace of the passersby told her just how warmly she need dress without having to crank open the bedroom window, always a struggle against the layers of old paint on the metal frames. If the pedestrians were hunched over and scurrying, she knew it was bitter cold. If they strolled by, she knew her lighter coat would be sufficient. A junkie, oblivious to any temperature, could throw her barometer into a tailspin. Dancers, too, with their toes outturned in permanent fifth position and chins jutted firmly and proudly forward into the air, could not be trusted. They were always bundled up within an inch of their lives, even on balmy spring days, to keep their overworked muscles warm, supple and ready for yet more torture.

Sue leaned closer to the blinds and looked toward Central Park West. Her pale blond bangs dusted to a dull shine a small spot on two of the aluminum slats. She smiled again. Here was a man she could trust. Mr. Shakespeare. Reginald Milford Saunders, actually, octogenarian actor, searching for the past fifteen years for the proper vehicle in which to give his "farewell performance." Sue wondered if he had not already admitted to himself that he had done his "swan song," unbeknownst to him at the time of course, a summer stock performance of *Bells Are Ringing*, in 1960. At any rate, his throat was open to the air today, which meant the temperature was well into the forties. No Charlie Brown type bundling required today.

She pulled back, worrying only momentarily about the light layer of dust on the blinds. She would get them bright and shiny

7

again when the construction was finished on the brownstone town house. *If* it ever was finished. It seemed as if they'd lived in a war zone for the past six months. One contractor had been fired already, and the new one was moving just as slowly and was just as devious with his, "Well, since we're moving that wall back anyway, wouldn't you like to go ahead and . . . " To hell with the budget and the estimates. Pile on the extras. His suggestion of an open, common, through-the-wall fireplace between the master bedroom and the sunny, glass-fronted sitting room was, however, a masterstroke. It would be smashing, provided, of course, that there would be no side draft, which forced the smoke into the rooms rather than up the chimney. He promised not, but she knew by now how easily promises gush from the mouths of contractors and decided on the spot to lay him out physically if the huge hole had to be sealed up later. If it worked properly it would "make" the third floor.

Sue glanced at the clock and tripped on the end of the brown comforter at the same time. She grimaced at the noise of her stumble and looked quickly to see if she had awakened him.

Nick Arcomano hadn't moved a muscle, not the slightest twitch. He slept on his side, facing her, with one thick arm draped over the outside of the covers, the comforter resting just below his hairy, well-shaped chest. His breathing was quiet and easy, which told Sue that he wasn't too deeply asleep. She'd move about quietly until nine-thirty, then wake him up. An extra hour in bed should make up for the unusually late hours he had spent at the ad agency last evening.

Poor baby, she thought, as her eyes lovingly devoured his sleeping face. She was constantly amazed that she still desired him as much as she had when they had first met seven years before. Where was that itchy yearning for a different body that married couples were supposed to experience after seven years?

"You're all I want or need, my little Nicky baby," she whispered quietly across the king-sized, thickly foamed platform. "You didn't hear that!" she said quickly, placing her hands on either side of her tightly swollen abdomen as if to cover the ears of the seven-month-old fetus growing inside her. "You are my littlest baby and I want you desperately," she cooed, smoothing her hand lovingly over her pushed-out belly button. She caught her image in the mirror. She really looked slightly overweight rather than pregnant. But then most of the growth would occur in the next two months, her doctor assured her.

She sighed and glanced again at the soft, curly black hair on Nick's chest, mentally projecting them both four months into the future when she could once again snuggle against him with a stomach as flat as his. She was feeling very horny this morning and considered, only briefly, crawling back into bed with his warm body. Coffee would have to do, she thought, as she padded softly through the large bedroom toward the stairs. Two thoughts filled her head at the same time as she headed for the kitchen. The wool, oatmeal-colored carpet was outrageously expensive but would look fabulous *and* why didn't coffee ever taste as good as it smelled?

Sue heard him coming down the stairs and quickly assumed her commercial model's pose against the counter, holding the saucer in one hand and raising the cup of coffee toward her lips. As soon as he came through the door she flashed a dazzling smile and went into her sales pitch.

"Finally," she beamed brightly, "a coffee that tastes as good as it smells! Copa de Brazil! To smell it is to love it!"

"Where were you and your clever copy last night when we needed you?" He kissed her lightly on the lips while reaching behind her for the glass beaker on the Braun coffee machine. "Any word from my son this morning?"

Sue's hand moved immediately to her belly. "*Our* son . . . or daughter . . . but in any case, our."

"Okay, our . . ."

"Not even a twitch," Sue said with a sigh, settling in a caned chrome chair. "Dr. Bronson tells me some women just don't feel the movement until the baby really gets rambunctious. He says I'll be punched and kicked from every which direction soon enough. And he does let me listen to the heartbeat through the stethoscope just to reassure me. Not to worry, he says, not to worry." Still she couldn't help worrying a bit.

Nick smiled at the glow of contentment registered on her pertly freckled face. "Why no banging from our rip-off artists?"

"You're the one who told them not to start until ten o'clock, remember? Your beauty sleep. Nick, can we afford all this? Shouldn't we maybe start shaving corners. . . ."

"Of course we can't afford it," Nick said as the cold, hard butter on his knife ripped a hole in his toast. "Look at that," he said, letting the knife drop noisily to the table. "Why don't you buy those neat little tubs of soft margarine? There's absolutely no difference in the taste and it doesn't tear your bread to shreds. Why . . ."

"You guineas have no taste," Sue said, smiling warmly.

Nick raised his eyebrows and snorted. "Listen to the WASP talk about taste. At least I don't go to the Stage Deli and order a roast beef on white with mayo and a glass of milk."

"I like what I like . . . and I'm *not* intimidated by tradition." She brought her knife across the top of the stick of butter, then placed the yellow curlicue of dairy fat on the end of her tongue. She waved the rich glob at Nick for a second, then ate it behind a wide "so much for you" grin.

"Now, that's disgusting," he said, laughing. "And fattening, Chubbo."

"Nick," she whined, "you promised. No fat jokes. *Can* we afford all this?" she repeated.

He poured more coffee for them both. "Nobody lives within his means. Why should we be any different? I just want a firm completion date from those clowns."

"Dream on, my darling."

"I'll just have to work longer hours at the office, that's all, more clients, more trendy Arcodan campaigns, more glittery, up-to-date buzz words. You won't see much of me, but at least you can watch your 'soaps' behind these walls of luxury I'm constructing around my two babies." He smiled and patted her hand.

She pulled her hand back and pouted lightly. "That's not funny."

Nick ran his hand through the shiny dark, medium-length curls which framed his squarish face and flashed his best smile at her. His teeth were so white and perfectly aligned that often people assumed they were caps, and the deep creases down his cheeks gave him a rugged, matinee idol handsomeness which most women found irresistible. He was well aware that his good looks had made some not-so-good campaigns more palatable to more than a few admiring clients. Female *and* male. He was also aware that the beautiful brown eyes which studied him at the moment were not immune to his charm. He loved her too, after years of marriage, and if anything she got more beautiful after the minor trauma of her thirtieth birthday. Sue had a variety of looks, none of which seemed worked on, from supersoft to dazzling. She looked simply perfect for every occasion. And talented and intelligent to boot. Nick knew he was a very fortunate man, and not only in love.

The Arcodan Agency, which he and his partner, Jonathan Daniels, had formed after they both left good-paying jobs at Grey, was now one of the "hot" small advertising houses. It had been a struggle. More than once they had been so close to going under that both of them were ready to throw in the towel. Then one campaign had turned their near-failure into the promise of success. It had been hard work in the beginning, and Nick knew he would have to work even harder now that Arcodan had become a viable competitor in the ad market. But he really didn't mind the long hours and the kid-glove handling and kowtowing to clients who really didn't know what they wanted. "Just a certain something . . . you know what I mean?" He enjoyed the challenge and reveled in the success. Nick Arcomano was quite content, and the arrival of a first son, hopefully, in two months would push him over the hump to "ecstatically fulfilled."

"I'm sorry about tonight," Nick apologized, suddenly remembering the importance of the occasion to Sue. "If there were any way . . . you know I would. Maybe I could catch the end. . . ."

"I know," she said, implicitly aware of his sincerity, "but don't plan on it." She flushed lightly, embarrassed by the importance she was granting the performance and by how much she had hoped that Nick could attend. "I'm making much too much of this whole thing, I'm afraid. After all, it's just another concert . . . you know? . . ."

Nick smiled at her with affection. "In that case, I think it might be wise if you considered skipping this one . . . you know, being seven months' pregnant and all . . . maybe even retiring your bow altogether until after the baby. . . ."

"Okay, you bastard," Sue said with a laugh, "enough of the bullshit. I wouldn't miss this performance if I were due to deliver tomorrow. He is the most universally acclaimed musician alive." She no longer attempted to modulate her elation. "Pedarius, Nick . . . can you believe it? The most glorious violin virtuoso since Paganini! Can you hear me?" she said, and laughed. "Pedarius! A living legend, my dear. And me and my cello, backing him up, contrapuntal, then harmonizing, then . . ."

"The rest of the Philharmonic has the night off, huh?" Nick kidded.

"Oh, them," Sue said with a laugh, tearing a soft slice of white bread in two and reaching for the butter. "They'll be there too, I suppose, but in my fantasies . . . Oh, God, I can't stand it!"

Nick got up and kissed her on the top of her head as he passed behind her chair. "I'll try to catch the last of it, I promise." He stopped at the door and turned back. "And no more bread and butter. You can't play with Pedarius with your zipper down"— he paused and waved his fingers à la Groucho toward an imaginary cigar—"not music, anyway." He disappeared into the hallway. "Tell the workers they can begin now. The Prince is in his bath."

Joke or no, she just might not be able to squeeze herself and the baby into that dress. It was very snug the last time she worked her way into it. Sue leaned toward the door and raised her voice. "There's no soap in the shower. Get one from the cabinet before you get in, okay?" Perhaps she should call Mandy and ask to borrow her black Halston, the one with the Empire bodice. With the gathered front, she might not look pregnant at all. Then again, she really wanted to look pregnant. She could dash out and buy a new gown, but she thought she could make do with what she had until she really got into her maternity wardrobe. Besides, there would be the hassles about alterations. What she probably would do is laze around all morning, savoring the anticipation of the glittering gala at Lincoln Center. However, if the dress was *too* tight . . . and only four hours until rehearsal.

The maestro barely wet his lips with the warm brandy, then brought the piquant fumes into his mouth with the tip of his tongue. As the aromatic stimulant drifted through his nasal passages, he returned the crystal snifter to the dressing table and leaned toward the mirror encircled with small bulbs.

His vanity hated what he saw. He had never intended to grow old and wondered briefly if anyone, ever, really dealt successfully with his own aging process. Not possibly, he quickly decided. Why was he not, as the critics sometimes wrote, "the ageless maestro, incomparably gifted . . ."? His peerless talent should be imperishable. Fans, mesmerized by his virtuosity, perceived him as godlike and handsomely distinguished. But to strangers on the street with no idea of who he was, and to himself, he was only a pathetically vain man, calling even more attention to his advancing age with the jet-black dye in his hair and the thin but obvious coat of pancake makeup over his sallow complexion.

With a heavy sigh, Pedarius turned his head slightly to make sure the age spots on his temples were camouflaged with healthy color. Satisfied, he then began to apply the same makeup to the back of his hands. Liver spots notwithstanding, his hands had never felt more lithe and supple. He then carefully brought a dark eyeliner pencil to his eyelid, his eyes locked on the eyes reflected in the glass. Not now! he pleaded with his subconscious, Not now!

. . . the green grass carpeted the rolling hills, sweet, fiercely fragrant. White and yellow flowers dotted the landscape, alone, then in clusters. Air, fresh and cool, clear in the warm August sunshine. Muffled laughter, gay and carefree, drifting up from the other side of the hills, coming closer . . .

Pedarius blinked rapidly, his eyes wide and fixed on his image, and tried to clear the tightness from his throat.

. . . the laughter and the young voices were becoming more and more distinct. Any second now, they would appear over the soft, grassy knoll. Faces, distinct words, familiar . . .

Pedarius started and the pencil dropped from his fingers as the knock came at the door. Relief!

"Half hour, maestro," the stage manager called through the closed dooor.

Pedarius cleared his throat. "Yes," he said in a moderate tone. He reached for a tissue and dabbed at the perspiration on his forehead and upper lip as he heard the stage manager move away from the dressing room. Pedarius wadded the tissue and dropped it into the basket beside the straight chair he sat on. He noticed the slight tremble in his hand as he started to retrieve the eyeliner. The old man cleared his throat again and leaned back against the hardness of the chair, folding his hands softly in his lap. A few deep breaths and then he would continue. And he mustn't forget the color on the back of his hands. With his eyes softly closed, he could *feel* the presence of the Stradivarius, which rested against the pillows of the sofa five feet behind him.

The dress hadn't felt so tight before, but now as Sue tried to settle herself comfortably in the chair, the black crepe seemed to bind her everywhere, even under the arms. The excitement,

13

she told herself, as she leaned forward and adjusted the back of the dress. And truly, the concert hall had never seemed so elegant, so impressive, so electric.

Avery Fisher Hall, home to the New York Philharmonic at Lincoln Center, had opened in 1962. Later, the concert hall was gutted and redone to improve the acoustics. It was now one of the most satisfyingly resonant halls in the world, and on this pleasantly chilly December night the huge room was filled to brimming with a glittering, bejeweled crowd dressed in hundreds of thousands of dollars' worth of expensive materials, cut and stitched carefully to the sketches of the world's most respected and most trendy fashion designers. Tickets to the performance by Pedarius were *the* hot item for December. Celebrities galore, the cream of New York and Washington society, Cabinet members and senators, the famous and the outrageously infamous, all elegantly coiffed and bedecked in costly finery, swept from limos, past the spectacle of the immense lighted fountain gurgling sixteen thousand gallons of water a minute, beneath the five-ton polished copper space sculpture suspended over the entire length of the Grand Promenade, seeing and being seen amid the continuous popping of flashbulbs, kissing and smiling and helloing before finally settling in one of the hard-to-come-by cushy seats in the golden light of the hall.

Sue Arcomano loved being onstage, a part of one of the world's great orchestras, but on this night would have dearly loved to have been part of the audience to glimpse close up the scores of celebrities. As she looked across the orchestra, then up, across and around the first, second and third tiers, she knew the hall had never before been more stunningly impressive. Even the murmur of the crowd had a strange, electric excitement, anticipatory and thrilling. When she glanced toward the wings and saw Leonard Bernstein standing in the shadows, goose bumps erupted on both her forearms. People still were coming down the aisles looking for their assigned seats. Better hurry, folks, Sue admonished them in her mind. Once Bernstein appeared in the wings, he never waited more than a few minutes before making his entrance. And the doors were closed upon the entrance of the concertmaster and the tuning of the orchestra. Latecomers would not be seated until the conclusion of the first piece. Just as Sue was hoping that Nick would catch the end of the concert, the concertmaster came onstage and tuning up was at hand.

Sue Arcomano shivered and the shy grin of embarrassment mixed with pride, which was so often the expression frozen in childhood photos, pulled at her cheeks. It was one of those "can this be me? here?" moments. Little Sue Ella Goodwin, girl cellist, onstage with the New York Philharmonic *and* Pedarius! Where were Wally O'Keefe and Maxine Finley now? Why couldn't they be there to see how far "spindly legs" had come from "Honest Abe L. Grade School" in New Orleans? Mean Wally used to love to humiliate her by comparing her pitifully skinny arms and legs to her violin bow. "My, what long arms you have, SueYeller," he would tease, quickly adding, "oh, I'm sorry . . . she's carrying her fiddle bow!" Hee, hee, hee. And then "Hot Maxine," with her premature ba*zooms*, would add gleefully, "Well, it's the *only* beau that Toothpick will ever git!" Hee, hee, hee. Sue could laugh about it all now, of course, but oh, the pain of it all back then. She'd hated being so thin and had always thought how much better it would be if they shouted, "Fatty, fatty, two-by-four, can't get through the kitchen door" as she walked by. Anything but skinny jokes. She also now knew that all adolescents had tons of insecurities and that it was part of growing up to pick at and tease everyone outside "your group," but it had seemed to Sue Goodwin that she never would be part of any clique. *Nobody* took music lessons, and especially did *not* play the fiddle. She felt destined to be alone, lonely and skinny. She remembered walking home from afternoon music lessons, hugging her violin case close to her flat chest, quietly singing to herself, "I'll go my way by myself. . . ."

Then, and it seemed almost overnight, she was a senior, invited to the senior prom by star quarterback Rick Olsen, and more than capable of supporting a gorgeous white satin *strapless.* She was most popular this and that, a cheerleader, and suddenly being an accomplished musician was just one more of her many enviable assets. And how she would gloat when "Fat Maxine" Finley showed up at the prom with no date! But Sue hadn't been able to gloat at all. Instead, she had felt so sorry when Maxine walked in alone, she spent the entire evening trying to make sure the lonely girl had a good time. Funny how things work out.

Sue realized, amid the discordant sounds of the instruments tuning up, that she had a wide, silly grin plastered on her face and that Jimmy Higgins to her right was staring at her.

"What?" the fellow cellist mouthed silently, curious as to what was causing her Cheshire cat grin.

15

Sue shook her head, "nothing," and flushed slightly that she had conjured up those particular memories at this particular moment. She brought her bow across the long strings and glanced at the front row of the orchestra. Stranger things had happened. Maybe Wally O'Keefe would be sitting there.

The recognition almost caused Sue to drop her bow. Not Wally O'Keefe, but four rows back, Jacqueline Kennedy Onassis was taking her seat, directly in the center of the house. And wearing *her* white satin strapless from the prom. Sue looked excitedly back to the man on her right, caught his eye and nodded with her head toward the world's most famous woman. Jimmy recognized her too and looked back with a grin.

"Who's she with?" Sue mouthed toward him.

Jimmy looked back toward the audience, squinted his eyes, then turned back to Sue and whispered a name.

Sue wrinkled her brow and leaned toward him. "Richard who?"

The cellist leaned closer and grinned mischievously. "Nixon!" he said in a gravelly whisper. "They both can use the notoriety!"

Sue grinned wider and shook her head appreciatively. His humorous reply surprised her. Higgins was a first-class musician and a nice man, but she never had given him credit for having a sense of humor. Probably an accident. One good crack in five years did not a sense of humor make. Perhaps . . .

The sudden sharp pain caused Sue to lurch forward a bit. Her mouth dropped open and she sat very still, slowly bringing her hand up to the left side of her swollen belly. She swallowed purposefully, then took a couple of deep, quiet breaths to allay her concern. Not to worry, she told herself calmly, not to worry. Just at that moment, she felt a little hand or foot push outward against the hand she held against her side. The very movement she had been waiting so impatiently for only served to alarm her further. Then, once again, a kick or a push on the other side. She felt a small smile, though a bit quavery, pull at the corner of her mouth. *That* you've definitely inherited from me, she thought, beginning to feel a bit relieved. An extraordinary sense of bad timing! But he or she actually moved. Dr. Bronson had been right. There was nothing to worry about. But what about that awful, ominous pain? Probably nothing more than gas. Sue tried to appreciate fully the experience of the baby's first movement and, at the same time, remember what she had eaten which would have produced enough gas to cause the pain. But

16

whatever caused it, the baby was alive and moving and would hear the wondrous music about to surround him. With such an auspicious beginning, his musical genius would no doubt bring him renown surpassing even that of Pedarius. The applause brought Sue back to reality, and she watched with pride as Leonard Bernstein moved crisply toward the podium.

In the wings, Pedarius adjusted his tails, cleared his throat and lithely drummed his fingers against the neck of the Stradivarius. As the applause for Bernstein began to die down, Pedarius watched the conductor dip his head one last time to the audience, then turn and extend his hand toward the wings. Pedarius artfully turned away, momentarily ignoring his entrance cue, as he pretended to make a last-minute adjustment to his clothing. The audience, anticipating the appearance of the living legend, began to applaud wildly. Then, just at the right moment, Pedarius turned and walked out into the lights. The applause became thunderous. Slyly, the maestro almost stopped in his tracks midway across the stage and flashed his carefully rehearsed "can all this be for me?" expression of surprise. As he knew it would, this expertly displayed touch of humility brought the audience to its feet and the house fairly shook with the roar of approval. Pedarius walked the few more feet to his position, bowed to Mr. Bernstein and then turned back to the sea of clamoring fans. Finally, when the outpouring of adoration showed no signs of subsiding, the maestro raised his arms over his head, the rich, warm patina of the priceless instrument glowing in his left hand, held the victorious pose while the cheers rose yet another decibel, then bowed low from the waist. Pedarius straightened himself, then smiled his appreciation to every section of the house as the most tumultuous ovation of his career began to ebb.

Toward the end of Bartok's Violin Concerto No. 2, Sue experienced a moment of dizziness but it passed. The Empire waistline of the dress seemed to be cutting off her breathing. She tried to adjust it during the applause. Then, two minutes into the Tchaikovsky concerto, a hot sweat literally burst from every pore of her body. She was stunned that it seemed to happen so quickly. One moment she was bone dry beneath the binding black silk and an instant later soaked through. The near-debilitating wave of nausea caused her to slump back in the chair, then the dizziness again, which made her feel as if she might slide off onto the floor of the stage. A quick, sharp pain caused

17

her to straighten up again and cleared her head for an instant. Something wildly wrong was happening to her, stupefyingly frightening. As she stared at the music on the stand in front of her, the notes blurred out, came back into focus, then fuzzed again. Somehow she played the passage but held the last note too long. She tried to swallow the mounting panic as she glanced at Bernstein. Was he looking at her? Help me, she thought, as another pain caused her right foot to kick involuntarily against the music stand. The metal base screeched against the wooden floor. She couldn't be having a miscarriage, she just couldn't. Where was Nick? What was she doing here? The dizziness again. Why was the music so soft and quiet? She felt her shoulder leaning to one side and barely regained her equilibrium before tumbling off the seat. Why wasn't the orchestra playing? The solo. Pedarius was in the middle of the soft, melodious solo passage. She should ask Jimmy Higgins to help her off the stage. But how could she? How could she totally disrupt . . . The baby, that's why. The baby was much more impor—

The excruciating pain forced a loud, agonizing scream from Sue's throat as her head whipped back, then forward again. She grabbed the neck of the cello firmly but knew she was slipping into unconsciousness. It was useless to struggle, and the pain was so awful. As Sue slumped forward against the cello, her arm drew the bow across the strings and a distinct six-note passage echoed through the silence of the hall, stilled momentarily by shock. The audience and orchestra members alike gasped in unison as Sue Arcomano tumbled heavily to the stage floor, spilling her cello and music stand noisily around her.

Jimmy Higgins was the first to reach her side. He knelt quickly beside her and tried to straighten her crumpled body into a more comfortable position. One did not need medical training to know at once that the pale young woman would require immediate professional attention.

"Somebody call for an ambulance . . . quickly!" Higgins shouted as he peeled off his jacket to fold into a cushion for Sue Arcomano's head.

The quiet of the hall suddenly gave way to a din of shocked murmurs. Members of the audience stood to get a better view of the strange happenings on the stage. But they all looked toward the fallen cellist, missing the strangest sight on the huge stage.

Pedarius stood frozen, his eyes locked in a terrified stare toward the young woman who had ruined his concert. He was unaware that the beads of perspiration had become rivulets coursing down his temples and cheeks. His chest was tight with sudden terror. His mind raced as he tried to remember distinctly the sounds which caused his fingers to petrify on the neck of the violin. Perhaps he had only imagined that she had played *those* six notes. Yes, he must have. How would she have known? How *could* she have known? No possible way. It was all in his head. He only imagined he heard those notes. Pedarius was suddenly aware that he was paralyzed by fright amid the mounting confusion onstage. He felt a tug at his arm.

The conductor was taken aback by the violinist's glazed, blank stare. "Are you all right, maestro?" Bernstein said, not attempting to mask the concern in his voice. When he got no reply save a brief twitch at the musician's throat, he deduced that Pedarius might be suffering mild shock at the bizarre, unexpected disruption. "If I may," Bernstein said without further hesitation as he took the old man by the elbow and led him toward the wings.

Pedarius did not fully realize how infirm his movements must have appeared to the stunned audience until they were a few yards from his dressing room. Embarrassed and furious at his own loss of control, he prissily removed his elbow from the handsome conductor's grasp.

"Thank you very much," he said crisply, dipping his head stiffly before moving rather quickly toward the dressing room. Pedarius paused with his hand on the brass doorknob and turned back. "The performance will not continue!" He stared at the conductor for a moment as if to make sure his orders were understood, then disappeared into the small, tastefully decorated suite.

Pedarius locked the door behind him and with an angry intake of breath raised the Strad above his head, gripping its throat with both hands, fully intending to smash the wondrously crafted instrument against the wall. But as he stood poised for the strike, his chin began to quiver and he felt the hot tears of self-pity and fear begin to cloud his vision. Feeling helplessly wounded and piteously alone, he allowed the violin to drop back to the cushions of the sofa, then brought his forehead to rest against the cool smoothness of the pale yellow wall. He relaxed his prideful façade and released the agonized moan which he had contained tightly in his throat. The pain, the fear and the humiliation were unbearable. As he began to sob he became aware of the increasing stiffness in his hands. It had all become too much to bear. He no longer had months between the crippling attacks. The stiffness was upon his joints much more frequently now. Only a week ago in San Francisco it had . . . and now tonight.

Pedarius cried out again and moved across the room toward the dressing table as he remembered being led across the stage like a half-paralyzed old man, dazed and almost comatose, in full view of some of the most important people in the world. It was all too humiliating. He could not go on. He pulled a tissue from the box as he dropped heavily into the chair. The tears had caused ugly, dark smudges around his reddened eyes, and the intense perspiration had caused the pancake to harden into powdery flakes above his eyebrows. Had he not been so frightened, the image reflected in the mirror would have been pathetically laughable to him.

But he only snorted as he raised the tissue to wipe away the mess from his face. The great Pedarius, it slowly formulated in his mind, had given his last performance. Ruined as it was, it was his last performance. He had tortured himself enough. His hand stopped as he stared with blurred eyes at nothing. Now the real torture would begin. More intensely now, he *felt* the violin behind him. Then he knew what he had to do.

The maestro leaned into the mirror and went at removing the stains from his face with renewed vigor. He had to see this girl before they took her away. He had to see her, to look into her eyes. That was the one way he could be sure, to be positive that he had only his own overworked imagination to blame. Besides, his concern as to the stupid girl's condition would be good for his image. He would assure her that she and her well-being were of more importance to him than any frivolous concerns over a ruined concert. The little bitch! He almost smiled as he pictured the human-interest stories the newspapers and magazines would carry. It was more than his incredible talent that had made him a legend. He knew instinctively when and where to create publicity. A nice explosive mixture of temperament, charitable warmth and vulnerability. That was how legends were made. Pedarius became feverishly excited about seeing this girl, looking directly and deeply into her eyes, daring her to *be* the challenge he only imagined her to be.

He would know!

* * *

When she opened her eyes, Jimmy Higgins was leaning over her with a look of concern, cupping both his hands over her right hand, which rested on his thigh. He smiled, warm and comforting, as he brushed a stray strand of hair off her forehead.

"Don't worry, baby," he reassured her softly, "you'll be okay. They're on the way."

Who's on the way? Sue thought just as a dull pain caused her abdomen to contract. Oh, my God, the baby! She was going to lose the baby. Her left hand moved to the bottom of her swollen trunk and she pushed up, not intending to let the baby slip out prematurely.

"I can't lose the baby," Sue said through gritted teeth.

"Don't worry," Jimmy said firmly. "Just relax."

"I can't relax," Sue said, laughing weakly, suddenly made giddy by her predicament, the pains, the increasing panic. "He might just slip out." She called the baby "he" without adding "or she." She always said both to ensure not being disappointed whether she had a boy or a girl. "Or . . ."

"I'll keep an eye out for him," Jimmy grinned. "He won't get by me."

Sue laughed right on top of another, sharper pain. He *did* have a sense of humor. "He might be a girl, Jimmy."

"So what?" he said, patting her hand. "You think I can't handle girls?"

"Oh, I didn't mean that, Jimmy," Sue said quickly, realizing at once that her eyes revealed that *that* was exactly what she meant. He flushed only slightly. She hoped he knew that his sexual preference would not alter in the slightest way her feelings toward him. She smiled and squeezed his hand to confirm it.

Jimmy Higgins's smile widened, acknowledging their secret exchange. "I know exactly what you meant. Now relax. If you'll tell me your husband's number, I'll call him when we know where they'll be taking you." Then a kindlier gesture occurred to him. "Or would you like me to come along with you to . . ."

"Oh, please," Sue gratefully interrupted, pressing his hand again. "I don't want to go alone. Ask someone else to call Nick." Poor Nick would be beside himself.

Only when she was on the stretcher, being wheeled across the downstage area near the cacophonous rumble coming from the curious crowd of disappointed devotees, did Sue realize the enormity of the spectacle she had caused. She had personally

21

made a shambles of the most eagerly awaited concert event of the season. She laughed at the unlikely absurdity of the whole thing.

When she heard a voice from the audience ask if she was all right, without thinking she raised her arm heroically and waved a clenched fist. The applause started in the first rows, then spread throughout the house as the milling crowd saw the fallen woman's triumphant gesture.

Sue felt herself blushing. "His first standing ovation," she giggled, patting her mound of a belly.

Jimmy Higgins leaned down toward her, smiling in relief at the flush of color in her cheeks. "Or her," he reminded her.

She felt another pain as they came into the more subdued light of the backstage area, but it passed quickly. Perhaps she wasn't miscarrying at all. But a premature birth, *two months* premature, would be just as bad. What chance would the poor little thing have? She tugged at the arm of the young doctor who moved alongside the stretcher's tediously slow progress. She needed to know what the baby's chances would be. The somber young man shook off her request for attention with a quick shake of his head and signaled her to remain quiet. Screw him, she thought. He probably wouldn't know anyway. Even if he did, he wouldn't tell her. Doctors were not supposed to be candid and sincere. It was part of their training. But Dr. Bronson wasn't like that, she quickly reminded herself. He was professional, knowledgeable, trustworthy, efficient . . . not to mention, expensive. She felt tense again. Time to crack a joke.

"So what did the applause meter say, Mr. Mack?" she said to Jimmy Higgins. "Who got the biggest ovation, us or Pedari . . ."

The stretcher stopped suddenly, and she was staring directly into the eyes of the incomparable artiste. *Held* by the eyes, which momentarily threatened to bore into her very soul. The eyes blazed coldly down over the long, straight nose and the thin lips, the entire face frozen into an authoritarian sternness. She suddenly saw him as Svengali and herself as Trilby, wondering if he was infusing her with a portion of his genius. Then she realized he was more likely to rip her to shreds for having spoiled his glorious night. But whatever it was to be, one of them had to say something. You first, she wanted to say, but somehow felt he was waiting for her apology.

"I'm so sorry, maestro," she somehow managed to get out. "I . . . and I couldn't even faint quietly. I'm sure I remember saw-

22

ing my bow across the strings as I fell . . . producing some God-awful . . ." When in hell are you going to let me off the hook? she almost screamed. Then, quite suddenly, a smile curled the thin lips and the astounding transformation was instantaneous.

"You mustn't concern yourself with the inconsequential post-ponement of a concert, my dear," the old man said warmly, reaching for her hand. "Concern yourself only with the safety of that wondrous creation you have been blessed to carry." Pedarius was now aware of a lone photographer who had his camera poised and waiting for just the right moment. Now that he was certain he had no reason to fear this pregnant *Hausfrau* and musical aspirant, he may as well ensure a color photo of himself in the "People" section of *Time*. With the most kindly expression of benevolence registered on his face, he moved his hand gracefully toward the woman's full belly, pausing just before touching her and asking, "May I?"

By now, Sue felt as if she were in the presence of a long-lost grandfather. She didn't know whether to say "Please" or "Be my guest," and so they came out together as "Plebe." She was about to correct herself when she realized that the old man was not satisfied by the light touch of his hand on her big belly. He was bending his head down to kiss it! She laughed just as the photographer's flashbulb exploded. This should pretty well guarantee the baby's musical genius.

"Be well, both of you," Pedarius said, just loudly enough so that nobody could miss the caption for the photo. "Take good care of her," he said to the young doctor and ordered the stretcher on with a wave of his hand.

Pedarius watched the curious procession move away. He'd been a fool to be alarmed by the notes the foolish woman had produced on her instrument. But the mere fact that he had been terrified by the possibility that she was some instrument of re-venge was a clear enough signal that he should remove himself from the public eye. He had reveled in a glory few men are for-tunate enough to know. And now, *unfortunately*, the Piper's demand for payment must be considered. He shivered involun-tarily as he briefly pondered his bleak future. But there would be no changing his mind. This would be his last performance. More reason, then, to pull some order together out of this chaos and give them something to remember. There had been no an-nouncement yet, and at least not one he had heard, that the con-cert would not continue. Pedarius felt the adrenaline pumping.

He was ready! He would give the performance of his career! He whirled about and took quick strides toward the stage manager's table in the wings. In his excitement, he was already formulating the outlines of his farewell speech. The stage manager stood up behind the table as he approached.

"Get Bernstein!" Pedarius ordered grandly. "Tell him I will continue." The maestro turned sharply to leave, then turned back. "And tell him that I will . . ." No, why tell him that? The secret would be his alone. "Make the announcement before we are faced with an empty house." He left before the amazed stage manager could reply.

On his way back to the dressing room, he vividly imagined the awesome theatricality of his surprise ending. At the completion of the prepared program, he would stand alone on the huge stage, lit by his two spots in the otherwise darkened house, and dazzle them with his favorite Bach unaccompanied violin sonata.

His farewell speech would be stunning, both literally and figuratively. Stunning!

Two and a half hours after Sue Arcomano was wheeled into the delivery room at Lenox Hill, and at precisely the same moment that the stunned audience at Lincoln Center learned that they had been witness to an historical performance, Severin David Arcomano, two months premature and a weakly four pounds eight ounces, made his debut. He was immediately given residence in the incubator.

Nick was with Sue when Dr. Bronson wearily made the pronouncement that the boy had a fifty-fifty chance of survival. Though he was on the verge of tears, Nick leaned down and kissed his wife, then flashed a none-too-convincing smile of reassurance.

Sue's smile was heartfelt and confident. She should be the one reassuring him, she thought. She *knew* Severin would make it.

II

DECEMBER 1980

The first "major" storm of the winter had been a dud. The mayor had announced the night before that the Big Apple's crack Clean-up Team had been reinforced and was standing by to ensure that the world's greatest city would not be paralyzed by a few feet of snow. The warmish "blizzard" dropped a scant two inches of damp flakes, leaving the city with a major problem nonetheless. How would they pay the reinforcement crews from the near-depleted budget? Indeed, how would they cover the cost of the vats of coffee consumed during the all-night vigil waiting for the white stuff to pile up on Broadway? That breezy, toddlin' town to the west hadn't been so lucky. Chicago was closed until further notice.

The streets were clogged with slush, but the small playground of The Ryder School looked like a picture postcard with the brightly dressed kindergarteners dashing here and there on a thin but beautiful carpet of snow. For one peering in from the street through the tall, spiked, black-enameled iron fence, Ryder might appear to be a fat farm for well-to-do preschoolers. Each little body seemed ten to fifteen pounds overweight dressed in trendy goose-down jackets.

Thinking of it, Sue Arcomano laughed suddenly. "It's been a great year for geese, hasn't it? Nobody would think of cooking one anymore, when there's so much money to be made from plucking them."

"I . . . uh . . ."

Sue turned and saw the blank, questioning look on Miss Fryer's face, which made Sue laugh again. "That did come out of left field, didn't it? I was referring to the run on down-stuffed jackets. Thick, bulky, puffy . . ."

"Oh, yes!" the teacher chortled, relieved that she didn't have another mother spaced out on diet pills, or worse, on her hands. "Our closets explode when you open them. As a matter of fact, since all the children have them, Mr. Davis is thinking of ordering a batch of Ryder emblems that can be sewn on. Make them into a sort of school jacket, as it were. Help instill pride in the children, you know?"

Well, let's not make them too uniform, Sue thought, while saying, "Good idea." She smiled as she watched, through the tall, paned windows, a struggle for a soccer ball. Her son, taller and stockier than the other children, came up with the black-and-white ball and took off, with four boys and a girl in pursuit of him. He easily outran them. Then to make it more interesting, he would stop, wait until they were almost upon him, then scramble agilely just out of their grasps.

"We named him Severin Arcomano," Sue said, rolling the name off her tongue, "in anticipation of his becoming a great musical genius. It appears we should have dubbed him O.J."

Miss Fryer adjusted her pinkish, plastic-framed glasses, then wrapped her arms protectively about her waist, hoping that what she was about to say had already been realized by the cellist. "I'm afraid I have to agree with you, Mrs. Arcomano. While Sev sings with great gusto, often drowning out the other children, he . . . well, it's just that, I'm afraid . . . drowning out. He . . . doesn't seem to have a great sense for musical tone. I hope you . . ."

"Don't be embarrassed," Sue reassured her, laughing again. "I'm well aware. He takes after his father in that respect. They are both tone deaf . . . excruciatingly so, and take great pleasure in driving me up the wall with their perfectly *awful* serenades. But I would like you to confirm," Sue said with mock seriousness, setting the teacher up, "that he's the brightest, quickest, most exceptional lit . . . and cutest . . . little five-year-old you've run up against!"

Miss Fryer's easy laughter indicated to Sue that the teacher was now more relaxed and comfortable, no longer self-consciously fiddling with the bulky knit cardigan. Now they could talk openly and honestly about the boy.

Severin was vibrantly healthy now, but he had gotten off to a very shaky start. The tiny babe had stayed in the incubator for two weeks, and then it was three more weeks before Dr. Bronson would allow them to take him home. It was just as well, Sue thought when they finally got Sev home, that they had the five

26

weeks in the hospital. The progress the builders were making on the brownstone was laughable, though one couldn't laugh about it. Nick waited until the workers had the place to a conceivably comfortable stopping place, then fired the second contractor in the most explosively emotional fashion. Sue had never suspected that he was capable of such violent anger and quickly padded down the stairs in her bathrobe to make sure Nick didn't kill the man *and* to relish the shocked expression on the asshole's face as he got his long-overdue comeuppance. Even when Nick had ordered the red-faced contractor out of the house, telling him that his payment would be as timely as the three promised completion dates, the man dared not challenge the outraged, well-muscled Italian. When the man was gone, Nick had gone to the freshly painted wall in the foyer to vent his anger by pounding his fist against it.

"Not there, Nick," Sue had said, quietly but firmly, from her position on the stairs. "That part they got right."

Nick stopped, with his fist poised in midair, then slowly lowered his forehead against the wall, nodding slowly up and down. "You're right," he said and began to laugh. "Why fuck up the one thing they got right?" Nick turned around slowly. "We'll just entertain in the foyer, that's all." Nick looked up at her, suddenly aware of that warm "aren't you something" smile on her face, and was at once excited. It was a moment of perfect timing, when their feelings of desire meshed completely. "We just won't let anyone upstairs," he smiled sexily, moving toward her, "maybe never . . . but most certainly not right now." Nick picked her up in his arms and whirled her around on the steps. "The Arcomanos are not receiving," Nick whispered, nuzzling her neck as he slowly and easily carried her up the steps.

Sue clung to his neck as the warmth of eagerness spread through her belly. She felt well enough now to be ravaged and felt not unlike Scarlett as she playfully whispered, close to Nick's ear, "Oh, Rhett . . . Rhett . . ."

But Severin's bad timing had interrupted the ravaging, and other things as well, later on, including her cherished career. It had been tough, in the beginning, taking care of the baby practically alone. Arcodan was suddenly swamped with new accounts, everybody seemed to want them, and Nick was ridiculously overworked, precariously overextended and loving every sweaty moment of it. Profits piled up, almost too quickly to bank, and Nick insisted, since he was never around to help

27

with Severin, that Sue find a nurse in addition to the part-time housekeeper she now shared with Mandy. Sue always had considered herself a spendthrift until Mandy had gleefully pointed out her mistake over a very expensive lunch at Regine's.

Mandy had leaned forward, covering her mouth with her freshly porcelained nails so as not to guffaw in the chic surroundings. "Spendthrift does *not* mean penny-pinching and miserly. Just the opposite, in point of fact," she said, assuming an exaggerated, comical grandness and delighting in their continuing, friendly competitiveness. "A spendthrift literally *throws* his money around . . . his, of course, referring to one's husband's, never one's own . . . spending the old moola as if it . . . uh . . ."

"You're searching for something as trite as 'if it grew on trees'?" Sue teasingly chided.

"Precisely," Mandy said with a laugh. "Don't feel too humiliated, my dear. It does *sound* as if it might mean miserly. But, as I've often said, a southern education does tend to fail one at the most inopportune moments." She laughed mischievously. "And don't worry. You *know* I wouldn't *dream* of telling a soul about a tiny grammatical error," she said, her laughter rising.

"Careful, Mandy, you're liable to laugh yourself *cosmotose*."

"What a cheap shot," Mandy said with a sharp intake of breath. "You know I was drunk when I said that . . . comatose, as a matter of fact." They both broke up, then decided that one more Gibson was in order.

But then, finally being in the position to become a spendthrift comfortably, Sue found herself uncomfortable at the thought of having a housekeeper *and* a nurse. And so she managed the first year with Severin alone, thoroughly fascinated by the almost daily changes in him. The two of them spend wondrous days together, never to be forgotten. Not by her, anyway. And then there were the other days, days when the baby would cry and complain for seemingly endless hours, days when she would feel so tired, so cooped up with every freedom taken away from her, so irritated by his squalling that she felt like dumping him in the clothes hamper and letting him scream himself to sleep. On those particular days, it would seem to Sue that he would never be able to take care of himself, that she would never again be able just to relax in a hot tub, never again have a long, hot, uninterrupted session of lovemaking with Nick, that she had a millstone permanently encircling her neck which could only pull her down, down and farther down.

And then he was pulling himself up in his crib, then crawling, then taking a few unsteady steps before plopping on his rear. His progress from then on was amazing in its swiftness. Sev raced around the house, jabbering wildly, entertaining himself for hours at a time. Sensing a glimmer of freedom, Sue began to think about returning to the Philharmonic.

She had become close friends with Jimmy Higgins, who was delighted to have a female friend who accepted him with no notion of trying to "cure" his homosexuality and who posed no threat to him sexually. They began to meet once a week, with two other friends, a sort of impromptu chamber quartet which served to keep Sue ready for her return to the orchestra. Jimmy was sure that Sue could get her seat back anytime she wanted, but she felt uncomfortable about bumping someone.

"You're too nice to be in this competitive business," he had gently scolded her. "You've got to scratch and claw your way. Don't you know this is a dog-eat-dog world?"

"So I've heard," Sue sighed, "but I refuse to play by those rules. And you really don't believe it either. You're all talk."

"Maybe . . . probably," he said with a grin. "But in any case, I'm sure one of two seats will be open soon. Two possibilities for us to run you back in. I'm watching out for you. Hey, Severin, how's my widdle baby boy?"

Mandy was around a lot too, almost constantly some weeks. Sue valued her friendship and welcomed the companionship most of the time. They had much in common, not the least of which was not seeing enough of their respective husbands. Nick was not only keeping very long hours at the agency, he also was beginning to spend a lot of time traveling to the Coast, where Arcodan would be opening another office. But they still had a good relationship when they were together. They *did*, Sue would emphasize to herself when she felt slightly neglected. It was a new phase of their relationship, what with the addition of Severin, and it could be even better than what they had before. More *things* to enjoy with their increasing financial freedom, sharing the new challenge of parenthood, watching Severin metamorphosing, constantly, surprisingly and wondrously. Just less time together, that was all. Paradise when compared to Mandy's imagined dilemma.

Amanda Broughton had married Kerry Buchanan two years after he had launched a small, independent record company, Bulletproof Records, and five years after she had graduated

29

from Wellesley and had already become disenchanted with a less than meteoric modeling career. Her family was well fixed financially but never accepted by Boston society, thanks to the generations-old Broughton Fish Cannery business. Her family's resentment at the lack of acceptance and a sturdy defiance because of it were instilled in Amanda. She wanted desperately to have her name recognized and respected. That was the main reason behind her brief fling at modeling. She was beautiful and saw this as the quickest, easiest way to make a name for herself. She found out rather quickly, however, that she was usually treated more like a piece of meat than a beautiful and talented young woman. So she would have to find another, more accessible route to celebrity. There was a sensuous quality to Buck Buchanan's rather gruff manner, but beyond the physical attraction, Amanda was attracted by his willfully relentless desire to succeed. Nothing was going to stand in Buck Buchanan's way, so when Amanda decided to marry him it was not a gamble, really. She knew from the outset that there would be money. And maybe lots and lots of it.

There was more than enough money from the company, since shortened to Bullet Records, but Buck Buchanan had no interest in mingling with the social elite, was bored by the mere thought of it. He liked the music business and musicians. He was both an extraordinarily gifted producer and a masterly businessman. That combination, coupled with an iron will, guaranteed his success. He lived for those late, late hours in the studio, laying down tracks with a new group, adding the background voices, shaping, working toward yet another "top ten with a bullet single," another platinum album, a sixth Grammy. He was quite comfortable with his homelife, secondary as it was, and would always be, to his career and ultimate fulfillment. He had a showplace in the co-op on Central Park South, ideal for "hanging out with," rather than "entertaining," the near-constant but ever-changing group of bodies he needed to have around him. And he had a wife.

Mandy was a beautiful woman and he loved her in his own way, needed her even more. He knew she felt neglected, maybe even unwanted at times, and with good reason. Buck Buchanan didn't have enough time for her, but he definitely wanted her there when he needed a few hours away from the madness. He hated sleeping alone and worse, for some strange reason, he felt a terrible insecurity about waking up alone. He also knew that

30

his wife suspected him of a long series of affairs. He denied it, of course, and, for the most part, he was telling the truth. He was guilty of a few indiscretions, no more than casual sex, but the truth was his sexual urges were not that urgent at all. It was a secret shared with no one, but sex was low on his list of priorities. His work was more exciting to him than any woman he had ever known. Kerry "Buck" Buchanan wanted his wife to enjoy his success and didn't care how much money she spent on designer clothes, redecorating the apartment, all eight rooms at once if she wanted, whatever. But if she felt neglected, she'd have to find a cure for that herself. His life was just the way he wanted it. And that, quite simply, was fact.

Mandy had, on occasion, considered the possibility that Buck was a latent homosexual. On other occasions, feeling totally alone and unwanted, she was almost positive that he was a practicing *faggot!* Why else wouldn't he want her? She was young, beautiful, talented. Hadn't she established herself as an accomplished decorator of unquestionable good taste? And she could have established herself as one of *the* hostesses around town if only he'd have cooperated. But all was not lost. She did like spending money and he never, ever questioned how much and for what. What she hadn't realized, when she gradually let her decorating distractions dwindle, was that spending money could become boring. She realized one afternoon, while trying a new makeup at Lord & Taylor, that spending Buck's money had become a chore. She realized further, while staring into the small, round mirror, that the makeup was not covering the crow's feet at the corners of her eyes, not even coming close. At that moment she finally faced the fact that she had only a year and a half left on the good side of forty. She quickly gathered her things, smiled a "No, I don't think so" to the saleslady and walked out onto Fifth Avenue. And the only good side to forty, she thought as she tried to find a cab, was not a minute past twenty-five. Amanda Buchanan spent the rest of the afternoon in bed with a headache.

It was not a question of *wanting* to get the decorating going again. She had to get it going again or simply relax and go crazy. The spectacular transformation she had pulled off on the four-room apartment of a rather infamous writer got her attention when he was featured in a *New York Times Magazine* article. She got two much more elegant apartments to do from that, then the beginnings of a minor reputation. She began to have fun again. And then she met a wonderful new friend, Sue Arcomano, a warm and giving woman, with whom she could relax and be herself. With Sue she even could find humor in her panicky "I won't go" slide toward forty.

After a third contractor finished the construction work on the brownstone, Sue and Mandy set about decorating. It was a constant though good-natured battle as to whose taste should prevail. Sue appreciated, welcomed Mandy's assistance but was determined that her home reflect *her* taste. Sue's initial announcement that the entire house was to be ultramodern but cozily comfortable was met with Mandy's incredulous, "Oh, my God." Sue wanted no lacquered Chinese cabinets, Mandy's current craze. They spent hours at Sotheby's auctions without bidding once, despite Mandy's "How can we possibly *not* buy that?" Sue wanted the lines of the rooms to be sleek, low and clean, earthy tones of brown, pale yellows and lots and lots of healthy greenery. But the furniture had to be comfortable and inviting. Mandy finally got her drift and began coming up with just the right things. Their last major battle was over the Steinway Grand, which Sue selected for the Music Room. Mandy wanted the Yamaha because it was precisely the right color for the carpet and bookcases. To appease her, Sue agreed to a huge modern abstract painting which she really wasn't sure of. At least the colors were right. All in all, they had a wonderful time doing the house. They were both thrilled with the final result. That last day, when they both agreed that they were finished, at least for a while, Mandy finished her coffee and was pulling on her Oscar de la Renta silk eyelet jacket as she gave the room one last once-over. "It is fabulously right," she assessed proudly, adding, "I do wish you were on Central Park West, though."

July 1977 was a very lucky month for Sue Arcomano. She found a wonderful live-in cook-housekeeper-nurse in the person of Anna Polanski, a forty-five-year-old Polish woman who was wonderful with Severin. She had the entire fifth floor to herself, and her only demand had been a color television with remote control, "hooked up to that cable." Then, in late July, Sue was asked to rejoin the orchestra. She was indeed living a charmed life. What more could she ask?

Playing with the Philharmonic was even more fun now that she and Jimmy were such good friends. The teasing about how she "single-handedly ended the greatest musical career of the decade" died down after the premiere performance in September, and things went well until late November. *Well*, that is, excluding the fact the Sue and Nick saw even less of each other now that she had resumed her career.

Then, as December approached, Severin began throwing the most violent temper tantrums whenever Sue would leave for a performance with the orchestra. And *only* at those times. He was a near-perfect child otherwise, even-tempered, amazingly independent, cheerfully happy and keenly aware, for a two-year-old, of things going on about him. The fits of temper were so violent and unappeasable that Anna Polanski had, on two occasions, called for a doctor. One evening, Mrs. Polanski had become so frightened and distraught that she begged Sue not to go to the performance. Sue did go, but only after insisting that Nick cut short a meeting and come home to help the governess keep the boy quiet.

Nick, constantly exhausted from overwork, felt somewhat rejected when his arrival home did not serve to soothe the "fits" at all. He blamed himself, of course, for not spending more time with the boy. Sev, he would scold himself, probably thought he was a visiting uncle rather than his father. But he couldn't slack off at Arcodan, knowing he was holding the reins of runaway success. Nick also was aware that if the tantrums continued, Sue would give up the career that meant so much to her so she could stay with the boy. Feelings of resentment toward Sev were unconscionable but, nevertheless, present.

Aside from being terrified by the strange changes in the boy's disposition, Sue felt a heavy guilt because she secretly believed that the emotional outbursts were no more than desperate cries of insecurity, fears of abandonment, Sev's particular needs for a full-time, special relationship with her. And so for the second time, Sue gave up her career to become a full-time mother to the boy.

The temper tantrums stopped immediately. The weekly, more often lately biweekly, string quartet sessions with Jimmy Higgins and their friends started up again, and Sue practiced almost daily, telling herself, but not really believing it, that she could go back to the orchestra when Sev was older and more secure. She missed performing, but she realized how much her son needed her and she accepted the sacrifice.

Nick commiserated with her and, for a while, held his resent-

33

ment toward the "crybaby spoiler." But the great change in Sev's disposition and behavior so pleased him that he soon forgot about Sue's loss and was content that he was the father of such a robustly healthy, intelligent son.

Near Stonington, Connecticut, an eight-inch layer of snow was kept crusty by six days of below-freezing temperatures. Around the big house, ten miles out from the main section of town, the white landscape still was pristine, save for the tracks left by the handyman, Raymond Hines, and his sister, who were on their way to inspect the cottage off to the rear of the house.

Inside the house, the temperature was neither warm nor cold, just annoyingly wrong. But it was more than the slight chill that made the old man uncomfortable. The pain was not so severe at the moment due to the injection Hines had administered to him after lunch, but his joints were so stiff as to be hobbling. He wanted to get a look at Hines's sister but was not sure it would be worth the effort of a trip to the window.

It was probably a mistake to offer to sell the cottage to the woman, but it was well outside the walls of his domain and it seemed too frivolous simply to allow it to crumble. Besides, he probably would never use it again, nor did he care to. He would never even know the woman was there.

Five years ago, almost to the day. It seemed an eternity had passed that he had exiled himself to a different world. But *that* night he would never forget. The stark terror brought on by the strange turn of events, then the supreme heights of exaltation as he held the audience spellbound, breathless, in the palm of his hand. It was the performance of his career, made more memorable by the chaotic disruption. Single-handedly he had turned a near-disaster into an evening of total magic, a farewell performance that had stunned the few fortunate enough to have been in attendance, and the following day the entire world had read of his unexpected retirement.

He'd never forget the silence of the hall as he made the announcement that this was to be his last public performance. All the right dramatic words had come to him effortlessly, as though he had worked them out over many long hours. And as if on cue, a tear had gathered at the corner of his eye, then slowly worked itself down his right cheek. His delivery had been flawless, a normal tone of voice and yet every ear in the house had heard each word.

34

And then, alone on the great stage, every light in the house darkened except the two spots, which hit him from either side. He had raised the violin to his neck and made it sing as it was meant to. He was the only musician alive worthy of the magnificent instrument, the only one who could bring forth the wondrous sounds waiting to be unleashed. They were made for each other. They were! It was meant to be his! No one, alive *or* dead, could have hoped to play . . . It *was* meant for him, no matter that . . . He had no peer! The instrument was . . .

. . . the laughter floated gaily over the rim of the green hills. The tops of their heads bounced as they ran toward the very top. They giggled and fell, then jumped up, chasing one another in the warmth of the sun. "Hurry, David, let's hide from her over here!" "Yes, we can . . . no, Hans, we mustn't. She'll be frightened." "You're right, of course. Anya! Up here." "Here, Anya, we'll wait for you." And then the playful struggle begins. "Who's stronger? I think I am. . . ." "No, I am!" The sun is warmer as they lie panting beside each other, an arm draped across a heaving belly. "We'll always be friends, won't we?" "Always. We have . . . over here little Anya!" "Here we are." Three happy, carefree children, holding hands and turning in circles as fast as they can without falling. Laughter, the musical giggles of devoted friendship, perfect sounds for the warm, summer days, cool nights by the . . .

The coffee cup slipped from his trembling fingers and smashed on the floor. The perspiration ran into his eyes and caused them to sting as he painfully raised his legs and placed his feet on the ottoman, away from the broken china. He forced away the vivid mental images by biting down on his tongue. He could taste the blood inside his mouth and he opened his clenched teeth as an anguished gasp escaped his lips. It had been weeks since the memories had attacked him. Why now? Recalling the performance, of course. The glory . . .

"Ha!" he snorted with contempt, but the thoughts remained. Had the glory been worth the incredible torture he'd had to endure? Was the agony never to end?

How was it possible? How had that woman struck *those* six notes? He had seen her. He had convinced himself that he had only imagined that he heard those notes. Why now should he remember the sounds? And now the worrisome fright was upon him again.

It was two-thirty when Sue left The Ryder School with Sev. Miss Fryer had confirmed what Sue already knew to be true. Her towheaded son was exceptional. She smiled proudly as she ruffled his light-colored curls while strolling down Central Park West toward home. He had inherited Nick's curls but her color, though his hair did seem to be darkening somewhat.

"Don't you want to put your cap back on, Sev?" she asked casually. It really wasn't all that cold.

"Nun-uh," he responded with a shake of his head as he raced to the gutter to pick up a muddy, near-deflated balloon.

"Don't . . ." Sue began, then stopped herself. Why not? What was it that Miss Fryer had said that worried her a bit? Oh, yes, the stomach aches. She said Severin had been complaining recently about stomach aches. But he never did at home.

"Could we stop in the park, Mom?" Sev asked, walking backward in front of her. "The snow might be new there, too. Can we?"

"Just for a few minutes, okay? You've been out long enough. Promise you'll leave when I say?" He nodded his head and threw the scroungy-looking blue balloon in the air. "Sev, why didn't you mention to me that you had stomach aches at school? Sev?"

"I dunno," he said, kicking the balloon as it almost touched the sidewalk. Then he looked back at her and grinned. "I didn't want you being hysterical."

Sue laughed along with him. "Oh, you didn't, did you? When have you ever seen me hysterical?"

"When Daddy's on the phone and he doesn't come for dinner."

Rather shrill, she thought, but not hysterical. "Why do you call Nick Daddy, and you only call me Mom? Where's my 'mie'?"

"Oh, *Mom!*" he said, laughing at her silliness.

As they crossed into the park at Sixty-ninth Street, Sue wondered if she should check with Dr. Bronson about the stomach aches. Sev certainly *looked* healthy.

Maybe she's not as crazy as I thought, Raymond Hines thought as he and his sister approached the white brick guest

36

house. His feet were soaked from trudging through the eight-inch layer of snow. He stopped and looked back through the woods toward the main house. The smaller house was so far away that it really didn't seem to belong to the old mansion, and in the spring, when the trees began to sprout new leaves, you wouldn't even be able to see the high brick walls that surrounded his employer's house. He turned and walked the few more feet to the porch of the house his sister was about to buy. Maybe that's why the house suddenly looked better to him, because his sister was about to own it. She was five years older than he, so there was the outside possibility that he might inherit it someday. Not likely, though, he thought as he waited for the puffing woman to catch up to him. She was strong as an ox.

"You're sure you want to go through with this, are you, Emma?" he said, stomping the snow off his feet on the stone porch and laughing as his fifty-eight-year-old sister almost lost her balance on the slippery ground.

"Whew," she sighed in relief as she lifted her considerable bulk onto the porch. "As sure as I'm sure we're standing here," she said and puffed. "My only concern now is that the old fool will change his mind. Are you sure it's all set?"

"The papers are all ready for signing, that's what he said. I risked a lot, you know, botherin' him about somethin' like this," Raymond Hines reminded her, sticking the key into the lock and putting his shoulder to the thick mahogany door. "You know how he is."

Emma Hines shifted her weight in annoyance, knowing what her brother was hinting at. "No, I don't know how he is. I only know how you tell me he is. Don't worry, Greedy, you'll get your little fee just as I told you. Will you open the door, for Christ's sake? I'm freezing my butt off."

Hines laughed again as he pushed the door open. "And that's a lot of butt to freeze off."

Inside, after they had looked through the small, two-bedroom cottage, the man wondered why he had always seen the house as a rundown shack. Under the thick layer of dust, the house was in excellent condition. All it needed was a thorough cleaning and a fresh coat of paint. If the kitchen were modernized slightly with a new stove and a refrigerator, the cottage would be extremely desirable.

Emma Hines bent over with a groan and tried to look up the chimney of the stone fireplace in the living room, which

37

stretched across the entire width of the cottage. She straightened up slowly, holding both hands to her back. "I can rent this place for a frigging fortune," she said with a grin. "A tight little cottage like this, with a private beach right down the path there in the cove." She cackled out a laugh and slapped her beefy thigh. "Are you kidding me?"

"Well, then maybe, sister," Raymond said, rubbing the toe of his boot in the thick dust on the plank floor, "you'd like to slip me a little more than you . . ."

"A bargain's a bargain, Raymond," she said in a flat tone. "Now cut the shit. Let's just get up there and get this over with before he changes his mind." She started toward the door, buttoning up the cardigan she wore beneath the camel-colored wool coat. "I'll be more than happy to give you a little extra if you want to fix this place up in your spare time." She stopped at the door and looked at him over the half-moon glasses. "And since I know you like the back of my own hand, we both know that you will do it on *his* time, so you'll actually be being paid twice for the same time, won't you, Raymond?"

They made their way back toward the mansion along the ten-foot brick wall, making their own path where there was none through the crunchy snow. The sky was bright blue above them and the crisp Connecticut air was fresh and clean-smelling, if perhaps a bit on the cold side.

The three-story, antique white brick colonial mansion had been quite stately and grand some fifty years ago, but had now been allowed to decay into a faded impressiveness. Its elegant personality still had a breath left to it, but the lack of care had added an ominous quality to its overall feel. The great curving drive in front of the columned portico carried out the look of abandoned glory. There was not a clue that the grounds had once been meticulously manicured.

Emma Hines shivered slightly as they rounded the wall and she looked up at the house. There was something strange about the house. Not frightening, she thought, searching for the right word. "Forbidding"—that was the word. She clucked her tongue disgustedly as her brother led her past the front of the house and around to a side door.

They quietly entered a too-warm kitchen and her eyes immediately went to the rows of copper pots on the red brick wall of the tall fireplace. Her brother quickly moved over to the dying fire and poked at it with the black metal rod.

"You stay here," Raymond whispered toward her, "and I'll go up and see if he's ready."

"I'm *buying* the frigging place, you dimwit!" Emma said in a loud voice. "Don't you think you might show me into the sitting room?"

"Shhhh!" Raymond Hines shushed her, screwing up his face in alarm, bringing one finger to his lips and pointing with the other to the partially open paneled door to the dumbwaiter. "He'll hear you!" he hissed.

She clucked her tongue again and settled in a chair at the rectangular butcher block table as her brother left the hot room, shaking his head. She fished in the black patent leather handbag for her new lipstick as she heard him creaking up the stairs in the quiet house. She would make a fortune in rent from that cottage. She probably could get a shorter mortgage and still not have to use any money of her own for the monthly payments.

Raymond paused outside the tall door to the master bedroom, cleared his throat, then tapped lightly on the dark wood. Not a sound from within. He cleared his throat again, then knocked louder.

"Mr. . . ." he began, then stopped. Why couldn't he have a normal name like Smith or Jones? After working for him for almost five years, Raymond Hines still was not sure what to call him.

III

Pedarius sat on the commode, his elbows resting on his knees, staring down at the grotesquely gnarled joints of his hands. He moved his index finger only slightly and winced at the excruciating pain. Hines must have made a mistake with the injection, mixed the stuff too weak. The pain should not be so great an hour after the shot. And the man was gone now, wouldn't be back until morning. He'd heard the old pickup pull out at least half an hour before. He wondered if he could administer a shot to himself. The old man moved his middle finger and practically cried out in pain.

He turned his head and stared at the soft roll of pale green toilet tissue, half recessed into the black-tiled wall. Handle a hypodermic needle, indeed! There was a very good possibility that he would not even be able to clean himself. His lower lip began to quiver and he felt the warm tears welling up in his eyes. He was paying too great a price. The suffering was nearly unbearable. Of course, there was relief. Just up the stairs . . . waiting . . . waiting. But he couldn't even get at it, now, alone. And wasn't the relief even more unbearable, more unthinkable, than the pain? Pedarius let his head tilt back against the cool, dark tiles, opened his mouth and released his feelings of helplessness and self-pity in one long, loud scream. The sound echoed around the resonant room, howling back on him again and again.

He suddenly fell silent, staring transfixedly at the ceiling as the howl came back on him one last time. Were those the sounds that came from his throat? What had he heard? Was it possible? The pain! The unbearable pain . . .

"But Mehta has those dark, flashing eyes and . . . and he's so
41

handsome!" Sue said with a laugh as they left the elevator. "And he's much sexier . . . no, not sexy, hot. Zubin is hot! That name . . ."

Jimmy Higgins laughed, shaking his head in agreement. "He is . . . all that, but I still say you can't compare them. It's like trying to compare New York and Los Angeles. They're so totally different. Bernstein had . . ." He suddenly stopped short and grabbed Sue's arm, listening to the sounds of the party coming from the door at the end of the lushly carpeted hallway. "There must be two hundred people in there. You told me it was a small . . ."

Sue smiled and pulled his cheek down to kiss it. "You just played in front of two thousand plus . . . and you were wonderful. You know Mandy and Nick and you might even get to meet Buck if you're lucky. Look, you don't have to say a word all evening if you don't want. Just stand in a corner and get loaded. Now, come on."

"Do you think there'll be any single boys here?" he deadpanned.

"Probably," Sue said with a laugh, hitting him on the shoulder with the rolled-up program from Lincoln Center. "Some of Buck's musician friends have got to be gay. Oh, and Jimmy, promise me you'll tell Mandy . . . and Nick that story? Please? It's the funniest thing I've ever heard. You can make it a straight story, can't you, if you're embarrassed?"

Jimmy thought about it briefly as they headed for the sounds of laughter. "No, it doesn't work as well if they're straight. What do I care?" he said, trying to relax. "The whole world must know by now that I'm a faggot, right?"

"I haven't told *anyone* on the East Side, yet," Sue said, and laughed.

There were no more than forty people in the Buchanan apartment, but a group of ten or so in one corner were making the noise of two hundred. The cloud of smoke drifting about them could not have been mistaken for anything other than pot, and the blue jeans and T-shirts, plus a couple of expensive Rafael leather jackets, identified them unmistakably as Buck's Bullet Records crowd. Way at the other end of the room, cozily clustered on Mandy's beige velvet "playpen" collection, was the designer fashions crowd, the smoke above them a mixture of grass, Shermans and Joy. And here and there in between, combinations of the two, plus some tweed jackets, some jump suits and a

42

couple of sweaters and skirts. In most hands, the same tulip-shaped, crystal champagne glasses filled with Dom Perignon. Crossing the room toward them was Mandy, cleverly attired to make both groups feel comfortable.

Sue began to laugh at her friend's wonderful sense of humor as Mandy did her "runway walk" for them. With her cheeks sucked in, she whirled about in front of them as if introducing Valentino's new line of ultrachic. She wore a very expensive Halston top, a frilly concoction of burgundy-colored silk organdy tied at the waist with a bow, just diaphanous enough to show that she was naked beneath it, skin-tight Calvin Klein jeans on the bottom and thin, thin burgundy straps held the rhinestone-studded heels on her smallish feet.

"Wanna know what I wear next to my Calvins?" she cooed.

"Gallon and gallons of moisturizer?" Sue teased.

"You bitch!" Mandy laughed, pulling Sue's beige mink jacket open to check the pale lemon, long-sleeved, wool jersey dress. "Oh, it's wonderful. You and Anne Klein were made for each other."

"Is that a crack?" Sue laughed as Jimmy helped her out of the short jacket. "Jimmy, was that a crack?"

"She just can't take a compliment," Mandy said as she kissed in the direction of Jimmy Higgins's cheek. "How'd the concert go?" On top of Jimmy's "great" and Sue's "wonderful," Mandy continued, "Now that I've made the jeans and T-shirt crowd comfortable, I'm going to pull on the rest of my fitout. Wait'll you see the pants Halston did for this top. Throw your coats in the bedroom . . . that one there . . . and grab some champagne."

Buck pulled Sue down on the couch beside him and kissed her wetly on the mouth. "You look gorgeous, sweetheart. Do you fool around?" he said.

"I'll do anything for a record contract, Bucky," she said.

"You a singer?" the long-haired kid next to her asked, holding smoke in his lungs and passing the joint to her. She held her palm up toward the marijuana and shook her head "no." "It's okay, man," the kid said, trying to keep the smoke from escaping, "it's not dusted."

"She's a backup man," Buck said with a grin as he reached in front of her to take the roach.

"Oh, yeah?" the kid said and grinned, checking her out again. "You shittin' me, man? Where's your ax?"

"My ax is too big to carry around," Sue laughed. Buck

Buchanan put his arm around her waist and pulled her close up against him, hugging her affectionately.

"Her old man owns Arcodan," Buck said to the bleary-eyed kid. "Be nice to her and maybe you'll get some session work in TV commercials."

Sue suddenly was aware that Jimmy Higgins was standing across the table, holding a glass of champagne for her. She held out her hand toward him, an invitation for him to squeeze in beside her on the sofa. As he carefully moved in, Sue looked past him, quickly taking in every corner of the room. Nick should have been there before now. Maybe he'd stopped at home to spend some time with Severin. She could call, but then Mrs. Polanski had the number here if she needed her.

Buck leaned forward slightly and waved a hand toward Sue's friend. "Hey, how ya' doin' . . ."

"Jimmy Higgins," Sue reminded him.

"Jimbo," Buck continued. "How's things with the big band? You guys could use a top-ten single, you know?"

"So sign us up," Jimmy said with a grin. "Sibelius penned some pretty catchy tunes, Bucko."

"Is he the dude with that . . . uh . . . Japanese group? You know, they had . . . uh . . . 'Dancin' Fool' . . . or . . ." The kid tossed his hair back out of his eyes and took a hit on a fresh joint as he tried to remember the melody.

"No, no, no, dummy," Buck Buchanan said with a laugh. "Sibelius, don't you remember? He was lead guitar with Pink Floyd."

"Oh," the kid grunted as everybody broke up around him.

Ten minutes later, Mandy came across the room looking like Halston meant her to look when he took all that money from her. She held out her hand toward Sue.

"Come, I want you to meet someone. Buck, let her up," Amanda Buchanan ordered with a wave of her hand, praying that her husband would not tell her "Fuck off!" in front of everybody. "Is everybody doing okay? There's plenty of champagne and food enough for an army. You look wonderful, Henry. California sunshine?" She took Sue by the arm and led her across the thick, orchid-colored carpeting. "How can you just sit there and leave him alone with that gorgeous creature? Oh, if only I could be that secure."

Sue looked at her with a frown. "Who? What he? What . . ."

"Nick, of course. You haven't seen him?"

44

"Is Nick here? Where . . ."

"Oh, my God, have I ever opened a can of worms. We'd better get more champagne first," Mandy said with a mischievous grin. "Tara Dobbs. I told you, I'm doing her apartment . . . the model? I told you. . . . Well, she's divine-looking, but with a sense of humor. You'll love her. . . . Well, you would have loved her, but the last time I saw them they were in . . . here."

Mandy pushed open the white laquered swinging doors and moved into the large kitchen, with Sue following. Sitting in the breakfast nook, which overlooked all of Central Park, were Nick Arcomano and one of the most beautiful women Sue had ever seen, so beautiful that she could almost feel her own face fall.

Nick got up from the padded semicircle seat and hugged his wife. He could tell she was a little upset. And why not? Tara Dobbs was spectacular. "Hi, honey. How was the concert?"

"Nice," Sue said, trying to sound bright and cheery. She very seldom felt jealous, but she had been there for at least thirty minutes, and her husband had been secreted in here for all that time with that creamy complexion framed by an awesome cascade of dark, shiny curls. "Really nice," she added unnecessarily, stepping on Mandy's, "I'd like you to meet . . ."

Mandy waited, thinking that perhaps Sue might run on some more.

"That's all," Sue stammered, pausing just long enough for them both to start up at the same time again.

". . . just nice . . ."

"I'd like you . . ."

Nick laughed and took Sue's face in his big hands, kissing her on the mouth with a loud smack. He knew exactly what she was feeling and why. "Honey, this is Tara Dobbs. Tara, my wife, Sue. Tara's a model."

"No kidding," Sue said, and laughed, finally realizing how foolishly she was reacting. "I guess Eileen Ford's taking just about anybody these days." Being witty was a mistake too. The woman was even more beautiful when she laughed.

"He told me a lot about you," Tara Dobbs lied, "but not that you were funny. As a matter of fact, Eileen Ford wouldn't take me. She said my tits were too big for high fashion. Thank God for John Casablancas. I'm with Elite."

"Well, Señor Juan Whitehouses has very good taste," Sue said, trying to make up for a very bad start. "I think your tits are fine."

45

"Buck told me to wear a bra tonight," Mandy said, folding her arms across the sheer blouse. "Why do I never listen to that asshole?"

Sue couldn't squelch the thought whirling about in her head. They looked like the end result of David Merrick's open call for the world's most beautiful couple. Tara Dobbs and Nick Arcomano looked made for each other.

He stood looking at himself in the huge, gilt-framed mirror over the bureau. Alone and in severe pain, he really didn't care what he looked like. It was merely a shock. His eyes were red from crying and the puffy flesh underneath them was dark. He turned his head just slightly and saw a few streaks of the original blond in the thick, tousled white hair. He would never get used to the light-colored hair after years of carefully combing, and dabbing bits of brilliantine on, the thick strands of jet black. His eyes moved down to the frailty of his rather long arms. There would be no trouble finding a vein. But how was he to handle the needle when he was having difficulty grasping the small brass knobs on the bureau drawer?

Pedarius grimaced as he forced his fingers to close on the knobs, then steadily and slowly pulled the drawer open. He groaned as he saw the hypo enclosed in the oblong plastic box. It would be impossible! There were two bottles, with the gray rubber tops, sitting alongside. He would have to try, that's all. He would have to try.

He took the plastic box and one bottle from the drawer and moved toward the huge, mahogany-canopied bed. He had considered, more than once, requiring Raymond Hines to move in from town and live in the old house with him. Why hadn't he done it? Because he was somehow afraid the man would discover his awful secret, living in such close and constant proximity? Perhaps he would scream something out in his sleep. Or perhaps the secret would become too much of a burden and he would attempt to lessen the pain by telling someone. But he needed the man desperately at the moment.

Sitting on the edge of the bed, he managed to open the box and remove the needle. Then he sat for fifteen minutes trying to stretch his thumb far enough to be able to push the plunger down. Finally, with a scream of frustration, he threw the paraphernalia across the room. He sat hunched and watched the small, clear bottle of liquid roll across the dark floor and up

46

against the paneled wall at the far end of the room. The bottle rocked to a stop, but the sound of its roll seemed to continue.

The old man's eyes widened as he slowly raised his head and stared toward the ceiling. It wasn't the sound of the bottle. The strange sound was coming from up *there*. He sat quite still, listening intently. It was a small, crunching sound.

Then it stopped, and the only sound in the house was the old man's breathing.

Anna Polanski awakened suddenly, turned on her back and held her breath as she listened for a sound. Had she heard a noise from Severin's room? It seemed quiet enough now. Probably only a car from the street. Severin hardly ever awakened in the middle of the night anymore.

She raised her head and glanced at the picture on the television screen. TV made a wonderful night-light when the sound was turned off, as it was now. It also made a person feel less alone. Johnny Carson was still on, so it wasn't yet twelve-thirty. They probably would be home before Carson said good night to his guests.

Anna Polanski rolled back on her side and pulled the comforter up around her neck. No need to check on Severin. He was a good boy.

Sue hated the way she was feeling, but she couldn't seem to shake the paranoia. This was the first time in their marriage that she remembered feeling insecure about Nick's fidelity. She kept reassuring herself that she was being very silly, that it was all in her imagination, but it was that one, slim, outside possibility that prevented her from relaxing completely. And wasn't Nick being a bit too attentive to her now? It seemed to Sue that every time she would glance at him, he would bend down and kiss her. And here they sat now, his arm around her, his fingers playing idly against her shoulder. Mandy was sitting on the glass table in front of the three of them, telling some story that Sue had lost track of. Sue casually turned her head and looked up at Nick. He crinkled his nose with a smile, pulled her closer by the shoulder and bent to kiss her on the nose. She wasn't imagining it. Her face would be raw from his guilty kisses. You bastard, she thought, smiling brighter than she intended. She turned her eyes back to Mandy, but her attention remained on Nick.

". . . but the topper was," Mandy said laughing, "the best of all. To illustrate how insanely busy she had been, she told me . . . with a perfectly straight face . . . that she'd been running around like a chicken with its hat off! This woman is one big, walking, breathing malaprop."

The three of them, Mandy, Nick and Jimmy Higgins, were all laughing, so Sue joined in, although she had missed the story. But Nick seldom contributed polite laughter, so it must have been funny. She had to get rid of the paranoia.

"Jimmy," Sue said, still laughing, more to relieve the tension she felt than from amusement, "you must tell that story. This is truly funny," she assured Mandy and Nick. "Please?"

Nick squeezed her shoulder. "Sue has this wonderful way of making your balls shrink up inside you . . . even when you're about to tell your very best, can't-fail story . . . by announcing up front how truly hilarious it's going to be." Nick realized, even as he was saying it, that even this was too much criticism at the moment. He recognized her symptoms of jealousy and was both flattered by it and sorry for her that she felt it.

"I don't . . ." Sue began to protest, but was cut short by a kiss on the mouth from Nick. That was proof positive, she immediately decided. She had reason to be paranoid. "I do, don't I?" she said, and flushed. She reached out and touched Jimmy's knee. "But it is funny. Tell it."

Jimmy Higgins turned beet red. "I see what you mean, Nick," he laughed. "I think I just swallowed both my testicles."

Mandy was loving it. "Would you feel more comfortable if we hit you with a baby spot?"

What the hell, Jimmy Higgins thought, gathering his wits about him. Everybody was hysterical already and he hadn't even opened his mouth. These people didn't seem to care that he was gay, and it was a funny story. He cleared his throat and broke in just as the laughter died down.

"Well, this friend of mine . . . the whore of the world . . . went to this sleazy leather bar, one of those down by the docks, you know, that scares all the straight people as they drive by? They appear to be all these tough-looking *macho* types, but for the most part they're just silly queens. Well, anyway, he's standing around in there, already half in the bag, and there is not a soul in sight that he would be caught dead with. But as it gets closer and closer to 4:00 A.M., he gets drunker and drunker and decides he's going to take somebody home with him, no matter what he looks like. And so, about two minutes to closing, he latches onto someone and off they go." Jimmy paused to take a long sip of champagne and moved himself up on the edge of the sofa, suddenly beginning to enjoy the limelight. "Well, he wakes up in the morning with the hangover of all times. His head is throbbing, he's nauseous, and then he's aware of the body sleeping beside him. 'Oh, no!' he says to himself, too strung out even to want to see Richard Gere laying beside him. He carefully bends over and sees an absolute monster! I mean, he's in bed with Godzilla! He immediately decides that he can't waste any time being polite, he just has to get the guy out of there at once. Immediately! He taps the guy on the shoulder and says, 'I'm very sorry, but you'll have to leave right away. My sister's coming over in five minutes.' The guy rolls over, rubbing his eyes, with this incredulous look on his face. 'You invited your sister to *my* apartment?'"

Even Buck's stoned-out crowd turned to see who was having all the fun. Tara Dobbs chose the moment to excuse herself from two boringly stuffy but lecherous attorneys and moved gracefully across the room toward the sounds of fun. Nick Arcomano was the sexiest man she had met in a long time, probably because he wasn't falling all over himself and pawing at her like all the others. Here was a man very sure of his masculinity and obviously very much in love with his wife. Too bad, she thought with a smile as she approached the group of four, although she did like the pretty blond wife as well. They were *fun*. Why was it so difficult to find fun people anymore?

Sue found it difficult to sustain the laughter as she watched the exquisite beauty approach. How could anybody have that much hair without a sign of a split end?

"Do you think we should call Anna?" Sue whispered to Nick. "To check on Sev?"

Still laughing, Nick shook his head. "He's okay. We'll go soon, anyway." He felt very horny, which was quite lucky indeed. Sue would need a lot of attention tonight to quiet her insecurities, and Nick felt more than ready himself. He wondered if he'd think of Tara Dobbs at all.

He lay on his back staring up at the polished wood of the canopy, his eyes wide, waiting. Sure enough, the crunching sound began again. Pedarius scarcely breathed as he listened in total terror.

On the third floor, in the room directly above the occupied bedroom, a small fragment of plaster dropped to the floor as the hairline crack in the wall advanced another two inches. Bits of dry, white powder settled on the dark hardwood floor. Then, with an almost imperceptible groan, the crack advanced farther across the wall and behind the huge, glass-fronted walnut breakfront. A plate-sized chunk of plaster came loose and banged against the back of the credenza before crashing against the baseboard. The china and delicate porcelains inside the case tinkled spectrally, then one fragile goblet tilted and smashed against the glass door. Suddenly, like a lightning bolt, the crack in the plastered wall widened and raced across behind the breakfront and farther across on the far side.

A thick, heavy section of the plaster broke free and tumbled against the case, tilting it forward on its front edge. The expensive collection of china slid forward, crashed through the glass front and shattered loudly across the library floor. Then a second section of the wall gave way and the case was shoved forward, literally exploding against the floor in a loud, shattering crash. Plaster dust whooshed up into the air in a boiling cloud and floated for a moment before settling over the splintered disorder.

Some of the plaster dust drifted back through the gaping hole and into the small round alcove which had been sealed up behind the breakfront. The fine white dust settled on the leather violin case, which rested on the oval table in the middle of the alcove. Inside the case, the strings of the Stradivarius reverberated eerily, picking up the tremor of the huge crash against the hardwood floors.

Below, Pedarius lay frozen by the chilling terror of the last few minutes. He *knew* what had happened. There was no reason to go up to the library. He *knew* what he would see. And there was no reason to question the possibility of what had just happened. *Anything* was possible. That was fact, even if he was alone with that knowledge.

Pedarius took a deep breath, then screamed his defiance through the quiet of the house. The scream was based in agony *and* in relief.

At that same moment in Manhattan, Severin Arcomano sat up in bed and screamed in agony, clutching at the sharp pain in his abdomen. It was the worst pain he had ever felt and he folded his small, husky arms across his belly, hoping to prevent it from doubling him over again. He felt it start again and held his breath, hoping to cut it short. It wasn't as bad as the first one, but it scared him into tears nonetheless.

"Mom!" he hollered just as Anna came through the door.

"What, baby? What is it?" she said, tying the robe loosely closed in front. His expression alarmed her further. "What is it, Sev?"

"Here!" he bawled, pointing to his belly. "It hurts in here. Where's my daddy?" he screamed as the pain struck again.

Mrs. Polanski had imagined he might be staging another temper tantrum as she headed for his room, like he used to do when his mother went off to the Philharmonic. Perhaps he had imagined that his mother's visit to the Philharmonic concert tonight meant the resumption of her career and that he would be without her again. But now, looking at the glistening sweat on the boy's flushed face and the frightened look in his eyes, she knew it was more than a tantrum. Maybe something serious, like appendicitis. She gently pushed him back against the pillow and probed his belly tenderly with her fingers.

"Quiet, baby. Does that hurt, Sev?" she asked, trying to appear calm.

He shook his head as the tears flowed down his cheeks. "I want my daddy!"

The fact that he called for his father frightened Mrs. Polanski even further. The boy never called for his father in stressful situations. Always for his mother.

"Be still, Sev, and I'll get him for you. Don't worry, just lie still." She decided to call the doctor first, then call the Arcomanos. Thank God they weren't far away.

Nick broke into a run when they came out of the exclusive building and onto a near-deserted Central Park South. Sue knew he intended to run the ten blocks home, so she slipped her heels off and prepared to follow him, however far behind she might fall. But just then, a yellow Checker cab rounded Columbus Circle, and headed east on the wide street.

Nick was giving instructions to the driver when Sue climbed in beside him, carrying her shoes in her hand. "Sixty-ninth and Central Park West," he ordered, adding, ". . . and take a U-turn here and go back. We're in a hurry."

"Sorry, pal," the driver said lazily, pulling the flag down and

51

starting east toward the next downtown street, "but that's against the law. We'll have to . . ."

"Don't give me that shit!" Nick shouted, exploding with fury. "You guys don't give a fuck about the law unless you see a chance to make an extra nickel for yourselves by driving around three extra blocks. Don't give me that shit! Just turn this fucking heap around *now* before I knock the shit out of you!" The driver immediately turned the car around and quickly headed in the opposite direction, looking straight ahead. Nick leaned back in the seat, still fuming. "Not another goddamned car between here and Fifth," he muttered aloud, "and this cocksucker suddenly is worried about breaking the law. I ought to knock the shit out of you anyway!" he shouted again. "That greedy mentality of yours makes me sick!"

"Nick, stop it," Sue said, slipping her shoes on. "You've made your point." The driver was afraid even to glance at them in the rearview mirror. "Anna and I had the same thought, that Sev might be throwing another tantrum because he knew I had gone to Lincoln Center. But she says not. She thinks maybe appendicitis."

"He'll be all right," Nick said quietly, almost pouting as he continued to glare at the back of the cabbie's neck. Nick needed to punch something. His mood had changed drastically in the past twenty minutes.

Ten minutes before the call had come, he suddenly remembered the rather trying meeting he had scheduled for the next morning. Still he was eagerly looking forward to getting home with Sue, getting her into bed. He'd had just the right amount of Dom Perignon to make him erotically amorous, and a good sexual performance would help relieve the slight guilt he felt for giving his wife reason to be jealous. Then he, too, had been sure that Severin was throwing one of his old temper tantrums, and Nick saw himself falling asleep alone while Sue tried to soothe the boy back to sleep. And he was always infuriated with himself when he allowed some callous salesperson, or in this case an asshole cabbie, to cause him to lose his temper. All that, plus the picture he still carried in his mind. Tara Dobbs. Yes, he needed to hit something.

"Turn in on Sixty-ninth Street," he said quietly to the cabbie as they passed Sixty-seventh Street. "It's in the middle of the block."

For the first time that evening, Sue leaned forward and kissed him. "You look tired," she smiled wanly. "Don't worry. It can't be anything serious."

52

IV

"It's not fair!" Sue said sobbing, burying her face in Nick's shoulder. "No matter how rotten this fucking world seems to be at times . . . impossible to understand, let alone explain . . . it's supposed to be safe for children. He's a *baby*! He's supposed to be happy and carefree and . . . we were supposed to provide a safe haven for him. Us! You and me! We . . ." She pulled back, jerking with tears, and looked into Nick's reddened eyes.

"It's not our fault, Sue," Nick said quietly, attempting to soothe her mounting hysteria. "It's not our fault."

"Then you make him understand that!" she shouted, beating at his chest with her fists. "You make him . . . understand . . ." Her voice trailed off as she cried tears of bitterness and helplessness.

The doctor had ruled out appendicitis at once. Perhaps it was a blockage of the intestines which was causing the boy to cramp in pain. Then there were X rays and more X rays, then a casually ominous mention of carcinomata . . . not carcinoma but carcinomata, plural. Immediate exploratory surgery would be required, and the place for that would be Sloan-Kettering.

Then Sue and Nick had been stunned that the surgery had been completed in so short a time. They saw Sev briefly as he was wheeled from OR 7 into the recovery room. He was quite pale from the anesthesia and the ordeal of surgery, but he still had the appearance of an indestructibly healthy boy. Sue was mentally flogging herself for not following up on Miss Fryer's report that Sev had complained of stomach aches. Sue couldn't bring herself to tell Nick that she had ignored the warning, especially not now. The guilt she felt, however, was almost strangling.

Then they were seated in the small white office and the doctor had been mercifully direct. Cruelly direct, Sue had thought at the moment, unable to think clearly and realistically. Their son's abdomen was riddled with malignant tumors. Inoperable cancer. The boy's condition was obvious and indisputable, so he had been sutured up at once and taken to the recovery room. Severin David Arcomano, alive and seemingly healthy, was going to die.

Nick had buried his face in his hands and cried unashamedly. Sue could only stare at him and pat his back mechanically. Her tears had been dammed up by the paralyzing shock of it all, plus the overwhelming guilt she felt, but kept to herself, for not having Sev examined after the teacher's prophetic signal.

"We'll start him on chemotherapy at once," the doctor had said, "and of course, there are drugs for the pain, but . . ."

"What about Laetrile?" Sue asked dully.

The doctor removed his glasses and pinched the bridge of his nose as he shook his head. "In my opinion . . . and please feel free to have me second-guessed . . . in my opinion, it's no more than a placebo. Not that I'm discounting the therapeutic value of the placebo, you understand . . . far from it. Too many of my colleagues fail to understand that at times the most rapid cure can be obtained simply by having the patient *believe* that he is on the way to recovery. The human body is possessed of the most miraculous powers of healing itself. Interferon is perhaps the most important medical discovery of the century. Its healing qualities will boggle our minds when we have truly unlocked its secrets. The human mind knows already and it can release the wondrous substance as the situation requires. And if a placebo can trigger the release of interferon . . . I'm sure you understand. Laetrile has not been proven. . . ."

"How long does he have?" Sue asked quietly, finally feeling the warm relief of tears.

"His liver is . . . it's going to happen rather quickly, I'm afraid. A matter of months . . ."

It was half past six in the evening when they finally moved Sev into a private room. The young nurse told Nick and Sue that he probably would come out of the anesthesia shortly.

"What'll we tell him?" Nick said, brushing the hair off the pale, smooth forehead. "We have to tell him the truth, don't we?"

Sue nodded yes, but her mind shouted no! "But how can we?"

"We've got a very bright little guy on our hands. He'll know.

And I think we've got to be strong enough to be open and honest about it. He'll probably be able to understand it and accept it better than we can. He's only been here a short time and . . ." Nick let himself go completely again, for the third time that day, hoping to get all the crying out of the way before his son came to.

Sue threw her arms around him and they cried together. "Oh, Nick, I love you so much. I love you . . . and I need you even more." The thought of telling him stopped the flow of tears almost at once. She rubbed her cheek against the soft, dark curls, then pulled back slightly as she felt the rough stubble on his cheek. "You need a shave." But she had to tell him. She had to. "I hope you don't hate me . . . for what I have to tell you. It's all my fault, Nick. It's all my fault. If I had only told you . . . you'd have insisted that we take him to a doctor then. I know you would have . . . and maybe then, earlier . . . they could have . . . I don't know . . . stopped it." The tears started again.

"What are you talking about?" Nick asked, pulling back to look at her face. He rubbed his forearm across his nose, sniffing.

Oh, my God, oh, my God, oh, my God! "Sev's teacher told me . . . one day I went to see her to see how he was doing . . . and she told me that . . . that he'd been complaining about stomach aches." Sue broke into sobs again. "And I ignored it! I did nothing! He just seemed so . . . so strong and healthy that . . . I just couldn't believe that there could be anything *seriously* wrong with him. You know how kids . . . I used to invent stomach aches whenever I didn't want to go to school . . . and . . . it's all my fault!"

"Stop it, baby. You can't blame yourself for something like that. And I'm worse than you are, you know that. I won't go to a doctor unless my arm is hanging by a . . . whatever your arm would be left hanging by."

"A tendon?"

"A tendon . . . a ligament, whatever. And telling me about it would not have changed anything. I'd have told you to forget about it, you know I would have. Nobody could have known. Sev almost looked ready to sit on the bench for the Jets."

Sue pulled back and managed just a trace of a smile. "Not New Orleans?"

Nick laughed, happy that he'd cheered her, if only slightly. "He could have *started* for the Saints this year!" They both felt better for the small joke.

"Did they take out my appendicitis?" Sev asked groggily.

Raymond Hines leaned the broom against the fireplace and walked out onto the porch of his sister's newly acquired Connecticut cottage. He took a wooden match from the small box, struck it against the carved, four-by-four porch support and held it to the end of the Camel. He took a deep drag from the filterless cigarette, leaned against the post and listened. He could just make out the music coming from the main house.

"New medicine, my ass," he snorted to himself. Something weird was going on in that house. Three days ago, that old man could barely hobble about. Now he was wandering around the house, up and down the stairs, poking his nose into the kitchen. And stranger still, playing that violin, which he had ordered sealed up in that room. The swelling was almost gone from those joints, which had been sickeningly twisted by what he said was arthritis. Something unreal definitely was afoot up there.

Hines considered himself very lucky that the old man hadn't chewed his ass out when that wall fell down. He'd known when he put it up that he wasn't putting enough support under the plaster, but he had gone right ahead with it anyway. He'd been very lucky that the old man hadn't blamed him for the mess. All that glass and stuff that smashed all over the floor probably was worth a lot of money too. He would have to watch his step now that Mr. Pedarius was prowling around again, checking up on what he had been doing.

"Precious little," he laughed defiantly to himself, tossing the butt out on the wet ground. There would be a lot more to do up there now, so he had better make a quick job of getting the guest house in order. Emma wouldn't pay him a nickel until he got it just as she wanted it.

As he picked up the broom, he made a mental note to do something about the dumbwaiter in the old house. It was going to fall one of these first days, and probably with a load of that expensive china.

"Shit!" he spat out as he stirred up the dust in the cozy little house.

Sue pulled the flannel pajamas down, looked at the puffy, red stitches, then leaned down and kissed his belly as she settled on the bed beside him. "Still hurt?"

"Yeah . . . you're sitting on my book."

56

"Oh, I'm sorry," she said with a smile, pulling the thin book out from under her. "Well, you get to go home tomorrow. That should make you happy, huh?"

"Yeah, but I can't kick the ball though with this, can I?"

"Well, not right away . . . but very soon you can. You don't want to pull the stitches out of that sweet little belly, do you?"

"Oh, *Mom*. When can I go back to Ryder?"

"Well, soon . . . too." Sue cleared her throat, hoping he would jump at the chance not to go back. "Then again . . . I suppose you could take the rest of the semester off . . . that is, if you wanted to. You probably wouldn't miss that much, do you think? And we could spend a lot of time together . . . going to the park, and . . . you know, just having a lot of fun."

"Can't kids with cancer be with other kids?" Sev asked solemnly.

"Of course they can," Sue said, struggling to maintain a calm exterior. "It's not contagious like . . . it's not contagious."

Sev idly gathered the sheet into pleats with his fingers. "Mom, am I gonna die?" he asked flatly.

Jesus Christ, help me! Against her valiant efforts, a sound somewhere between a gasp and a heavy sigh escaped her lips. Sue quickly coughed to try to cover the rush of emotion. "What a question," she got out while failing in her attempt at a small laugh. Jesus Christ! "Dying is part of living, Sev. Everything that's alive will have to die finally. Flowers and birds and animals . . . people. Every living thing finally dies. That's the way things are. But not right away you won't . . . you're not . . ."

"Does it hurt?"

Oh, God, couldn't somebody please come into this room? Even that fat, crotchety nurse would be a welcome interruption. "No, I don't think so. Usually it's more like . . . like just going to sleep, I think." Sue forced a smile. "But why are we talking . . ."

"Does that keemothurpy hurt?"

Yes, it's awful! "Chemo*therapy*. No, I don't think it'll be that bad," Sue lied, unable to do anything else. "Besides, we don't have to worry about that for a week or so." Sue got up off the bed and walked over to the window. "I wonder what time it is. Your daddy should be here soon." Sue knew she was on the verge of an uncontrollable crying jag. She'd best get down to the visitors' lounge at the end of the corridor.

Severin knew that his mother was trying not to cry in front of

57

him and tried to think of something to cheer her up. "You and daddy can have another baby, can't you?"

It was useless to try to contain the flood of tears, and so she gave in to them.

Nick Arcomano had always hoped for success but in reality he had never really expected it. And certainly not on the grand scale of Arcodan's meteoric climb. He was, however, very careful that no one suspect he saw himself as anywhere but at the very top. His well-hidden insecurities, his lack of faith in himself were borne of his extraordinary good looks.

He was an excellent student in the lower grades, all A's, but then in high school he suddenly stopped trying. It was at this time that he emerged from plumpish boyhood into a near-perfect male, almost too perfect to be believed. His boyishly pretty face suddenly was strong and darkly handsome, and as the baby fat melted away an Adonis-like body was revealed. All the girls wanted Nick Arcomano, and all the boys compared themselves to him.

For a while, Nick relished the adoration and in fact adored himself. But sometime during his senior year he began to see his handsomeness as a liability, and the teenage insecurities which developed were almost crippling. People were content to look at him rather than relate to him, he felt. It was assumed, by grown-ups as well as by his peers, that his emotional stability was as well ordered as his exterior. Somehow his physical makeup was supposed to be a shield against ordinary teenage anxieties. How could anybody look like that and still feel insecure about anything?

Subconsciously Nick Arcomano was aware of his native intelligence, but on the conscious level he played it down. That was why he stopped studying for a while, stopped applying himself. He was embarrassed that he might appear too perfect. He hated being constantly in the spotlight. Everything was too easy. Girls threw themselves at him, and while he relieved his healthy sexual appetite often, he seldom felt emotionally involved. Nick always wanted the girl who showed no interest in him. If he could get her, he knew he was being touched genuinely, that she cared for the caring man inside the glossy exterior.

Sue Goodwin had shown almost no interest in him—sexually, anyway—and so he wanted her desperately. She was madly in love with being in New York, full of dreams about a career, wanting to do everything and be everywhere at once. It took him a full month to persuade her to have dinner with him, and by that time he was already in love with her. He would have married her after coffee on that first date but she took her time falling in love with him. She didn't know it but that was exactly as Nick Arcomano preferred their relationship to develop. By the time she finally said yes, he was sure she really loved him and wanted him. And so it seemed perfect.

Your son is going to die!

The unreality of it. Like the news was meant for some other couple. It didn't fit in with the fantasies that had become reality. What possibly had either of them done to deserve this? Sue was a perfect wife and mother and now she was suffering overwhelming guilt because she ignored a complaint of a minor stomach ache. Stomach aches were as common as headaches and not reason enough to rush to the emergency ward. Wouldn't he have ignored the complaint as well? In retrospect, knowing what he now knew, it was impossible for Nick not to see himself as being more concerned. But it was just that—second-guessing, not reality. He couldn't blame her. He wouldn't.

Your son is going to die!

More likely, he was being punished for cheating on Sue. Three times? No, four. But the casual sex had meant nothing to him other than a momentary escape from the pressures of reality. Each time he had been faced with a depressing situation and had used the body of a beautiful woman to postpone coping with a seemingly unsolvable problem. Each encounter, however, only brought him closer to Sue, made him realize his love for her all the more. And never was there the slightest possibility that she could be aware of his indiscretion. This knowledge and the guilt were his alone.

Nick stared at the boards propped on the easel at the end of the room. He had to snap out of this debilitating depression. Sev was going to die. That was fact and he had to accept it. He loved his work and he had to bury himself in it instead of walking through the days like a zombie. Arcodan was rolling, steamrollering, because of his creative instincts and his innate power of persuasion, but he was slacking off. He had to spend more time with Sev, he wanted to, but that only meant that he had to be twice as aggressive when he was in the office. Jonathan Daniels was good, the partnership worked well, but Jonathan would be quite happy with half the business they now had. Arcodan's drive was Nick Arcomano, and he had to rev it back up to full speed.

"Well, what do you think, Nick?" the young man said as he tossed the styrofoam cup in the white, cylindrical basket.

Nick leaned back in the chair and put his feet up on the long table. "The graphics are great. I don't think we could come up with anything better. Nice colors . . . perfect."

The chubby young woman in the wool, wrap-around plaid skirt beamed as she curtsied. "Thank you very much. I tried to keep it clean and uncluttered. . . ."

"Unlike your life," the copywriter teased. "Bev, could we get some more coffee?"

"What, do you think she's some kind of servant?" the fat artist parried. "Not so much sugar in mine, Bev, okay? I'm trying to diet."

Nick shook his head no to the girl's offer of coffee as she passed his chair. He reread the copy as the two staffers exchanged further put-downs. Finally they ran out of insults and stood staring at Nick, waiting for his appraisal.

"I don't think the copy's quite right, Teddy," Nick said finally. "It's good, you understand, but I think we're gonna have a hard time selling them on it. It's . . . you know, launching a new brand of coffee is a bitch. It's got to be just right. People tend to pick a brand of coffee and stick with it forever. We've got to come up with something fresh enough, strong enough to make them give up their Folgers and Maxwell House and give this shit a try. I don't think this is it. We've got to kick this around some more."

"Well, we don't have too much kicking time," Teddy complained mildly. "We have to face those fuckers at two-thirty tomorrow afternoon."

Nick got to his feet as the girl came into the room with the coffee. "That's time enough to come up with three trendy slogans, Teddy, my boy," Nick said, flashing the disappointed copywriter his most dazzling smile, "and I know you're the man who can do it."

"Yeah, but making the new boards is . . . well, let me know if you think of anything." He pulled the cover sheet over the display. "And not a word from you, you bitch," he said to the artist, "unless you happen to have a wonderful idea. Do you, sweetheart?"

Nick and his assistant, Sandy Brandt, shared a deli lunch on the coffee table in his office as he spoke for an hour and ten minutes with Jonathan Daniels in the Los Angeles office. Between bites of rare roast beef, Sandy filled three pages in her steno book. Every ten minutes, Nick had to reassure his partner that there was no way he could come out to the Coast that week. They would have to work out any problems over the phone. And every fifteen minutes, Nick would remind Daniels that they were on a speakerphone and that Sandy was not interested in his romantic escapades with Hollywood's finest.

Finally, Nick clicked off the speakerphone, leaned back with a sigh on the burgundy cushions and loosened his tie. He desperately needed a vacation from everything. Maybe the month of August. Suddenly his eyes flew open. They wouldn't have Sev in August. Poor baby Sev. Poor Sue. Poor Nick.

"Don't get too comfortable, my poor, tired friend," Sandy Brandt said. "You've got the Fleurama Perfume people in fifteen minutes. The room's all set and there's champagne in the fridge. It shouldn't be too hard to take, though. Selecting 'The Fleurama Girl' from a luscious collection of hopefuls? Me, I'll just spend the afternoon trying to decipher my notes amid all these greasy roast beef stains. Life is hard, isn't it, boss?" Wrong thing to say, dummy, she thought as she started to clear the remains of lunch. "How's little Severin?"

The two slick-looking types, both in gray pinstripes, were doing most of the talking, but Nick knew that the decision would be made by the carefully made-up older woman who sat back in her chair, legs crossed, with her immaculately manicured red nails drumming slowly and quietly on the leather arms. She probably was between sixty and seventy years old, but her hair was a pale blond and her skin was stretched taut from several expert lifts. Her extravagantly expensive wool outfit exactly matched the lightest gray of the fluffy chinchilla which was spread on the back of the molded leather chair.

"It's your show, of course," Nick said, smiling directly at the woman after the fourth girl had been thanked and dismissed, "but I think it'll be a mistake to select a girl who looks too modelly . . . too high fashion. These girls all have been lovely, gorgeous . . . but not one of them has had a body. They're all angular and straight and thin . . . not thin, skinny. Right now the trend is away from that look, toward a more healthy, realistic, uh . . . easier to identify with . . ."

"Tits and ass?" the woman said with a slight smile, getting right to the point.

Nick laughed. "T and A, exactly. But tinged with a worldly sophistication. Just a touch less natural than your average beautiful woman. A cut above, yet still reachable. Does that make any sense?"

"Well, uh," one of the men ventured while doodling on the pad in front of him, "I thought . . ."

"Precisely what we want for Fleurama," the woman said, smiling her agreement to Nick. "Don't you agree, Charles?"

The other man fingered his tie and straightened slightly, "Right on the nose. If we could . . ."

"Hand me those pictures, Charles," the woman said, pulling the chair closer to the table and setting the reading glasses low on her nose. "There was one dark-haired girl here", she said almost to herself as she examined the color shots, "who had . . . ah, yes. If she's anything like her photo, she may be our girl." She pushed the photo down the table toward Nick. "What do you think of her, Beauty?"

Nick, startled by her directness, smiled and opened his mouth to say something.

"Don't thank me, and please don't blush," she flirted. "You'll spoil my fantasies." She smiled wider as she placed a thin, brown cigarette between her lips. "Well, what do you think?"

Nick was taken aback when he glanced at the photo. Fate. He was both pleased and slightly disturbed. It was a photo of Tara Dobbs.

"Well?" the woman demanded, taking a light from an attentive Charles.

"She's stunning." And very right, Nick knew at once, as he remembered her crossing the floor at Buck and Mandy's. Nick picked up the phone and buzzed. "Is Tara Dobbs out there?" The girl outside checked her list, then told him she was not scheduled until four o'clock. "Let me know when she gets here, all right?" Nick replaced the phone and stood up. "She's not due for another twenty minutes. We can either see a couple more girls, or we can take a champagne break."

The woman gracefully rose from the chair and moved over to the window. "Don't you ever say or do anything wrong? I'll bet you even know that the champagne shouldn't be served too cold."

"Doesn't everybody?" Nick grinned as he moved across the room toward the concealed bar.

"Do they, Charles?" the woman said pointedly.

Nick decided that Charles was unaware that the woman was digging at him as he eased the cork out of the magnum of Taittinger. He tried not to think about seeing Tara Dobbs in less then twenty minutes, but he thought of her nevertheless. And it was impossible to think about her with thinking of Sue. Then he remembered what Sue had said that morning. It was perfect!

He poured the champagne, then excused himself as he picked up the phone and dialed.

"Teddy? Nick," he said, turning his back to the Fleurama threesome. "The coffee that tastes as good as it smells." He smiled and waited. "Of course it's perfect. How do you think I got to the head of the company."

Nick sent a mental thank you to Sue as he turned his charm back to the wealthy vamp. He also should have sent an apology to his wife for what he was thinking about Tara Dobbs.

The deterioration had begun almost at once and proceeded at an alarming rate. Sev lost his appetite just after the first chemotherapy session and never regained it. Anna made him all his favorite things five and six times a day, but he had no hunger for anything. The boy had a violent reaction to the chemotherapy and hated it almost worse than the pain.

Sue watched in horror as the flesh seemed to melt off the husky, five-year-old frame. Then she began to find tufts of hair on his pillow every morning, and his skin turned a dull, yellowish gray. It was much more heartbreaking than she had possibly imagined. That Sev was being so brave about the entire nightmarish decline made it even more impossible for Nick and Sue to face their imminent loss. Sue spent every waking moment with him. Then in the evenings Nick would lie on his bed with him and they would talk for hours. Anna Polanski's eyes were constantly red and puffy.

Finally, Sev was completely bald except for one scraggly tuft of hair on the left side of his head.

"Come with me," Sue said, taking his hand and leading him toward the bathroom. "We're going to do something about that wild hair of yours."

She cut the ugly strand off with the scissors, then rubbed shaving cream on the stubble and shaved it clean with Nick's razor.

"There," she said, wiping his head dry with a towel. "Now

63

you are quite handsomely bald. No more combs. You've got a wash-and-wear head."

Sev stared at himself in the mirror. "You like me better with that wig, don't you?"

"I do *not*," Sue said honestly. "You were quite right about not wanting that sleazy-looking rug on your head. You look much better without it." It had looked awful, but Sue had thought it might make him feel more comfortable.

"Don't I look like the space people in that movie?"

"*Close Encounters*?"

"Yeah, don't I?"

"You do not, silly," Sue lied. His head did appear much too large for his frail body. You could count every rib in his narrow chest, and his bony arms and legs seemed exceptionally long. More than a creature from outer space, he resembled one of Cambodia's starving children from the seven o'clock newscast. "You look like Severin David Arcomano, son of Nicholas and Susan, and we're proud of you, shiny head and all."

"Oh, *Mom*."

This was Buck's third evening visit inside a month and it was almost impossible to get him anywhere outside the recording studio. Mandy was over almost daily. And as usual, Buck brought along more expensive computer toys, two this time. Nick, Sev and Buck were stretched out on the carpet playing with some beeping toy, laughing as if they were having the time of their lives. Mandy and Sue sat on the padded seat in the bay windows, overlooking Sixty-ninth Street, sipping spiked coffee.

"You're certainly going to hold onto Anna, aren't you?" Mandy asked quietly. "That woman is a magician in the kitchen. Chicken Kiev is my new favorite. I want it at least twice a week for the rest of my life."

"You should see what she stirs up for Sev, seven or eight times a day. But he won't eat. I sometimes think he's trying to rush it along . . . starving himself, I mean."

"Poor baby. He looks . . . I'm sorry to say this, but you certainly see it for yourself . . . he looks much worse than he did on Monday, even."

Sue nodded her agreement. "I know." Sev's head was beginning almost to bobble on his reed-thin neck. Sue shook her head sadly. "I think I'm going to discontinue the chemo. Sev hates it so much he starts to cry the night before he has to go in. And it's obviously having little or no effect on him, aside from making him deathly nauseous, I mean. Nick told him earlier this evening that he didn't have to go for it tomorrow, so I think we may just as well call it off permanently." She turned and looked deeply into her friend's eyes. "I've also thought at times, more than a few . . . about giving Sev sleeping pills and just getting him out . . ."

Mandy took Sue's face in her hands and kissed her directly on the mouth, then pulled her close in an embrace. "Don't!" she whispered urgently in Sue's ear, beginning to cry softly at the same time. "Don't, Sue. Take him off the chemotherapy if you want, but don't"—Mandy sniffed and straightened up, wiping the tears from under her eyes—"don't . . . do anything yourself. It'll be much harder to reconcile yourself to the loss if you . . . do something like that. Promise me you won't?"

Sue got a smudge from under Mandy's lash with her little finger. "I'm not even sure I could . . . even if I thought it best for him."

"Don't!" Mandy said, her eyes pleading. "I promise you it would be wrong."

"Mom," Sev called in a rather weak voice, "see if you can do this. I can."

"Yeah, Mommie Sue," Buck laughed. "Let's see if you've still got your musical chops. All you have to do is repeat the notes this here machine plays for you. You think she can do it, Severino?" he said, wrapping his huge hand completely around the boy's thigh.

Even though the doctor assured them it would be easier for all of them, Nick and Sue absolutely refused to put the boy in the hospital to die. They would administer the pain-killer themselves and had more than enough on hand for when it was needed. But as Sev grew weaker and weaker, he complained less and less about pain. He just seemed to be slipping painlessly, closer and closer to death. Then suddenly one night, that dreaded moment was upon them. For months they had known that this night would arrive and still they were not prepared for it.

Nick had fallen asleep on the bed beside him and was awakened by the rasping sounds of Sev's breathing. One look at the boy's colorless face and the ominous rattle of his breathing told him that his son was about to die.

65

Nick didn't want to call loudly to Sue, so was just about to run to the bedroom for her when she walked into the room. One look at Nick's teary-eyed face told her everything. She rushed to the opposite side of the bed and knelt over the gasping boy.

"Sev!" Her voice was already choked with emotion and a tear dropped onto the boy's forehead. She wiped it away and felt the coolness of his skin. Sev was dying. "Sev, can you hear me? It's Mom . . . and Daddy . . . can you hear me? Sev!" She took his hand and pressed it to her lips as the tears rushed down her cheeks.

Nick cupped the cool cheek in his hand and bent close to the boy's ear. "Sev, we love you. We love you very much." He suddenly heard the sound behind him and turned to see Anna Polanski, standing in the doorway crying. "Come, Anna. Come and kiss your boy good-bye."

Nick draped his arm about the woman's back as she leaned down and kissed Sev on the lips. "I love you, baby," she choked out. "Good-bye, my sweet angel." Anna Polanski turned and moved away to the end of the bed. "Shall I call the doctor?"

Nick nodded his head and the woman left to place the call. Sue was stroking his forehead when suddenly Sev's eyes opened slowly. He looked first at Sue, then slowly his eyes moved to Nick. His body jerked sharply, his eyes widened into a frightened stare fixed on the ceiling and his breathing slowed to near stopping.

"You know how much we love you, Sev," Sue whispered lovingly, "I know you do. And you must believe me that where you are going is more wonderful than you could possibly imagine. More wonderful than any story I ever read to you. There'll be other children just like you and . . . and everything good that you could possibly dream of . . ." Sue held her breath as Sev's eyes slowly rolled up in their sockets and his eyelids slowly fluttered closed.

The boy lay very still. There was not a sign of movement in the bony chest, and Nick's fingers could feel no sign of life. Sue placed her hand lightly on top of Nick's, and together they shed tears of sorrow for themselves and tears of relief that their son's agony was at an end.

V

At first, it was a deep, black void behind Sev's closed eyes. Then tiny pinspots of reddish-orange appeared, here and there, suddenly running together, blending, spreading until the entire spectrum blazed with fiery orange. Up from the bottom of the infinite vision, a white mist began to rise, slowly at first, then churning up, around and across in great rolling clouds of white, blinding in their brightness. With one great whoosh the bubbling stopped, and everywhere there was a cool, soft whiteness, serene and inviting.

He heard his mother's quiet sobs for a few seconds, then they began to blend with the high-pitched voices echoing through the soft, opaque fog. Children's voices. She had promised him there would be other children. His mind smiled. But he couldn't make out what the children were saying, the voices were too shrill and muted.

Then the fog began to swirl and he could see their outlines moving toward him, running in slow motion, all of them clothed in the brightest white. They were waving their arms above their heads, and their hands left crystal trails in the bluish-white behind them. But they were all yelling at once and he couldn't hear. Then the voices began to blend into one and their figures became more distinct, but he could not distinguish features because of the bright backlighting.

"Goooooo backkkkkkkk!" The high voices reverberated around and back, then back again. 'Gooooooobackkkkkkkk!" Their hands, over their heads, whooshed toward him, trailing light, forcing a warm breeze around his entire being. "Goooo backkk. You must be our force, Severinnnnn Arcomanooooo. We will help you so that you may help us. Listen to us and you are our power. Believeeeee, Severinnnnn. Just believe and you

are. Hear us. Hear us! HEAR US!!!! GOOOOO-
BACKKKKKKK! Gooo back. Go back."

The voices faded as the fog swirled about them. The white
clouds boiled up again, then were sucked up quite suddenly,
leaving an inky void which stretched forever.

Severin felt a sharp jolt and was aware that his left arm had
jerked up to his face. He slowly opened his eyes and was at once
aware that he felt better than he had in months. There was that
gnawing in his stomach, but now it was familiar and welcome.
He was hungry. He heard the murmur of their voices just outside in the hallway.

He had strength enough to stretch and he knew his voice
would be stronger.

"Mom?" He listened as their voices stopped suddenly. Then
they were both in the doorway, staring at him, mouths agape.
"Mom, I'm hungry."

Closely akin to a miracle, the doctors all had agreed. Truly
astounding. Some of the carcinomata had shrunk to no more
than scar tissue, and the three remaining were now benign tumors and shrinking rapidly. And the original diagnosis and
prognosis were not innaccurate, that had been their first concern. The boy was making an inexplicable recovery. The only
possible explanation was that the boy had somehow convinced
his "cure center" to release massive amounts of interferon to
combat and defeat the invading killers.

Sue knew her way around the nine-building complex of
Sloan-Kettering as well as she knew the amazingly simple lay-
out of midtown Manhattan. And the red and brown cards that
identified authorized visitors at Sloan-Kettering were as familiar as her Bloomingdale's charge plate. She even knew her way
through the underground passage that connected the radiation
treatment building to New York Hospital.

She felt relaxed and confident, for the first time in a month,
as she sat with Mandy Buchanan in the visitors' lounge just up
the escalator from York Avenue. She was now convinced that
Sev was recovering, and she could watch a doctor approach
without feeling all the blood drain from her face.

"East Hampton would have been perfect ten years ago,"
Mandy said, tapping her cigarette against the stainless-steel
rim of the ash receptacle. "But now it's like a zoo out there in
the summer. Can you imagine? Bumper-to-bumper traffic . . .

for miles . . . in East Hampton? It's impossible to escape anymore."

The doctor had suggested that Sev's recovery might be speeded even more if they got him out of the city, into the peace and quiet of the country. Now Sue was trying to think where.

"It's got to be close enough so that Nick can come out on weekends . . . if he can tear himself away from the fluff factory long enough . . ."

"Bitchy, bitchy," Mandy teased. "Nick keeps us isolated, uninformed housewives abreast of the very latest in must-have products. . . ."

"All of them 'new and improved,'" Sue said with a laugh, "lemony fresh and packed with energy-producing sugar. Anna has discovered the perfect use for TV. She uses it as a nightlight."

"I hardly ever watch it myself," Mandy lied, digging about in her purse, "and when I do, I'm certainly not influenced by the commercials." She made a big show of spraying her neck lightly with the small, silver Fleurama atomizer. "I buy only those products I know to be . . ."

"Who's being bitchy?" Sue said, and grinned, snuffing her cigarette. "Nick had nothing to do with selecting her. The Fleurama people brought her. . . ."

"Do you still believe the Easter Bunny leaves those . . ."

"Mandy, you can't judge all men by the way Buck beha—"

"Time out! Tick-a-lock!" Mandy said, laughing. "Oh, you're so vicious. Why must you always retaliate? You know Nick loves you to pieces. You have nothing to worry about from . . ."

"Did I tell you?" Sue said smiling sweetly. "Nick tells me that Tara Dobbs wants to be a singer. Maybe Buck would be interested in hearing . . ."

"I'm getting just the slightest headache. Do you think we might . . ."

"I thought you might."

"What about Maine . . . or Vermont? Nick could fly up. Oh, here he comes."

Sue turned and waved at Sev across the room. He saw them and broke into a rather pathetic skip toward them. Sev still was bony but his color was much better and his hair was growing in again, light brown and straight. He looked like a small, thin Marine recruit fresh from the barber. Sue looked past him at the young doctor standing behind the glass doors, who smiled and held her hand up in an "A-okay" signal.

"Mom, can we go see Billy?" Sev said, resting his hands on her knees and kicking his toe against the floor.

"Sure," Sue smiled, rubbing the soft, short growth on his head. Now that he had some again, Sue didn't think she'd cut his hair until it reached his shoulders. "I'm sure Billy will be very glad to see you, Sev. You two are good friends."

"Do I want to go?" Mandy mouthed silently toward Sue.

Sue shook her head no, frowning briefly. It was heart-breaking to look at the seventeen-year-old football player. His once-bulging biceps were now pathetically stringy, and the last time Sue had seen him his right eye had almost been pushed out of his head by the malignant growth behind it. The tall, once-strapping youth seemed very much out of place in the children's ward, but there he was, wasting away slowly but surely. His parents refused to allow the doctors to tell the boy that he was dying, and the teenager could not survive surgery. So he lay there enduring what must have been excruciating pain, nauseating radiation treatments, maybe still hoping to walk out alive to resume his athletic career. Sue had been furious at first that they weren't telling the boy the truth, but now that Sev had recovered so miraculously she wasn't so sure anymore.

"Well, Sev," Mandy said, adjusting her skirt, "I'd like to meet your friend but I've got to run. And crosstown, too. Can you imagine the traffic at this hour?" She bent to kiss Sev. "Bye, baby. Call me later?"

The young athlete was receiving radiation. Sue let Sev watch him for a few minutes on the TV monitor outside the room, then convinced him that Billy wouldn't feel like talking to him after the session. They would visit him very soon, she promised.

What a wonderful staff they had here, Sue remembered as she watched the young volunteer carry a tray of three single flowers vased in Perrier bottles into the ward. And how heart-breaking it had to be for them all, watching so many children suffer.

She smiled as she noticed that Sev's calves were fleshing out a bit.

Anna Polanski stopped stirring the beef stew and rested the wooden spoon on the edge of the pot as she listened. He was doing it again. The first two or three times she had heard him she had gone in to see whom he was talking to. His mother had known about it and surmised that it was a result of those long,

70

lonely days alone. Anna smiled to herself as she moved quietly toward the music-room door to have a peek at him. She assumed she must have had imaginary friends when she was young, too, but she couldn't specifically recall. She certainly remembered talking to her corn-husk dolls.

Sev sat on the window seat, one leg folded under him and the other dangling down, kicking idly against the pale yellow paneling. The sun was bright outside the tall bay window and created an aura around the boy. Anna watched in amusement as he seemed to listen, then shake his head in agreement with an unheard voice. He rolled a soccer ball in front of him, controlling it with his right forefinger. Then she saw his lips begin to move and she heard a slight murmur but could not distinguish his words.

"I know numbers," Sev was saying softly. "I can count past one hundred. When you get there, you just start over again. It takes you longer to say them, that's all the difference is." He stopped and listened again. "And A, B . . . letters too." He nodded his head. "I can write them both, letters and numbers. Yes, I can too."

Anna pulled her head back and stealthily crept back to the kitchen to tend to her stew. Her good cooking would have that boy as strong and sturdy as ever and quicker than anybody expected. How would she stand it when Sue took the boy to a country place to speed his recovery? She'd have to stay there to care for Nick and the house, but she didn't know how she could get along without her little boy. Of course, she'd have him back in the fall.

She jumped and almost upset the pot on the stove as Sev ran through the kitchen and up the stairs. "Where are you going, Sev?" she called after him, wiping her hands on the white apron.

"I want a pencil and a paper," he called back. "Will you make some more cookies?"

Anna moved back to the stove, very pleased with herself and anticipating his surprise when she told him she'd already baked a fresh batch of the thin, crisp, vanilla-flavored wafers. She loved them even more than he did, but he was the one she needed to fatten up. But not too many of them, she thought, preparing to be stern when he seemed determined to eat the entire batch. She glanced up at the clock. Mrs. Arcomano wouldn't be back for another two hours or so. Anna almost hoped the house

71

on Long Island that Sue went to look at wouldn't be right either. She didn't want to lose them.

Fifteen minutes later, she dropped the pot holder and ran toward the music room. She didn't know what Sev had cried out, only that it was in an alarmingly loud voice.

"Sev, what are you doing there?" she called out as she saw him on his knees, looking out the open window down to the street.

"Up here, Mr. Saunders!" he called, waving his hand and laughing as he watched the elderly man try to determine who was calling to him. "Up here!"

He couldn't fall out of the window unless he wanted to, Anna thought as she knelt beside him, but still it frightened her whenever he pushed it open. She looked down just as the Shakespearean actor looked up.

"Ah, Severin, my boy," the old boy said, and laughed, tipping his tweed hat to them both, "how well you look. You'll be back with the soccer boys very soon. And a good afternoon to you, my dear Anna. We must have tea again very soon."

"We'd both like that, Mr. Saunders," Anna said with a quick smile, holding Severin around the waist.

"Did you see any kids playing over in the park?" Sev asked him, sitting back on the ball between his knees.

"Haven't made it there yet, my boy. I'll circle back that way. And if I see any of your friends, I'll tell them, 'Why, my very good friend, Master Severin Arcomano, can outrun the lot of you . . . and will be ready to do so very shortly.' How's that?" he called up, smiling broadly and affectionately.

"If you see Jimmy, would you ask him to come down to my house?" Sev asked.

"Now, which one is Jimmy again?" the old man asked. "Oh, never mind, I'll find him and you can be sure that I'll give him your message, er . . . your invitation. Well, I must be moving on . . . studying a part, you know . . . ta ta, both of you, and don't forget our tea. I'm available. . . ."

"Yes, I won't forget, Mr. Saunders," Anna said, pulling the window back. "Please don't open the window, Sev. I know you're a big boy, but still I worry. Are you getting hungry, angel?"

"Not yet," Sev said, rolling the ball over the printing on the page in front of him.

"Well, let me know when you are because it's all ready." Anna smiled at him and went back to the kitchen.

Sev moved his finger slowly along the numbers and letters he had carefully printed on the paper. He had printed smaller than he usually did and it didn't even look like his printing. He stopped to listen, then carefully folded the paper with the writing left on top.

"By the phone in her bedroom?" he asked softly.

Anna called after him again as he ran through the kitchen. "Now what?"

"I'm hungry," he called back as he climbed the stairs. "I'm going to wash my hands."

Anna shook her head in disbelief. Next thing you know, she thought, he'll be *asking* to take a bath.

"Well, it's about time I had a little luck," Sue said, backing the white Mercedes convertible into a spot directly in front of the town house. "Ooops, bite your tongue, Sue," she grimaced, thinking about Sev's recovery.

"I would think so," Jimmy Higgins said, knowing what she was thinking. "Your luck has been used up for the next twenty years."

"Tell me about it," Sue said, turning off the ignition. "Wasn't that place just the absolute pits?"

"They told you that place was quiet and secluded? Maybe at four in the morning, if you were lucky, it might be quiet. But secluded? Only a flash fire would have left you secluded."

"Jimmy, they've all been almost as bad. I'm so tired of looking at 'dream houses' . . . such phony, full-of-shit advertising. Forgive me, Nick . . . I just feel like screaming!"

"Go ahead. It's good for you. Honk the horn and scream at the same time. As a matter of fact, I could use a good scream myself."

Jimmy reached over and held the horn down, and the two of them screamed at the top of their lungs, then dissolved into raucous laughter.

"You're right, you idiot," Sue said with a laugh. "I feel much better. Come up for a drink? Please, Jimmy, it's Anna's night off and Nick probably won't be home for hours. Keep us company? Sev would love it and so would I."

Sev immediately trapped Jimmy into a game of Battleship, and while Sue mixed three Gibsons on the rocks, two of them with Boodles gin and one of them Seven-up with two cocktail onions, Anna gave her dinner instructions.

"The stew is on simmer, there's a nice salad in the refrigerator . . . just add the salad dressing . . . and bake the biscuits 12 minutes at 450. I'll see you in the morning." She stopped and smiled. "Sorry that the house wasn't what you were looking for."

"I know you, Anna," Sue smiled back. "You hope I'll never find anything. Well, I understand completely. Have a nice evening. I hear it's a good film."

While Jimmy Higgins mixed another round of Gibsons, Sue went upstairs to change and call Nick.

"Let's each have three onions in our Gibsons this time, Jimmy," she heard Sev say as she headed for the bedroom.

Sue cradled the phone between her chin and shoulder as she pulled on the tight designer jeans. "Oh, no, Nick . . ." she began to complain, then listened to the reasons why he couldn't get home for dinner. "I know . . . I do too understand . . . it's just that I've had a nice Gibson and . . . yes, from a water glass, you bastard . . . and I feel like having you." She did and she would, no matter how late he came home. "But I may be drunk by then. Oh, well, Jimmy's here so I may just seduce him instead." She laughed at Nick's immediate retort. "He does too like women, he just . . . oh, never mind." Sue wondered if Brooke Shields had this much trouble getting her body next to her Calvins. "The house sucked. I'm at my wits' end. I . . . okay, see you later. I love you."

As she hung up, she spotted the note on the nightstand by the phone. She picked it up and read the phone number. Underneath the number was printed, "Stonington, Connecticut." It didn't look like Anna's writing, or printing, but she assumed it must be. Or maybe Nick had left it there and she hadn't seen it until now. She pulled on a light blue T-shirt and carried the note downstairs with her.

"I'm winning, Mom!" Sev said with a laugh as Sue came into the room.

Jimmy Higgins looked stunned. "Winning? He's destroying me, if you'll pardon the pun. He knocked out both my destroyers and my cruiser with his first seven shots. Not a single miss, you understand? And only two misses in the last game. He's cheating somehow, but I can't figure out how. You are cheating, aren't you, Sev? It's all right, you can tell me. It's so clever I don't mind you're cheating. Just let me in on it."

"Nu-huh," Sev said seriously, shaking his head no. "I'm not neither cheating."

"Either," Sue said, settling on the sofa beside the cellist. "You're *not* cheating, are you, Sev?" Sue asked, knowing full well that the boy didn't cheat at games.

"*Mom*," Sev complained, screwing up his face in disappointment.

"Then how are you doing it?" Jimmy Higgins asked, handing Sue her second Gibson.

"I can't tell," Sev said with a grin. "I'll show you, though."

Each player in Battleship had a graph-type board in front of him with a hundred squares, each line identified on top by letters from A to J, and down the side numbered from 1 to 10. Each player "hid" his fleet on the board, two destroyers represented by two adjacent squares, vertically or horizontally, one cruiser represented by three adjacent squares, and one battleship, which was four squares. Then, taking turns, each player would have five shots in an attempt to sink the other player's fleet, calling out, for instance, "A 2, C 4, G 5," etc. At the end of a player's "shots," the other player would have to tell the shooter if he had scored any hits and on which type of ship. Each player kept a record of the shots he called on his own board and could, therefore, eventually track down his opponent's ships and sink them.

"Okay, Sev, Sev, have at my battleship," Jimmy Higgins said, sipping the Boodles gin. "Now, watch this, Sue. I think we can take this act on the road."

Sev concentrated for a moment, frowned slightly for an instant, then slowly nodded his head. "B 5, B 6, B 7 and B 8." He stopped and looked at both their faces, knowing from the double look of surprise that he had done it again. "Did I do it, Jimmy?"

Jimmy turned and looked at Sue's surprised expression. Sue looked behind them, knowing there was no mirror there, but looking for some explanation.

"And he didn't see my board," Jimmy assured her. "I made certain of that this game."

"How did you know to call those four squares, Sev?" Sue asked. "How could you possibly know those . . . eleven squares out of . . ."

"A hundred," Jimmy Higgins prompted.

"A hundred? How did you do that?"

Sev grinned and clasped both hands between his knees, rocking back and forth. "I don't know. I'm just good at this game, I guess."

"'Good' is not the word for it," Jimmy said, and laughed. "We've got a new Houdini on our hands."

"Tell me this, Houdini," Sue said, holding out the note. "Do you know who this is from and what it's about?"

Sev had to think a minute. He knew what to say. "It's . . . a nice cottage for rent . . . that Mr. Saunders told us to tell you about."

"How nice of him," Sue said, examining the note closer. "Do you know where Stonington, Connecticut, is, Jimmy?"

While Jimmy humored Sev with a pretend concert of piano and cello, Sue stretched out on the burgundy velvet contoured chaise at the far end of the room and dialed the number in Connecticut.

"Hello?" the woman on the other end said, rather gruffly.

"Who am I speaking to?" Sue asked, thinking that "To whom am I speaking?" always sounded a bit stilted.

"Who did you want to speak to?"

"Well . . . I don't know, really," Sue said, slightly put off by the woman's impatient sound. "Someone gave me this number and told me that you had a cottage for rent . . . in Stonington?"

Emma Hines was taken aback. She hadn't even placed an ad yet. The cottage was ready, but how could this woman have known about it? One of two ways. Either from her brother and his big mouth, or from Mr. Whatsizname. But what the hell, it was ready to go.

"Yes, yes, that right," Emma Hines said, intending to sound more friendly but not too eager. "It's a wonderful cottage, very private, with a private beach right down the path." If she could get a thousand dollars a month, she'd be able to furnish the place a little nicer. "I'm asking twelve hundred dollars a month."

Sue kept telling herself not to get too excited as she shoved the pan of biscuits into the oven. "Here I am believing the advertising again," she said, and laughed, "but Jimmy, it sounds just perfect. In the woods, secluded *and* a private beach. Of course, it is farther away than I had intended but . . . oh, it sounds perfect! Nick will just have to fly up if it takes too long to drive."

"Surely Arcodan has a private plane by now," Jimmy teased.

"Hardly," Sue said, slightly embarrassed by the thought that they *could* afford their own plane at this point. "I don't suppose you'd like a nice drive up to Connecticut?"

"Too much work," Jimmy apologized, pouring the dressing over the crisp green salad. "Take Sev along. He looks ready for it now."

"Hmmmm, maybe a bit too tiring for him yet," Sue said. "But isn't it amazing how healthy he looks? I still can't quite believe it. I'll drag Mandy along. She loves Connecticut." Sue suddenly became aware that Sev was standing in the doorway, rubbing one foot on top of the other. "Almost ready, Sev. Are you hungry?"

Sev nodded his head. "A cottage is a small house . . . cozy. And Houdini was more a es . . . scrape . . . escape artist than a mentalist."

Sue and Jimmy stared at each other, then she shrugged her shoulders. So perhaps he was even more exceptional than she thought. It was cause to feel proud, not to worry.

Sue turned the knob just slightly and the water was at once perfect. Now if no one flushed a toilet she could luxuriate in the steamy shower. Three contractors and the shower still was affected by a lousy commode. And after spending all that money, Nick now was making noises about a co-op apartment, a better location. Of course, the way real estate had skyrocketed they probably could turn a substantial profit on the town house. The neighborhood was becoming very chic, new restaurants popping up almost weekly. But she liked the friendliness of the area, and having the park one block away was perfect for Sev.

"Shit!" she complained as the stream of water from the shower head knocked the plastic cap off her head and wet her hair thoroughly. Oh, well, she thought as she reached for the fragrant shampoo, she'd just pretend she was Bo Derek rushing out of the warm Acapulco bay waters and into Nick's arms. She ran her hands over her slick breasts, imagining them against Nick's hard, hairy chest. She would miss him terribly up there. Weeks and weeks alone, except for weekends. Already she was preparing herself for those Friday calls, those "Sorry, baby, but I can't" calls. But the house was so perfect, fresh sea air, woods for Sev to play in and totally secluded. She would finally make her debut as a solo concert cellist . . . in the woods of Connecticut. Nick was right. It *was* too far away from the city, but it was right for Sev and he was their main concern for the immediate future. As for the immediate present, she wanted to run her tongue across the rippled belly of one, Nick Arcomano. And if he fell asleep in there with Sev . . .

77

Sue towel-dried her hair and combed it straight back, shaking it and loving the smell that drifted from it. Her skin was flushed and healthy-looking from the hot shower, and thanks to Mandy, her eyes looked perfect without makeup. Mandy had insisted that she come with her to Elizabeth Arden for a facial, then insisted that she have her eyelashes dyed. It was a masterstroke. Her lashes looked naturally thick and lush without having to bother with that messy brush. She also had Mandy to thank for talking Emma Hines into letting her have the cottage for a thousand dollars a month. Sue would have paid the twelve hundred dollars the woman had asked originally because the place was so right. But Mandy had insisted, again, that they dicker over the price, and the woman had agreed. Sue smiled into the mirror as she imagined herself and Sev laid out on the sand in the small cove, turning brown as berries under the hot sun. Then jumping up to greet Nick as he paid them a surprise visit, running down the path in a thin, yellow bikini.

Sue stood up, pulled the short, white terry robe around her and tied it loosely at the waist. You look fresh and clean and lovely, my dear, she thought, and very desirable. She was ready.

She stopped in the doorway and her heart sank. Nick was stretched out on the big bed on his stomach, on top of the comforter, sound asleep. His face rested on his hand, his mouth parted slightly and his breathing was slow and rhythmical. She felt like crying, or better yet, punching him. The brown briefs just covered his hard ass and his hairy, muscular legs were spread so as to take up most of the bed. Sue crossed her arms across her waist and sighed deeply, her shoulders slumping in disappointment. It seemed she could never get laid when she needed it anymore.

Nick could hardly keep from laughing. He knew precisely the expression on her face. Finally he opened his eyes and smiled up at her. "You like it?" he asked teasingly.

Sue felt her face light up as she broke into a wide grin. "Yeah, you bastard."

"Well, come and get it."

Sue knelt on the bed behind him, pulled the briefs down and bit him. Then she laid on his back, put her arms around his chest and nibbled on his neck and ear. "I thought you told me you didn't have time to go to the gym anymore."

"I don't," Nick groaned.

"You're full of it. You don't stay this hard without getting

78

out from behind that desk . . . and more than a few times. I'll bet you spend more time in the gym than you do with Sev and me."

"Wrong, you shrew," he laughed. He raised his head and looked over his shoulder. "And what was that you told me about Sev and Battleship? I don't think he even knows how to play it. He can't even keep track of . . ."

"I watched him, Nick. He called those letters off like he was looking directly at Jimmy's board." Nick shook his head, laughing. Sue pulled his hair playfully. "It's true, and you know Sev doesn't cheat . . . does he? And mentalist. What five-year-old kid knows things like Houdini was a *mentalist*? Huh? I ask you."

"He takes after me," Nick said lazily.

Sue sat up, slapped him lightly on the back and took off the terry robe. "I don't care how smart you are right now," she said, rubbing her bare breasts across his back, "I'm just hoping I've got a sex maniac on my hands."

Nick flexed the muscles in his back against her. "Ummmmm, what's that?"

"They're called tits, ape man," Sue whispered into his ear. "Roll over here and I'll show you what you do with them."

Nick rolled over on his back and gently rubbed his palms against her nipples as she freed his erection from the bikini briefs.

Severin smiled in his sleep as he saw the happy, carefree children vividly in his dreams. Everything was so green and the sun seemed to fall in giant rays on the softly curving hill. He longed to be in the circle, holding hands, as they went round and round, then fell laughing on the ground. Then they lay very quietly in a huddle as the woman's voice floated through the air, calling them down.

". . . Anyaaaaa. David, come down now, children. You must rest before dinner." The children giggled softly. "There's strudel baking." As one, the children leap to their feet and disappear over the rim of the grassy knoll.

Severin jerked in his sleep. The same three are now at a rather formal dinner table with adults. But the three children have grown taller, older, and Sev wonders why he has been left behind, still small.

79

". . . you must have more wiener schnitzel, Hans. I know it's your favorite." "He's feeding it to Rollo, under the table, Mama." "He is not, Mama!" the girl says adoringly. The boys snicker behind linen napkins.

Sev frowned as the children were suddenly coming toward him through the white haze, their loose garments flowing brightly around them.

You cannot tell them what we say to you, Severinnnnn. They will not understand. We are your secret and you are ours. Come. It's warm. There's no need to be afraid. Come.

The fog cleared and the children were standing up to their necks in calm, green water. Sev walked toward their outstretched hands, slowly and hesitantly. But the water was warm and he felt safe as he walked in up to his waist.

Come, Severinnnnn. You will float, soft and gently on the waters. Do not be afraid. Hear what we say and be safe.

Sev lay back and floated in the serenity of the warm, green wetness.

Sue sat astride Nick, her hands massaging his chest as she moved her body against the hardness within her, working ever closer to another orgasm. Soft sounds of erotic pleasure came from both their throats as Sue settled into a climactic rhythm and position. Almost subliminally she heard the click, then saw the movement of the door from the corner of her eye. Her head jerked around sharply as she grabbed for the comforter.

"Sev!" she cried out. "What are you doing?"

Sev stared wide-eyed and his thumb automatically came up to his mouth, something he hadn't done in years. He crossed his legs in embarrassment and stared as his mother pulled the cover over her nakedness.

Nick pushed the comforter out of his face, raised his head and looked at his son in the doorway. It was too funny. He fell back on the pillow, covering his face and laughing hysterically. "We're playing . . . we're playing Horsey, Sev."

Nick's body was jerking with laughter and Sue felt the movement beneath her. Then she began to laugh. "Sev, you're supposed to knock, you know that." She smoothed back her wet hair from her face and saw the hurt expression on the boy's face. "It's all right, Sev. Just remember to knock. What is it?"

He shuffled his feet. "I wet my bed." He wanted to add that it was "their" fault for taking him into the warm, green water. But they said not to tell, so he didn't.

VI

The newer leaves were a lighter green, but all of them had a waxy, fresh gleam. The birds chirped and flitted about, seeming to enjoy the bouncy ride they got on the weaker shoots of the elm trees. Everywhere was green and bark, new life stretching after the rather cold winter. Here and there amid the long blades of grass, clusters of Dutchman's-breeches sprouted, waving their delicate creamy-white double-spurred flowers. The warm sunlight filtered through the trees, creating bright patterns and different shades of green on the fresh dampness of the ground.

Sev sat cross-legged on the patchwork quilt in his private clearing, holding the soccer ball in his lap. Normally he would have chased the squirrel which stopped to eye him briefly before scurrying away through the undergrowth, but he was enthralled by the horrifying daydream they laid out so vividly before him. And frightened by it. He wished they would stop it.

. . . and once at Dachau, they were separated from their parents, huddled together in the gray bleakness. But these children were not victims of cancer. Their doomed look was the result of extreme cruelty, starvation and hopelessness. Their heads were crudely shorn, scratched and cut by the sadistically careless wielding of the shears. Packed like animals into boxcar trains and dumped inside barbed wire to rot with disease, drop from starvation or be suffocated with toxic gases, then charred in great ovens. The stench of burning flesh, the clouds of smoke in the damp, misty air, a glimpse of a loved one marching in a seemingly endless line of tattered skeleton-like creatures, the devastating sight made more surreal by the rapturous sounds of the violin floating on the thick air. Too many bodies in the graves to be real. It was only a nightmare and they would all soon wake in the fluffy warmth of their own beds to the smell of croissants and jam. . . .

The scream froze in Severin's throat as the large, black crow glided to a landing on the edge of his quilt. He kicked his feet wildly against the pallet, trying to get away from the ominous-looking invader. The bird squawked once, then flew off through the trees. Sev breathed a sigh of relief that he was back to reality. But then he froze suddenly and shivered again. The images were gone but the music still was faintly in the air. He was in his familiar clearing but the sounds of the nightmare remained. He stood up quickly, ready to run back to the cottage, to the safer reality of his mother.

As he watched the black-and-white ball roll away, he realized that the music was coming from the direction of the big house behind the walls, and it was so faint that he could barely make it out. But he couldn't shake the fright, so he decided to go back to the cottage. Besides, she would be calling him for lunch anytime now. He was very pleased with himself when he realized that he knew it *felt* like lunchtime.

Pedarius could not see them clearly, his eyes watery from the bitter tears, but he knew his fingers were slenderly agile as they danced about the neck of the Stradivarius. He brought the bow back and forth across the strings with effortless mastery, even though he was into the most difficult passages of the composition. He looked out through the open French doors toward the overgrown garden but he knew the hellishly tormenting images must play themselves through.

He sobbed out loud as he reached the trills which preceded the loud reports. He turned, almost defiantly, in his anguish and stared at the huge stone fireplace. Through his blurred vision, the stones become horrifically similar to the inescapable rocky entrapment. And then the first loud CRACK! tailing off eerily in a hissing ricochet. A cry of agony as the maestro steeled himself for the series to follow.

In the back of the garden, amid the dark tangle of lush growth, Raymond Hines froze in position, gripping the cane pole by its very end and listening to the sounds coming from the house. When the music stopped, he strained his ears to hear the emotional outburst that always followed.

"You are ready for the nuthouse," he said aloud, shaking his head in bewilderment. He always thought that the emotional involvement displayed on the faces of some musicians on television was faked and phony, but the theatrics that old fool went through really took the cake.

He took a puff on the wet end of the Camel and shoved the pole down until his fist was touching the top of the murky, green water.

"Goldfish pond, my ass," he said to himself in amazement, "this is a fuckin' well!" And deeper than fifteen feet too, since he still hadn't felt the bottom with the cane pole.

The "pond" was five feet across, round and rimmed by a low wall five bricks high. Tangles of water vines grew thick just below the surface and, he could tell by poking around with the pole, several feet down. It was dangerous and should be covered over.

"Shit," he said aloud again as he tossed the butt into the water and pulled the pole out. He knew there would be a lot more work now that the old man was out of his bedroom and wandering about again. *Now* he wanted the garden cleaned up. That weird old man, and Emma, would run him ragged this summer.

Sev sat stiffly in the chair at the table, gripping the seat on either side as hard as he could. He couldn't believe the awful pictures flashing in his head. He felt sick but he couldn't move. It really was going to happen!

Sue carried the pot of creamed spinach to the table and placed a good-sized spoonful onto Sev's plate. His whole body jerked just as she put the spoon back in the pan. She looked down at his face with a smile.

"Well, it's not that bad, Sev. I know it's not Anna's cooking, but I thought you liked spin . . ." She stopped in midsentence as Sev jerked back again, and for the first time she noticed that he looked a little pale.

Sev grimaced as he heard the loud CRACK! again. Then it was over. He swallowed hard and released his grip on the chair bottom. Then he was aware that his mother was staring at him.

"Sev?" Sue said, becoming more concerned. "What is it?" She set the pot on the table and bent down to feel his head. "Don't you feel well?"

Sev looked at her, then down at his plate. "I thought . . . we were having sandwiches."

Sue continued to look at him for a long moment, then followed his eyes back to the plate of food. She laughed as she realized that it didn't look particularly appetizing to her either. "Hmmmmm. I see what you mean. But it was a lot more trouble than sandwiches . . . and maybe it tastes better than it looks." She picked up the hot pot from the table and noticed the ring it left. "Oh, shit—pardon me, shoot—I've ruined her table." She rubbed at the mark with her fingers for a few seconds, then plopped some of the spinach on her own plate. "I admit I'm a bit out of practice in the kitchen so we'll just have to rough it until I get my chops back. Okay?"

"Okay," he said amiably, his mind having been distracted by the slight burn on the table. He picked up his fork and dug into the pile of creamed greens.

Sue sat down and tasted the food. Not bad at all. "It tastes pretty good, doesn't it?"

"Um-hum," Sev said, shaking his head and trying to swallow too big a mouthful.

"So what were you doing out there all morning?"

"Ummmmm, playing."

"Not bored yet?"

"No," he said, playing with the food on his plate with his fork as he chewed another bite. "Is Daddy coming this weekend?"

Nick usually hated *in* places, the ones that required clout to get into. Either celebrity, money, friends or a combination of the three. But Elaine's was different. He felt comfortable there *usually*. And it certainly impressed clients when he was ushered to a favorite table and afforded the friendly treatment of a regular. But tonight was different.

He felt comfortable knowing that the people who knew him and might see them there together would assume she was a client. And she was. But he felt uncomfortable knowing he was slipping closer and closer to making the mistake he knew he would regret.

Tara Dobbs felt guilty as well, but she wanted Nick Arcomano. Dating married men was nothing that bothered her unduly. They usually pursued her and she figured that this made it more their problem than hers. She hadn't met one yet that she felt any real involvement with. She had fun with men and on occasion she knew it would help her career. But this one was different. She liked his wife and she knew that he *loved* his wife, so

86

both of them felt guilty. But guilt or no, she was determined to have a go at this man, whatever the results.

Nick knew when she called him at the office with the impossible-to-get theater tickets that her "date" had not "fallen ill" at the last minute. He knew she was after him and that this was part of her plan. But the awful part was, he too wanted to see her.

"Can you believe he *wanted* to raise the top prices to fifty dollars a ticket? I mean thirty-five dollars is outrageous, but fifty dollars?" Tara tossed her perfect hair back and pushed a wild strand behind her ear. "Where do they expect to find people to pay those prices?"

Nick felt her knee brush against his. "I think Buck Buchanan is right. He thinks the theater producers are making the same mistake that the record industry made. They're pricing themselves right out of business." That wondrous scent floating around her had to be more than Fleurama. "People don't have that kind of money these days."

Tara Dobbs placed her hand on his and leaned closer. "Except us," she whispered jokingly. "Don't you feel the least bit uncomfortable slopping all that money away? It's indecent what they pay me. But the funny thing is, I never feel so guilty that I want to give any of it back."

They both laughed. "I know what you mean," Nick said. "Once you've made a little you forget the times when you struggled just to get the rent together. Suddenly it seems so *easy* . . . like, why can't everybody do this? And it is so easy you just want to get more and more. It doesn't mean as much as it once did, but getting it becomes an obsession. You just want to see how much of it you can get, you know?"

"I know," Tara Dobbs said, and smiled, looking directly into his eyes. "Do you think you could get me . . . if you wanted?"

Nick laughed to rid himself of the discomfort. "It hadn't crossed my mind."

Tara grinned wider. "Nor mine." She continued to watch Nick's face as the waiter slipped a plate of crepes onto the table in front of him. "And even if it had, I have a friend staying with me this week." She lowered her eyes seductively, picked up a fork and cut into the crepes.

The food suddenly reminded Nick that he hadn't called Anna to tell her he would not be home for dinner. "Oh, Christ," he said, lifting his napkin off his lap and standing up. "I have to make a quick phone . . ." He stopped in midsentence and flushed at being so flustered. Anna was off for the next two weeks. He was in more trouble than he thought. He wasn't thinking properly. Tara Dobbs had him just where she wanted him. And if he was totally honest with himself, just where he *wanted* to be. He thought briefly about going back to the telephone anyway, since he was already standing there like a fool. That *was* foolish. Instead he grinned rather self-consciously and sat back down. He reached for the fork and discovered that he was still holding his napkin in that hand.

Tara Dobbs knew she was very close. "You're not trying to get away from me, are you?"

"I'm not sure," he said softly. He hated remembering that the town house was empty and waiting.

When she smiled it was genuine, not the one she worked up for the cameras. "The crepes are delicious."

Sue was furious when she hung up the phone. Furious that she had tried to sound so understanding when Nick said he just couldn't make it this weekend. She had felt like screaming at him and she was furious with herself for not doing it. She was beginning to feel like she was in this thing alone. Her son was running around the woods talking to himself like some loony, and her husband didn't care enough about either of them to put off some of those "must-see people" to attend to the needs of his family. And she was furious that it was such a glorious day outside because now she knew she wouldn't enjoy it. Furious! She laid back on the pillow and made up her mind to stay in bed all afternoon to pout.

And now *he* wasn't listening to her. She jumped off the bed when she heard the screen door creak, and she ran through the living room. Her voice stopped Sev just as he was stepping off the porch.

"Sev!" she shouted irritably. "I told you to take a nap before you go back out there and I meant it. I insist that you rest for a while. That sun will be out all afternoon. Now, come right back in here."

Sev glared at her for a moment, twisted his mouth into three different expressions of defiance, then stomped back across the porch and through the doorway. "This is like being in Dachau!" he muttered as he passed by her.

Sue's mouth drooped in amazement as she continued to hold

the screen door ajar. She must have misunderstood him. "What did you say, Sev?" she asked as she watched him stomp across the room.

"I said it's like being in Dachau . . . or Auschwitz around here, you know?" he pouted. He turned back to her, his eyes both angry and hurt. "I don't need a nap."

Sue was stunned. She let the screen door close but stood riveted to the spot. "What did you say?"

"I said, 'I don't need a nap,' Mom," he whined. "I'm not tired. Please, can I go out?"

She forgot about being angry with him and moved over to him, unable to believe that he would know about those places. "No, no," she said, kneeling in front of him. "What did you say before that?"

"I don't know," Sev said, twisting his T-shirt, "I was just talking. Mom, could we get a dog?"

Sue ran her hand through his hair, marveling at its silky texture, remembering when it had not been there at all. The scraggly remnants she had finally shaved. He seemed healthy enough now, but he was acting strangely. "Do you know what Dachau is . . . was?"

"No," Sev fidgeted. "Can I have a dog . . . please?"

Sue racked her brain as she tried to imagine where Sev had heard about those places, much less remembered them. Granted, he was very bright, exceptionally so, but there was a limit to the exposure he had had in his short five years and there had to be a limit to his retentive abilities as well, assuming he had overheard someone talking about the concentration camps.

Tell her you're sleepy. "Mom, I'm sleepy. I want to lie down now, okay?" He pulled away and headed for his bedroom.

This startled Sue even further. He was consciously avoiding giving her the explanation she wanted. Needed. He wasn't sleepy and both of them knew it. He had cleverly lied when he felt she was pinning him down. What was going on now?

Sev was already in bed when she came into his room. She walked over and sat on the edge of his bed and began stroking his hair again. His eyes tried to avoid hers. Perhaps he was feeling guilty over the small lie he had told her.

"Can I have a dog?" he asked quietly, rolling on his side to face away from her.

Sue took a deep breath and sighed. She would get to the bottom of this later.

"We'll see."

Sev hadn't been that close to the wall before for two reasons. Sue had told him that he should stay close to the house, not to disturb the old man who lived in the big house and *never* to go down to the beach without her. Second, he was frightened by what might wait for him behind those walls.

"No," he said, shaking his head, "my mom said not to go down by that wall."

He booted the ball with his toe and it rolled ten feet and bounced back off a spindly sapling. The high brick wall was visible through the trees, some thirty yards away. He started to punch the ball again, then stopped and listened to them.

Take a short run and use the side of your foot.

Sev smiled in anticipation, backed up four steps, then ran at the soccer ball and brought his foot into it. His mouth dropped open as he watched the ball rise in an arc through the trees as if it had been booted by Pelé. Then he began to jump up and down laughing, thrilled that they had taught him so easily and quickly how to propel the ball like a professional.

"Wait'll my daddy sees me!" Sev laughed. "Yippee! Yippee! Yippee!" He giggled, jumping up and down and around in circles. Then he ran toward the wall to recover the ball to test his new technique again, skipping and swinging his arms around in circles.

He forgot his mother's warnings and his feelings about the wall as he waded about in the tall grass searching for the leather ball. *They* were becoming so much a part of him that he really didn't realize that he probably would not have seen the ball without their subliminal signals.

The ball had come to rest in a rather small, crumbling hole in the wall which otherwise would have been hidden by the tall grass. Sev stopped suddenly as he came into the shade of the brick barrier, realizing he was within three feet of the forbidden place. He looked up at the thick green vines growing over the top of the wall, then back down to his ball. He shivered and felt the gooseflesh rise on both arms. He wanted to get the ball quickly and get out of there.

He made a run toward the ball, tripped and fell headlong toward the wall. His hand just touched the black-and-white ball, which sent it rolling inside the garden and out of sight. He lay on his belly in the grass, panting. He felt a damp coolness come from inside and brush against his face. Cautiously, he pulled himself closer on his elbows and peered into the garden.

He could see his ball inside but it was too far away to reach. The green growth inside was lushly dark and shaded, and the smell of damp earth was heavy. He pulled back slightly and examined the hole in the bricks. It was too small to squeeze through.

Sev got to his knees and pushed on the two rows of bricks just above the hole. The bricks moved slightly, then three rows gave way and fell rather noisily to the ground. He could now easily crawl through the opening if he could muster the courage to do so. He took a deep breath and leaned inside for a better look.

It resembled a jungle inside, like the ones he had seen on TV, except it felt cool and darker than he would have imagined a jungle to be. Any second, he expected to hear the shrill cry of elephants, then the chattering of monkeys as some *thing* crashed through the growth toward him.

It's all right, Severin. Don't be afraid.

Warily, Sev moved through the wall, then crawled quickly to his ball. He sat back on his heels, picked up the ball and held it close to his pounding heart. It was very quiet inside the garden but not nearly as scary as he had expected. He began to relax.

Tall cones of Japanese yew, once carefully sculpted, now grew scraggly and wild, and the spirals of juniper just barely retained outlines of their once-careful pruning. Euonymus and gentians mingled with miniature conifers among the shale rocks now all but concealed by wild grasses and slick mosses. Thick vines of variegated hops grew on the walls and over the branches of leafy trees. Pale yellow marguerites grew in seemingly unplanned clumps and lush azalea, sporting their scarlet corollas proudly, splashed vivid color amid the green. And everywhere, the cool, heavy dampness.

Sev explored cautiously as first, then began to enjoy the quiet "jungle." He picked up a stick and began to skip through the growth, hitting vines out of his path with the stick like the jungle explorers. He almost yelled with joy when he spied the round "goldfish pond." He ran to it, knelt on the low brick wall and looked at his reflection in the dark green water. He couldn't see any fish beneath the surface but guessed that they had to be there, hiding among the vines. He poked the stick into the water, hoping to scare the fish into view. He streched out on his belly, rested his chin on his folded hands and waited for the small, circular waves to subside so he could see the glint of the fishes.

His head jerked slightly and his legs tightened to almost cramping when he saw the reflection in the pool. He held his breath and raised his eyes as much as he could without moving his head. He saw the man's legs standing directly across the pond from him. He was caught!

This is the man, Severin!

Sev panicked. He had to get away from him!

Don't be afraid, Severin. He cannot harm you.

Sev slowly brought his knees up under him and sat back, his legs folded under him. He trailed the stick across the water. The man was very tall, and old, and the eyes were strange. But he was smiling and not snarling, as Sev had expected him to be.

"You must be the boy who lives in the guest house," the old man said pleasantly.

Sev stared up at him. "The cottage," Sev said self-consciously, wondering why the old man didn't look scarier.

The man smiled more broadly. "Ah, yes, the cottage. I've heard you playing in the woods back there. I was wondering when you might pay me a visit." The old man turned and looked about him. "It's rather frightful about the garden, isn't it? I mean the way we've let it go wild and unruly. Of course, I always thought it rather sadistic to cut the junipers into those unnatural spirals. Rather degrading for them, don't you think?"

Sev stared at him, smiling slightly, without an idea of what he was talking about, as he moved the stick in the mud at the edge of the pond. "I like it," Sev said, moving the stick carefully against the ground.

Across . . . now down . . . now to your right.

The man looked back toward the back of the wall. "Perhaps you're right. Wild and natural may be better than formal. But it must be somewhat manicured so that one may move about without being jabbed and poked by it all."

Down . . . now to the left . . . now down. There.

"Is it yours?" Sev asked, lifting the stick and washing the mud from it in the dark water.

"Yes, it's all mine," the man said, clasping his hands in back of him. His strict posture made him seem even taller. "What do they call you?"

"Sev."

"Sev?" the old man said with a slight frown.

"Severin."

"Ah, Severin," the man smiled, nodding his head. "A nice name. Unusual, aristocratic, pleasant to enunciate. I, too, am called by an unusual name. I am Pedarius."

"Pe . . ." *Pedarius, Pedarius.* "Pedarius," Sev said with a triumphant smile.

"Very good, Master Severin. I think you are a very bright lad," Pedarius said, lifting a low-hanging branch and stepping under it. They both laughed when the branch swung back and tapped him on the back. "And I think you may be right about the garden remaining *secundum naturam* . . . according to nature's plan, that is."

"Can I see the violin?" Sev asked, getting to his feet.

The short hairs rose on Pedarius's neck as he continued to stare at the burgundy azalea. His eyes blinked and fearful thoughts raced through his mind. But it was ridiculous, he told himself, to be made paranoid by the remark of a small boy. Ridiculous! He slowly turned and stared at the boy's face.

He said it wrong. "*May* I see your violin?" Sev corrected himself. But the man suddenly looked very different, more like what he had expected.

The boy had heard him playing, of course, across the wall. That's how he knew. But how could such a small boy know one instrument from the other? And why did he say *the* violin rather than *your* violin, as he had said the second time? "You've heard me playing, I gather? How did you know it was a violin you were hearing?"

"My mom is a musician too," Sev said, jumping up to touch the limber, low branch. "But me and my daddy are tone deaf."

He was a very bright boy, Pedarius thought, and he was being very foolish about a silly, offhand remark made by the precocious, curious lad. Why not show him the instrument? After all, he was playing it again, regularly, necessarily. Maybe the boy's presence would relieve the suffocating loneliness he felt.

"You may see the violin," Pedarius said, preparing to enjoy the boy's company for a half hour or so. "As a matter of fact, I have it out in the gazebo. I was planning to play this afternoon. Come, I think you might enjoy the gazebo."

Sue stepped out on the porch and leaned against the post, enjoying the warm sun on her face. She brought the cigarette up to her lips, then paused, listening. The music was faint but more audible than she had heard it before. It was very familiar.

93

"Brahms," she said to herself, finally puffing on the cigarette. "Brahms's Violin Concerto." And being played with the touch of a master. It had to be a recording. Then a thought crossed her mind and she listened more intently. The violin was unaccompanied. A recording of Brahms's Violin Concerto would have an orchestral arrangement. Perhaps the unseen neighbor was an accomplished musician, in which case she would have to arrange a meeting. They could have wonderful concerts together, provided, of course, that he wanted to be that social. She certainly could use the company.

"Sev!" Sue called, getting back to matters at hand. "It's time to eat!"

When he didn't come, Sue walked back to his play area in the clearing. As she approached, she walked softly so she might see if he still was talking to his imaginary friends. That part was very normal, she decided. It was the strange things that popped out of his mouth lately that worried her. Who would have told a five-year-old boy about the horrors of World War II? The Ryder School was very progressive, but she doubted seriously that Miss Fryer would have told the children about Dachau. She could have mentioned that Houdini was a mentalist, however.

The quilt pallet was spread in the clearing but both Sev and his soccer ball were gone. Sue listened for sounds of him moving about in the woods nearby. Nothing. She should have checked on him earlier but he had been very good about not wandering off.

"Sev!" she called louder than before. "I'm over here in the clearing!"

Fifteen minutes later she was panic-stricken as she ran down the path to the cove, calling his name between pants. Dark stains appeared on the green T-shirt, under her arms where the perspiration flowed from both nervousness and exertion. Why had she left him alone and unattended for so long a time? A mental picture of his small body tossing about in the sound popped into her head and she began to cry. If she found him on the beach alone she'd make him stay inside for a week. Two weeks!

After calling two or three times, she left her clogs at the edge of the cliff and descended the rocky path to the sand in her bare feet. She knew she was bruising her feet by hurrying down too quickly, but she scrambled down nonetheless. Once she reached the warm sand, she realized he would have left tracks if he had crossed the thirty-foot beach to the water. The sand was smooth and untracked.

She moved out a few feet from the rocky cliff and looked both ways in the small cove. The cliffs curved down to and into the water on either side, forming a crescent-shaped beach no more than forty yards across. The beach was deserted and quiet and there was hardly any wind at all. The small waves lapped lazily across the strip of wetly packed sand, washing silently back and forth.

"Sev!"

She knew he wasn't there but she called out again anyway before turning to climb back up the cliff. At the top, she grabbed the leather clogs and ran back on the path toward the cottage. She called his name as she ran but she was beginning to get hoarse from the frantic shouting. Then, as she neared the cottage, she heard the sound from within. A perfectly clear, resonant chord as someone brought the bow across her cello. Sev had to be inside, he just had to be! And someone else as well.

Sue bounded across the porch and threw open the screen door. There, standing in the middle of the room, was Sev, holding her cello against him as if it were a bass, and holding the bow in his right hand. Sue was too startled to ask him where he had been. She looked about the room to see who was there who could have played the chord. He was alone. Then she realized that there had not been time enough for someone else to transfer the cello to Sev. He had played the chord. He must have. Standing there panting, she all but forgot her anger at his failure to answer her frantic calls, and was, instead, amazed that he had produced that perfect-sounding minor chord.

"Let me hear that chord again, Sev," she said breathlessly.

Sev grinned sheepishly and brought the bow up to the strings. He almost lost control of the big instrument, regained its balance, then drew the bow across the strings in a particularly awkward fashion, producing the most God-awful screech.

Sue winced and shook her head slowly. Obviously, the good chord had been an accident. "I thought for a moment that some of my musical talent had finally bubbled to the surface of your little body," she said, and smiled, wiping the beads of perspiration from his forehead with the back of her hand. "Oh, well, you'll probably be a whale of an advertising whiz, just like your dad." Then she remembered her vision of him drowned in the

95

sound, and her frantic calls. "And the next time you hear me calling for you, you'd better answer me, you understand? Where were you?"

"Playing," he said, plucking a string with his finger.

"Well, you must have heard me call you. I had supper all ready and now it's all cold." She ran her hand across his cheek as she passed him on the way to the kitchen. "Just answer me when I call to you, you understand?" She heard him giggle to himself as she came into the kitchen. She shook her head and smiled to herself. "You understand?" she called back to him.

"Ladies and gentlemen!" she heard him say, and she laughed at his playful inattention as she reached for the coffee cup. "The fabulous"—what now, she thought—"artistry of the incomparable"—nice word—"Pedarius!" Then the perfect chord again, this time followed by a perfectly executed two-chord ending.

The cup fell from Sue's hand and shattered on the floor around her. She steadied herself against the counter so that she would not stagger barefoot into the broken glass. What was going on here? What was happening to Sev . . . or to her? Maybe it was all in her head? No! No, not in her head. These things actually were happening. But how? What had happened to him as he lay near death? Was that it? Had something . . . strange and inexplicable happened to him as a result of the near-fatal disease? Something that might explain the miraculous recovery? How could he know of Pedarius? There had been little or nothing written about him for at least a year after his sudden retirement. Of course, Sev could have heard her tell of the way she single-handedly caused the retirement, the ruined concert and all. They had joked about it for a long time, but he had been a baby then. But they must have told him about it later on, how he had been the cause of her falling over in the middle of the concert and how he had been born a few hours later. And he had somehow remembered the name Pedarius. Then she shivered again. But how did he produce those chords? Three rather difficult chords could not have been accidentally produced by a five-year-old *un*musical child. Then another thought occurred to her as she stood frozen against the counter, demanding a logical explanation from her addled brain. The music from the old house that afternoon. Could the resident of the house be the legendary Pedarius? It was more than a remote possibility, she decided instantly, remembering the quality of the music she had heard float through the woods. And had Sev been visiting him that very afternoon? Perhaps that's why he hadn't heard her calling to him. Could the maestro have taught her son the three chords in a single afternoon? Maybe the two of them had visited before. But why would Sev keep it a secret from her? She had a lot to ask him about over dinner.

Sue had just bent down to pick up the broken glass when Sev burst through the kitchen door, tears streaming down his cheeks.

"Mom!"

"Be careful, Sev!" she shouted at him, waving him back with her hand, "there's broken glass all over the floor. What's the matter, Sev?"

"Mom, Billy's dead!" he cried out, rubbing at the corners of his eyes with tightly doubled fists. "Billy's dead."

"No, Sev," she said, trying to calm him. "Why do you think that?"

"I know," Sev said, his mouth square with emotion. "He just died. My friend Billy just died."

The phone had not rung all afternoon. Nobody could have told Sev that the young athlete had just died. Why was he carrying on so? "Who told you that, Sev?"

"Nobody told me!" he screamed almost hysterically, "I just know! Billy just died!"

At that particular moment, looking at Sev's wild eyes, Sue *believed* that the young, pathetically ill football player had just died at Sloan-Kettering. And that Sev somehow knew it.

VII

Pedarius sat staring into the fireplace, rubbing the swelling around his knuckles in an attempt to ease the dull ache he knew would grow much worse in a matter of hours. The boy had seemed so innocent, and, in fact, probably was. Pedarius had enjoyed the naïve company, the relaxed, rambling chatter as they sat in the gazebo sipping lemonade. The white enameled wrought-iron dome with its covering of rustling ivy had never felt more peaceful, more serene. The boy had been very attentive when he played and seemed genuinely to enjoy the Brahms concerto, played as it was meant to be played. It was, to be sure, the most memorable afternoon Pedarius had spent in years.

And then the boy had heard his mother calling for him. Pedarius was ready to show the boy out through the front of the house but the boy wanted to leave through his "secret entrance." Pedarius was enchanted by the boyish excitement, and memories of his own secret places and things stirred his emotions. He had walked with the child back to the hole under the wall near the well. They said their good-byes and then the boy flashed him a strange glance, which he had immediately interpreted as an "ours is a secret friendship" pact. Pedarius had leaned against the wall smiling, briefly imagining the boy to be the grandson he would never know. Then with a sigh he had taken a few steps back toward the deep well.

How wondrous it was, he had thought as he saw the stick on the wet ground by the pool, that a broken and brittle limb could be a magic wand in the hand of a boy. It was at once a sword, a scepter, a cane, a baton, anything the holder wished it to be. He had bent to pick up the short stick and had frozen with his fingers inches above it.

It was crudely scratched out in the mud but there was no mistaking it. He had stared at it, incredulously. Then he remembered seeing the boy moving the stick on the ground beside him as he knelt by the well. There was no question about it. The boy had left the mark there. Was he their messenger? Or was the mark made by an innocent young lad as part of his war games, soldier games? It was a Nazi swastika!

Raymond Hines's voice startled him and brought a momentary interruption to his tortured speculations. The fire was almost out in the fireplace. It didn't matter. He would go upstairs in a few minutes anyway.

"What did you say?"

"I asked if you'd like to have your dinner now," Raymond Hines repeated, heading for the fireplace.

Pedarius waved him off. "Don't bother with the fire. Just put it under a warming cover and place it in the dumbwaiter. I'll eat upstairs later."

Hines thought at first the crazy old man was telling him to put the fire in the dumbwaiter. "Oh, the food, you mean?" he said with a slight laugh. His chuckles ended abruptly when he saw his employer's disgusted look. "Yes sir, I'll . . ."

"Then you may go. I won't need you further."

"Yes, sir," Hines stammered, praying that this would not be the time that the faulty lift crashed to the bottom of the shaft. He had to get that thing fixed. "Well, good night, then, Mr. . . . uh . . ."

"Good night!" Pedarius said with unmistakable finality.

"What's the old man like, Sev?" Sue said casually, pretending to be engrossed in tossing the salad that she knew he wouldn't touch.

"What old man?" Sev asked, picking at the string beans with his fingers.

"The old man who lives in the big house, of course. What's he like?"

"You don't want me over there, do you?"

"Did I tell you that, Sev?"

"Do you or not?"

"Not especially, but I . . ."

"Well . . ." Sev smiled innocently. "Can we have meat loaf tomorrow?"

He was being mischievously coy, Sue thought, thinking of a more roundabout way of approaching the subject. "We should
100

have the veal cutlets tomorrow. I don't want to keep them too much longer. I'll bread them and . . ."

"Oh, good, wiener schnitzel. I wish we had it today."

Sue's heart bumped again. "Wiener schnitzel?" That's what it was, all right. "Did Anna make wiener schnitzel for you?"

"Nuh-huh."

"Then how did you know about it? I've always called it breaded veal cutlet."

"Oh, *Mom*." He held his hands up and waved them frantically. "I don't want any of that, I don't want any of . . ."

"Okay, okay," she said, putting the salad onto her plate instead. Her mind was whirling a mile a minute. "Are you lonely up here, Sev?" He looked at her as if he didn't understand. "I mean, you don't have any kids to play with and all, and I thought maybe . . . I remember when I was a little girl, if there was nobody to play with, I used to make up my own little friends. I'd sit my dolls around and we'd just talk and talk. Do you ever do that? Make up your own friends, I mean?"

"Ummmm, yeah," he said, wrinkling his nose. "You know, sometimes we talk . . . I talk to . . . yeah, sometimes."

"What do you talk about?" He simply shrugged his shoulders and picked up a piece of potato skin. Sue decided that this was the time to throw him a curve. "I hope you don't talk about Dachau a lot."

Sev tilted his head and wrinkled his nose again. "Da . . . what?"

"Oh, come on, Sev," Sue said with a laugh, making it seem very unimportant, "you mentioned Dachau and Auschwitz to me one day, remember? I just hope you don't spend a lot of time dwelling on those places with your little friends."

"No," Sev shuddered. "They were bad. They killed and . . . could we not talk about that, Mom? I don't want that dream again. I don't . . ." He stopped suddenly and jabbed his finger against the newly frosted cake on the table. "Is that cake chocolate inside or just white?"

It was shortly after ten o'clock when Sue made the call. She purposely waited until she was sure Sev was sound asleep. "Hi, stranger. Guess who?"

"Hi, baby," Nick answered. "I miss you."

"Not so's you'd notice."

"Come on, Sue. You know. How's my boy?"

101

"Strange. And growing stranger by the minute."

"What's the matter?" Nick asked with concern.

"His new buzz words. Are you ready?" She paused to make the effect as dramatic as she found it to be. "Dachau . . . Auschwitz . . . wiener schnitzel . . . what else? I can't even remember."

"What?" Nick said in astonishment.

"Dachau, Auschwitz and wiener schnitzel. Now, where is he coming up with that . . . those places . . . words? And he's being very coy and secretive all of a sudden. Answering my questions with questions . . . I can't tell you how deviously clever he has become at avoiding truthful answers. I'm worrying myself crazy. Nick, I need you up here for a while."

"I know, I know," he said.

"'I know, I know,' is not an answer, Nick," she said, feeling a bit annoyed. "At least we know where he picked up his clever evasive action."

"Thanks for the guilt trip," Nick said sullenly. "I really need that right now."

"I'm sorry, Nick, but you keep promising and promising and in the meantime I'm left to deal with this . . . this . . . whatever it is, and I don't think I'm doing such a hot job."

There was a brief pause before Nick spoke again. "Maybe he picked that stuff up at Ryder."

"That occurred to me, too. But I hardly think they're teaching a bunch of preschoolers history at this point . . . not history to that extent, at least. I'm going to ask his teacher, anyway. I think I'll call her in the morning."

"Oh, that reminds me," Nick said. "I got a very sad phone call a while ago. The big kid at the hospital . . . Sev's friend, Billy? . . . his mother called a while ago. He died late this afternoon. Maybe we shouldn't tell Sev. What do you think?" When she didn't answer he thought they might have been disconnected. "Sue?"

Sue could literally feel her heart pounding at her temples. That was what she had forgotten to tell Nick. Sev had known! Sev had somehow sensed . . . ESP, whatever . . . that his friend had died in New York City! There was no doubt about it. Sev's close brush with death had changed him somehow, granted him some extraordinary mental capability, some secret knowledge, something!

Sue forced herself to take a breath and clear her throat when she heard him clicking the phone button up and down. "Nick," she said quietly, "that's what I forgot to tell you." Maybe he'd have the explanations that eluded her. "He came in crying late this afternoon, shouting at me that . . . that Billy had just died."

"Maybe she called out there first," Nick said immediately, "and told Sev that . . ."

"Nick!" she almost screamed. "Do you think the woman would have told a five-year-old boy . . . on the phone . . . that his friend was dead? No!"

"No," Nick agreed, "she probably wouldn't have."

"No, she wouldn't have!" Sue said emphatically. "He *knew*, Nick. Somehow he knew without anyone telling him. I'm not being hysterical, Nick. He's not acting normal. He's acting . . . he plays perfect chords on my cello! He's acting very weird and I'm scared." She was determined not to cry but she felt it would be a futile attempt.

"There's a logical explanation to all you've told me, Sue," Nick said, though he couldn't think of one at the moment. "We're just overlooking it somehow. How does he look physically? Is he still gaining weight?"

"He looks fine," Sue said, swallowing a sob. "He just acts weird."

Nick took a deep breath, hating what he had to say. "I know you're going to hate me for this but . . . I have to, Sue. I have to go out to Los Angeles on Thursday, I have to. I promised Jonathan. It's a very sticky problem and I have . . ."

Sue's urge to cry left her as soon as she realized that he was not coming out, yet again. She heard the toilet flush in the background as he was talking. "Who's there with you?" she said in a flat, uninterested voice.

"What?" Nick said, a bit surprised. The toilet flush. "Oh, it's Teddy. We've been working on the copy for . . . oh, you don't care about that. I brought him home with me so we could finish it up tonight."

"I hope you didn't try to cook anything," Sue said, wanting to get off the phone. "How're you making out without Anna?"

"Okay," Nick said. "Not eating as much. Keeping my belly hard, you know, the way you like it."

"Yeah, well, have a good trip. Call me when you get back."

"Sue, don't be this way," Nick pleaded. "Why don't you have Mandy come up for a few days. It'll be good to have someone to talk to."

"Yeah, maybe I'll do that."

"And don't worry about Sev. He'll be all right."

"No," Sue said, quietly sarcastic, "no, I won't worry about Sev."

After she hung up, Sue pulled up the blanket around her chin and let the tears spill out. She didn't need Mandy, she needed Nick. Sev needed Nick. And Nick was being an asshole.

Just as she was beginning to feel drowsy enough to fall asleep, the thought struck her. Suddenly she was wide awake and she stared into the darkness. Finally she sat up in bed and lit a cigarette, which meant she would not be able to fall asleep for at least an hour. But it was true. She carefully went through the whole house in her mind.

The only room in the entire town house where she would have been able to hear the toilet flushing as Nick talked on a telephone was their bedroom. She knew it to be true.

Why would he and *Teddy* be working in their bedroom?

Mandy was aghast. "So what did they say at Ryder?"

"Miss Fryer, his teacher, seemed shocked that I would even ask," Sue said, pausing for a sip of her morning coffee. "So I don't know where he's picking it up. Out of the air, I imagine . . . and I'm not altogether kidding."

"I can understand," Mandy said, quite seriously. "Maybe he's got it from Anna. Wasn't she born in Poland? Maybe she was in one of those camps. Perhaps she thinks they're never too young to be taught the . . ."

"I thought of that too," Sue said. "But she never mentioned anything about it to me and we talked openly about almost everything. No, I think I would have known about it too. I can't think why she would tell only Sev. No, that's not it."

"You poor baby," Mandy said, genuinely concerned. "Why not bring him back in for a checkup? Maybe a child psychiatrist?"

"No," Sue said, "if I'm going to take him to a shrink I'd rather take him to a grown-up."

"Oh, you're so bad, Sue," Mandy said, and laughed. "A *child's* psychiatrist, then. Well, at least you've still got a sense of humor about it. Sue, I'm really sorry that I can't come up right now but I'm dreadfully busy. I'm still not finished with . . . *her* apartment and I've already started on Sven Lebak's apartment. Do you know him? The director?"

"No," Sue said, quickly adding, "but I do know *her*. Did she get any zits yet?" Sue decided to tell her about the phone call.

"You should see her closets," Mandy said breathlessly. "Well, my dear, Halston need never work again thanks to that. Let's be totally honest, Sue. I don't think I've ever seen a more stunning creature. She makes Lauren Hutton look like a wallflower."

Just what I needed to hear, Sue thought. "I was just about to tell you something but you just scared me out of verbalizing my foolish suspicions."

"Stop with the editorializing already," Mandy said, her curiosity up. "Tell. That's why we get on so well with each other. We have no secrets that we can't share. Let me light a cigarette."

Sue told her about the late phone call to Nick and about hearing the toilet flush in the background. And how she had deduced that he had to be in the master bedroom *with* someone. Sue finished the story and took a deep drag on her Tareyton. "Well, what do you think? Is he cheating on me?"

"Why, you sly fox," Mandy whispered into the phone. "Miss Marple has nothing on you. What a brilliant deduction. But I can't believe it. You think Nick is having a homosexual thing with this Teddy? You know I've always told you I thought Buck might be latent."

Sue laughed again. "No, you idiot. I don't think . . . I *know* Nick is not having a *thing* with Teddy. What I'm asking you is, do you think there's a possibility that . . . that he's having a *thing* with someone else?"

"Oh, I see," Mandy said, genuinely confused. "You think Nick might be having . . . a *thing* with . . . her?"

"Tara Dobbs," Sue said straight out, not feeling quite so amused. "We've done enough of that *her* shit. Do you? Have you picked up any vibes from her?"

"Well, I . . ."

"Don't tell me! I don't want to know."

"NO!" Mandy said truthfully. "No, I have not picked up on anything from her . . . Tara Dobbs. Nor do I consider it a possibility even. Nick loves you, I know he does, and he would not cheat on you even if the opportunity were laid out before . . . oh, shit, Sue. How would I know? I think Buck screws everything in his path, but I don't have any definite proof. I just think that. And you know what? I think I tell myself he is screwing around just so I won't have to face the fact that maybe he's not doing anything at all. That maybe he just doesn't want to take me to

105

bed. I really think that's it, Sue. I really believe he'd rather jerk off than touch me. Sad, huh? Oh, well."

Now Sue felt sorrier for Mandy than she did for herself. "Mandy, you mustn't think that. You're a beautiful, desirable woman and Buck loves you. You know that's true. We both just made the mistake . . . no, not a mistake . . . we just happened to marry workaholics, that's all."

"Yeah, I suppose so," Mandy said with a sigh. "It's just that my poor body is in desperate need of touching, that's all. Oh, God, Sue, I miss you."

"Then come up. You can put off those . . ."

"I can't. I promise you I can't. But I will, soon, too," Mandy said, sounding like her old take-charge self again. "Why don't you just call this Teddy and get it . . ."

"Absolutely not," Sue said with a laugh, though she had already considered it. "I'll just wait to read it in the papers."

Ten minutes later, Amanda Broughton Buchanan was on the phone to Arcodan.

"May I speak to Teddy, please?" she said in a confidently demanding voice.

"That's 236," the receptionist said. "Just a moment, please."

Mandy was all ready when he answered the phone. "Hello, Teddy, this is Amanda Buchanan, a friend of Sue Arcomano's . . . Nick's wife?"

"Yes?" the copywriter said, wondering what this strange interruption would be about.

"Sue asked me to call you," Mandy continued rather quickly. "I found a watch over at her town house the other afternoon and she thought that perhaps you had left it when you were over the other evening."

"Nick's place?" Teddy said, thoroughly confused.

"That's right. Is it yours?"

"She must have meant some other Teddy. I don't think I've ever been to their apartment."

"Town house," Mandy corrected, forgetting for a moment that she wasn't selling her decorating skills. "Aren't you Teddy Frazier?"

"No, Teddy Baer," he said, relieved that he could get back to work without further hassles, "and don't say it."

Mandy Buchanan laughed. "I wouldn't dream of it. And don't you say anything to Nick about this call. He already thinks I'm a little dizzy and this will only give him more ammunition to use against me. How could I make such a mistake? Oh, well, forgive me for bothering you."

Oh, my God! she thought to herself as she hung up the phone. Now she had another problem. Should she tell Sue or not?

How could they get any work done out there? Nick thought as he drained the last of his martini. Every day felt like Saturday afternoon, what with the bright, constant sunshine, the casual dress and the laid-back attitudes. Jonathan Daniels had been very defensive about it.

"You work just as hard in L.A., get just as much done as you do in New York," he had said. "It's just the illusion of everybody being very laid back that's throwing you off. We get a hell of a lot done here. You gotta remember, Nick, a lot of big deals are made on tennis courts out here."

Perhaps it was true. But it seemed to Nick that there were an unacceptable number of "flakes" on the Arcodan staff in the "Big Orange." And how dare they do a takeoff on Manhattan's nickname? Which posed another question.

"Why do they call it 'the Big Apple,' do you think?" he asked the stewardess who smiled down at him.

"Well, because it's . . ." She started out very confidently, then stopped abruptly when her answer seemed not to fit at all. "Hmmmm, good question." Then her smile brightened. "Because it's the core of the entire world?"

Nick laughed. "Not bad. It's better than I've come up with. I'll have to mull it over while you bring me another double martini. What's the weather like at Kennedy?"

Hot and muggy, what else? Just like the mess he had gotten himself into. He never meant to become involved with Tara Dobbs, and that was the absolute truth, not a subconscious lie to ease his guilt. He loved Sue Goodwin, had always loved her and imagined he always would. And he loved his son enormously. Why then had he betrayed them, their trust? Perhaps the resentment he felt toward Sev when he forced her to give up her career was greater, deeper than he knew. Everything had been so perfect, then Sev came along and their world fell apart. Maybe Nick was blaming them both for that. He certainly was doing his part, building an extraordinarily successful business from nothing, amassing a small fortune beyond his wildest dreams. They had let him down. Sev had gotten sick and almost died, and wasn't it really Sue's fault for ignoring the warning signs? The stomach aches.

"No," Nick said aloud to end the foolish thoughts. "Absolutely not!"

"Well, I won't force you," the stewardess said, and smiled, holding the drink above the small platform, "but you did order it."

"No, no," Nick apologized, "not you. I was . . . that woman over there, across the aisle, keeps after me to move over there with her." Nick laughed, both at the ridiculousness of his small joke and at the Freudian connection with his thoughts. Adultery.

The stewardess glanced at the woman in the opposite window seat. She was sound asleep. "Vamping you through ESP, huh?" she said, and laughed. "Why is it that every beautiful man thinks that *all* women lust after his body? We're all very different, you know, have different tastes, hate being fitted into that stereotypical mold and detest being taken for granted."

Nick laughed. "I know all that and you've got me all wrong. That was a small joke. I'm a very happily married man."

She smiled her best smile and looked deeply into his eyes. "Good, I'm glad to hear it. My name is Marcie Warren, I live on East Thirty-fourth, and I'm in the phone book."

That's why he had done it, he thought as the woman wiggled away. It was so easy. Tara Dobbs had done all the work, carefully arranged the "chance meetings," just happened to have theater tickets. He hadn't done it because he loved Sue and Sev any less. He had just stepped willingly into the carefully laid trap. Now he had to pry himself free. He could do it, *had* to do it, but it wouldn't be easy.

Tara Dobbs was, without question, the most luscious woman he had ever laid eyes on. Why couldn't he have stopped with the visual satisfaction?

Sue watched him as he skipped down the path in front of her. His shoulder blades were still a bit prominent but he was filling out nicely. His hair, bouncing and shining in the sun, made her smile. Still, that vivid picture of her shaving the last locks from his head never would leave her. But he hadn't come up with any more shockers in the past five days, was eating well and acting as normal as . . . what kind of pie was it that Nellie Forbush felt as normal as?

Sue sang through the lyrics of the song from *South Pacific* until she came to it. Blueberry pie. That's how Sev was acting.

As normal as blueberry pie. Then another thought struck her. But how normal was blueberry pie? They never had blueberry pie at home when she was growing up. Apple, yes, cherry, yes, but blueberry? She laughed at her own silliness and because she felt really good for a change. Nick was driving up on Friday. "We'll be brown as berries when Daddy gets here, won't we, Sev?"

"Did you tell him to bring me that Atari?" Sev said, stopping to turn and face her.

"I told him," Sue said, shaking her hair and smelling the lemon juice she had squeezed on to lighten it a bit. "But I wouldn't count on it working too well. We get such lousy TV reception that . . ."

"That has nothing to do with Atari," Sev said, turning and breaking into a full run toward the cliff. "All you need is the TV set. Don't you know anything, Mom?"

He was a genius, that's all, Sue told herself. There was no point worrying about anything he said. She had to stop coming up with her ominous speculations about what a five-year-old boy would know and what he wouldn't. They had an exceptional son and that was that. But even as she thought it, she knew there was much more. She had never heard that Einstein could know when a friend had died, in another city, without being told. But people did have premonitions, feelings that something might be wrong with a loved one, intuitions. Then again, Sev had *known* that Billy had died. A premonition usually does not make one hysterical.

Pedarius watched Hines work his shoulders through the square opening in the paneled wall of his bedroom, then twist his body to look up. He had to get him out of there. The pain in his hands was excruciating.

Hines fooled around with something inside the shaft, then pulled his body back through the opening. He brushed a cobweb off his forehead and took a couple of steps toward the old man. Hines shuffled his weight self-consciously, then stood with his weight on one foot, his arms akimbo.

"It's that main pulley, up there," he said finally. "It's bent over a bit and that's what caused the cable to slip off and the stuff to break at the bottom. . . ."

"Well, now that we know," Pedarius interrupted, "let's forget about that problem for the moment. I want you to go into

Stonington and get those prescriptions filled. I need them at once. The pain is very bad. And while you're there, you may as well take the list and get the supplies we need." It was a very long list of supplies, Pedarius remembered, and it would take quite a while to buy everything on it. A smarter man would have wondered just how urgently he needed the medicines if he would allow him to spend extra time filling such a long list of household needs. But with Hines, he need not worry. The man was little more than a cretin.

Twenty minutes later he was in emotional agony but the physical pain was subsiding. The bow bounced with precise accuracy, creating the small, staccatolike breaks before the difficult trills.

"No, no, no," the teacher said, tapping her stick against the stand. "David, play the passage for him," she said. "This is how is must be played." The instrument seemed to glow in her hands as she held it out, the patina breathtaking in its perfection. "I've always known it should be yours." "Why him" is reflected in the other boy's expression, "Why not me?"

The tear seemed to fall in slow motion from Pedarius's eye and its "splat" against the Stradivarius was deafening.

"But it can't be true, Father! Why them? What have they done?" "It's nothing they've done, my son, it's merely what they are." "But there's no sense to it. How are they different from us? We're all . . ."

Sue wished she had brought her watch down to the cove. But it felt like thirty minutes had passed, so she rolled over on her stomach. The sun felt wonderful but she had to be careful. She wanted to be tanned but not burned when Nick arrived Friday night. She wanted those strong hands all over her. The erotic scene she was reading in the paperback made her wish it was Friday afternoon instead of Wednesday.

She glanced up at Sev, who was standing with his back to her, ankle deep in the water. Sue wondered briefly how the waves could be so high when it felt so warm and still where she lay. The cliffs probably were sheltering her from a wind that was whipping the water. Sev was standing very still. Probably talking to himself again, she thought, as she went back to the novel.

110

Sev stood terrified as the horrible daydream progressed vividly in his head. It was so real, so scary, and by then he knew what was coming next.

"But he's like my own brother. *You* can do something to prevent this outrage, Father. We must help them. I can't believe that there are no reasonable men who . . ."

It would be different this time, Sev prayed. It had to be! He could not bear to go through that horrible ending again. He couldn't! Maybe they would get away this time. No! No, it was going to be the same! He was going to do it again!

"I won't watch!" Sev said in a choked, quivering voice. He saw nothing but the horrible pictures as he began to move forward into the water. "I won't watch!" As the sound of the first shot echoed in his head, Sev tried to run through the waves, which were already lapping at his knees. "No! Run away!!"

Sue looked up and saw him waist deep in the waves and moving farther out. Her voice froze in her throat as she scrambled to her feet. As she dropped the book on the blanket, Sev stumbled and disappeared under the water.

"Sev!!!" she cried out as she ran across the warm sand. "Sev! What are you . . . doing?!!" Halfway across the sand she felt herself grow lightheaded from sheer terror. Her right knee collapsed under her and she sprawled headlong onto the tightly packed sand at the water's edge. The breath went out of her and she felt for an instant that she couldn't pull herself back to her feet. With a terrible ache in her stomach, she forced her arms to lift the trunk of her body. She saw a wave wash over Sev's head and he was gone again.

She fell again as she tried to run before she was fully standing. Then she was on her feet and fighting her way through the onrushing waves. But where was he?

"Sev!!! Where are you?" she screamed, feeling the gritty grains of sand in her mouth. She stopped with the waves washing around her waist and frantically pounded the water with her fists. "Where are you, Sev?!!"

Her arms crossed around her and her nails dug into her hunched shoulders as total panic swept over her. She couldn't even remember what color his bathing suit was. What color was she supposed to look for in the greenish-gray water?

"Greeeeeen!" she cried out in agony, remembering the small

stretchy bathing suit. She would never see it in the water. "Severinnnnnnnnnnn!!!!"

And then she saw him, five feet away, and then he was gone again. She ducked under the surface and pushed off against the sandy bottom toward him. She felt the bottom of her bikini wash down around her knees and then she felt his small body. She grabbed at him wildly and pulled him tightly against her. She couldn't tell if he was breathing or not as she struggled to get them both to the surface.

She gasped for breath as they broke the surface. Sev's eyes were closed and his head wobbled about on his neck. The water was only about a foot over her head but she was having trouble keeping them both afloat. The bikini bottom was right at her knees and she couldn't move her legs freely. She kicked her legs wildly but the Spandex hobble wouldn't move. Finally she took a deep breath, sank back to the bottom and shoved off again, this time toward the shore.

When they reached the surface this time, Sue turned on her back, held Sev's limp body on top of her and kicked furiously, propelling them toward safety. When she felt the sand against her naked bottom, she flipped over and managed to get her footing. She gathered Sev in her arms and hobbled up onto the hard sand. Sue dropped to her knees and gently stretched Sev out on his back. At first he didn't appear to be breathing, but then his chest heaved and he gulped in a great mouthful of air. His chest rose and fell steadily but he still appeared to be unconscious.

She pulled her bikini up and turned Sev over on his stomach in one continuous motion. She immediately began applying pressure to his shoulder blades, hoping to force out any water he might have swallowed. She watched his mouth to see if any liquid was draining out.

"Sev? Sev? Can you hear me?" she asked as she continued the regular pressure on his back. She glanced up to the top of the cliffs knowing she wouldn't see anybody there, but hoping nonetheless. Then she looked frantically back to the water. Maybe a boat passing by.

After five minutes, she stopped the artifical respiration and turned him over on his back. His breathing was perfectly normal. Perhaps he had just fainted from panic. But she had to get help. She'd wrap him in the blanket and take him up to the old house. Someone there could help her with him and they could call for a doctor.

* * *

Pedarius sat in the big overstuffed chair, drained of all energy. His eyes felt irritated from the crying but his hands grasped the arms of the chair without the slightest sensation of pain. He leaned farther back into the softness of the chair and lifted his legs effortlessly onto the ottoman.

The banging on the front door startled him. He listened for a moment, then closed his eyes again. Probably some drunken friend of Hines. But the knocking persisted. He opened his eyes again when he remembered that Hines was in town. Surely the unwelcome intruder would wear himself out and go away.

But the banging became even more insistent and he heard a woman's voice crying for help. And it sounded like she was kicking the door rather than banging at it with her hand. He'd have to see what it was about.

"You've got to help me!" Sue Arcomano said quickly as soon as the old man opened the tall door. "My son almost drowned in the cove down there." Sue started to move forward with Sev in her arms, but the white-haired man didn't move out of the way.

Pedarius felt all the color drain out of his face and his knees went weak when he opened the door and saw *that* woman with *that* child in her arms. Her face was etched permanently in his memory and he had wondered constantly about the boy since their first meeting in the garden. Now here they were together. There was no cause for further speculation. They were part of a vengeful plan. He was face to face with his destiny.

Either the woman or her child was *their* surrogate.

VIII

Sev opened his eyes the moment Sue lowered him to the long, mauve-colored sofa. He blinked his eyes a bit but there was no coughing or sputtering. He took one deep breath, then grinned sheepishly at Sue.

"I went out too far, didn't I?"

"Are you all right, Sev?" Sue asked in a rather shrill voice. "How do you feel?" She couldn't stop stroking his cheek and rubbing his chest.

"I think I could swim if the water was nicer."

"The water wasn't nice," Sue said sternly, her terror turning to anger. "The water was very choppy, there were waves and ... you can't swim! You don't know how to swim and you know better than even to go into the water without me right there beside you. You know that, Sev!" Then his expression scared her again. "What is it, Sev?"

Sev stiffened when he saw the old man walk up behind the sofa and look down on him. His eyes were cold and glaring. *Don't be afraid, Severin. He won't harm you. Don't be afraid.* Sev relaxed a bit and forced a small smile. "Nothing," he said. "I just thought we were at home, that's all."

Sue followed his eyes and was suddenly aware that the man was standing at the back of the sofa. Kneeling beside Sev, she sat back on her heels, totally drained of all energy, and weakly smiled up at the tall, white-haired man.

"I think he's all right, don't you?" she asked, suddenly aware of his familiar features. "I don't think there's any reason to . . . call for a doctor. . . ." Sue brought both hands up to cover her open mouth as she recognized the maestro. "Oh, my God, it's you again! I mean ... Pedarius! It's you. . . ."

Pedarius forced a smile, hoping that the facial tic was not obvious to the two most unwelcome intruders. "Yes, my dear. I find it extraordinary that you manage to seek me out in moments of crisis. What is it you say . . . uh . . . we must stop meeting this way." But we won't, will we? he thought.

Sue all but forgot about Sev's narrow escape as she pondered the unlikeliness of their being thrown together again, the second time as bizarre as the first. "I can't believe it," Sue said, completely nonplussed. "We seem destined . . . I seem destined to . . . belabor you with my problems. I . . . oh, my God," Sue blurted out, feeling the fabric of the sofa under her fingers, "this is silk. We've ruined your . . . Sev, get up. You're wet. . . . No, sweetheart, stay there," she said, feeling his forehead again. "Do you feel all right, baby?" She knew she was babbling, embarrassed and probably in mild shock, but she couldn't stop talking. "I'll pay you for the damage, but . . . oh, shit! I'm like that chicken . . . with it's hat off." Suddenly she started to laugh. "Are you all right, Sev?"

Sev laughed too, because she was laughing so hard. "Oh, *Mom*."

"Then get your ass off"—she lay her head on the sofa and guffawed—"the man's silk . . . sofa."

It was the boy, Pedarius decided, as he watched the strange scene play itself out before him. It had to be the boy. Twice now he had seen the woman, observed her closely, looked deeply into her eyes and sensed there was nothing threatening about her. The only thing she had done was give birth to this child. *He* was the one. If he watched this boy closely, he'd get another sign. Sooner or later, the boy would give himself away.

"Don't worry about the covering," Pedarius said, knowing he had to give the performance of his life. "It is inconsequential. We'll have some tea and you'll tell me what mischief this young lad has gotten himself into. We're fast friends, you know, he and I."

Half an hour later, they were chatting easily, Sue curled up in one overstuffed club chair and Pedarius in another, facing her across the low, green marble table. Sev wandered aimlessly around the huge sitting room, curiously examining dozens of antique gewgaws placed here and there. Sue watched him closely, ready to stop him immediately if he looked likely to pick something up. She was unaware that the violinist was scrutinizing her son's movements and expressions even more closely.

"But how could you have possibly remembered me?" Sue asked, genuinely amazed.

"A more appropriate inquiry might be, 'How could I possibly have forgotten you?'" Pedarius said, expertly displaying unfelt amusement.

"True," Sue laughed, "true. But please assure me that it was not *entirely* my fault. Your retirement, I mean. I can't tell you how guilty I felt when I heard."

"Then you have punished yourself unnecessarily, my dear," Pedarius said, wishing they were out of his house, his life! "It was not your fault at all. I had planned to announce my retirements for weeks, and during that very concert," he lied. "You did me a great favor, in point of fact. Mine was undoubtedly the most dramatic farewell performance in the history of . . ."

"Legendary virtuosos," Sue inserted, though she doubted he would be modest about self-descriptives. "You're very kind to let me off the hook."

"Not at all," Pedarius smiled. "Do you still play? I assume, since you're here, that you are not with the orchestra still. However, that doesn't necessarily follow, does it? You might be on hiatus, mightn't you?"

As Sue told him of the circumstances of her retirement and her occasional string quartet sessions at home, the musician kept his eye on Sev, who had wandered over to the fireplace, behind his mother's chair and out of her sight. Pedarius grew more nervous and sensed something was about to happen when the boy glanced back at him before stepping up onto the great stone hearth.

Staring at Sue but, at the same time, watching the boy's movement behind her, Pedarius saw Sev pick up the heavy black iron poker in his small right hand. Suddenly the boy planted his feet wide apart on the stone hearth, extended his left hand before him and effortlessly lifted the heavy poker, holding it in his fingers like a fiddle bow poised over an imaginary violin "held" in his left hand. And just as suddenly the boy's eyes grew hard and cold-looking, hatefully locking onto Pedarius's astonished stare.

Before his horrified eyes, the boy's lips curled in a knowing smile and he *knew*. The innocent game-playing was at an end. Now the real game was at hand. The boy *was* their instrument of revenge. The six notes from that woman's cello that had disrupted the concert had not been imagined. They had been a warning, an eerie "*en garde*" from *them*! He could not believe that the boy's innocent face now looked so sinister, so frightfully

117

vengeful. The boy's eyes seemed to burn into his very soul. He could almost hear their voices, echoing, laughing at his paralyzing fear. He was almost relieved that the prophecy had come true. Anything would be better than the torture he constantly endured. Defiantly, his survival instincts declared war. If they wanted him dead it would not be so without a struggle. And how could they hope to win? His adversary was a small boy. Disposing of him would be child's play. He almost laughed, hysterically, at his near-pun. But what assurance was there that they wanted him dead? None! Perhaps there was even greater torment in store. But even now, as the dark eyes bore into him, he began to plan the boy's death.

Sue suddenly was aware that the old man's face had paled and that he stared, transfixed, at something over her shoulder. She stopped talking in midsentence and turned to see what held his attention. It was then that she saw Sev standing on the hearth holding the poker in his hand.

"Sev, what are you doing?" she said, very annoyed that he was behaving so badly. She gritted her teeth and grimaced as she saw the poker fall from his hand and clang loudly on the flat stones. Sue set her cup on the marble table, jumped from the chair and ran over to Sev. "Get down from there at once. What's gotten into you, Sev? I'm very upset with you." As she leaned down to pick up the poker, she looked back toward their host and said, "I'm very sorry, he's not usually so . . . My, God how did you lift this thing?"

How indeed? Pedarius thought as he glared at the boy. At once, the boy went all shy, flushed slightly and smiled self-consciously at him. He studied the now innocent-looking face for a moment. So that's how it was to be? All friendly-like, cat and mouse. Interesting. Challenging. The mother never would know that the deadly game was afoot. He'd be very friendly with her and she would bring the boy around often, never knowing the danger he faced. Pedarius suddenly felt very much alive and was determined to stay that way.

"Don't worry so much, my dear," Pedarius said, rising so that she would know it was time to leave. "All boys are naturally curious. Exploration garners knowledge, and knowledge is the stuff that kings are born of. Encourage his curiosity." Pedarius strolled over to Sev and placed his hand on the back of the boy's neck. "It's the old saying that a little knowledge is a dangerous thing." He smiled and stared directly into the boy's eyes. "But

118

here is a lot of knowledge . . . in a little thing. And that's not so dangerous, is it, my small friend?"

Sev looked back up at him. Now he seemed nice again, like a grandfather. Sev felt very confused. "Yes . . ." he stammered. "I mean no . . . I guess so."

"I hope you'll bring your cello over," Pedarius said to Sue, "and we can make a wonderful concert together. I can send Hines to help you with it. I'd like it very much, and I know already that the boy . . . Severin is fond of music. Would you be our audience, our critic, our conductor?"

"Yeah," Sev said, delighted to be invited back into the wonderful garden. "Yeah, I would. Can we, Mom?"

Sue was beside herself with pleasure. "Oh, please tell me you're serious and not just being nice. There's nothing I'd like more."

"I'm quite serious," Pedarius assured her, "and I will be very pleased myself. I'll assume your schedule is as flexible as my own, so we'll just play it by ear, as they say."

"Oh, wait'll you see the yard, Mom," Sev said excitedly. "It's like a jungle."

"And you have an open invitation to play in the garden any time you wish, my friend, and before you say it," Pedarius said, turning to Sue, "please be assured that I welcome his company and that he'll be quite safe within my walls."

When they were gone, Pedarius built a fire in the big stone fireplace, though it was really too warm for it, and sat staring into the hot, orange-red blaze.

He had had many thoughts, had made many plans but had scarcely moved a muscle when Raymond Hines arrived back at the big house an hour later.

The following morning, Friday, Sue practiced on the cello for an hour and a half, excited as a child but believing all the while that she probably would freeze and saw the instrument like an amateur when the great maestro invited her over for a duet. Every time she thought about it, she'd stop what she was doing, stare off into space and giggle like a schoolgirl. What a wonderful day it was going to be. Nick would be there later on and they'd make mad, passionate love after Sev was asleep. She had started, three times to be exact, to call him last night to tell him about Sev's episode in the waves but she decided it would be pointless to have him worry about it. And almost as badly, she

119

had wanted to tell him about her meeting with Pedarius and that he actually wanted to play with her. But tonight would be soon enough for everything. They would have a lot to talk about. Sev. Pedarius. She wasn't sure, yet, whether she'd bring up the toilet flush or not.

Just hurry and get here, she thought as she picked up the paperback and glanced at the clock. It still was only ten-thirty. Almost everything else had changed completely since she had grown up, but important days still dragged on interminably, just as they had as a child when she was waiting for something wonderful to happen. She dropped the book back on the table as she realized she would rather fantasize than read. This was the perfect time to work on the patchwork quilt. As she sewed the scraps of material together, she could fantasize about Nick's body and about her duet with the great Pedarius. Then she remembered Sev's shocking pronouncement.

"The incomparable artistry of Pedarius," she said out loud to nobody, then pretending to be Sev, ". . . and my Mom!" Now that she knew he had picked up the phrase from the maestro himself, it didn't seem so scary at all. But still there was plenty to worry about. Nick would have all the answers. He had to.

Fifteen minutes later, Sue was just about to put her sewing aside to check on Sev, when he came bounding across the porch and into the front room.

"What'cha doing?" he said happily, skipping across the room to her chair.

"Making a wonderful quilt for you." She smiled. "What have you been doing?"

"Playing." He knelt beside her chair and started digging through her basket of scrap material. "Can I have one of these?"

"I guess so," she said, not really paying attention. "What did we decide you would do if something happened to sting you again?" He had told her that something in the water had stung him on the foot yesterday, and that was why he ran out into the water.

"I dunno, what?" he said, still digging in the basket.

"Yes, you do know, Sev," she said, perhaps a little too sternly. "You run *out* of the water, not farther into it, right?"

"Right," he said absentmindedly, choosing a scrap of bright yellow material and standing up. "How much time till lunch?"

"About an hour and a half, I guess. Is that okay with you?"

He nodded yes and turned to go outside again. "Stay in that clearing, all right?"

After she put the lunch on the table, Sue went outside to bring back Sev to eat. As she approached the clearing she noticed that he was talking to himself again. She left the path and came up behind the big tree, hoping to hear what he was saying. She hated spying on him but felt justified in light of the strange changes he was going through. He was talking to himself and gesturing, but she couldn't make out the words. The words had a strange guttural sound to them. She leaned closer to the tree and strained her ears.

Just then, Sev turned around and Sue's mouth dropped open in astonishment. Tied around his upper arm was a yellow armband with a red Star of David on it. First Dachau, Auschwitz and wiener schnitzel, and now that armband! Immediately, without actually hearing, she assumed that the guttural sounds coming from her son's throat were German. Sev was walking around with a Jewish armband and speaking German. What on earth was happening to him? Whatever it was, it had gone quite far enough!

Sue startled him as she jumped from behind the tree and ran into the clearing. "Where did you get that?" she shouted, grabbing him roughly by the arm.

"What?" he cried out, having no idea what she was so mad about.

"That armband," she demanded. "Where did you get it and what were you talking about?"

"You gave it to me," Sev said, now frightened by her anger and the rough hold on his arm. "I took it out of your basket. Ouch, you're hurting . . ."

"Don't lie to me, Sev," she said, shaking him. "You didn't find a yellow armband with a red star on it in my scraps. You didn't!"

"I did too!" he yelled, beginning to cry. "I put it on because I scratched my arm and you're hurting it!"

Sue released her grasp on his arm and looked closely at the yellow strip of cloth. Sure enough, it was a bloodstain that had seeped through the cloth, and close up it only vaguely resembled a star. At once her anger changed to remorse and she knelt quickly beside him and held him close to her. Then she started to cry, and they both cried for a long minute.

"I don't know what you're so mad about," Sev said, jerking with sobs. "You said I could have it."

"I'm sorry, Sev," Sue said, sniffing and holding him at arm's length as she wiped his tears with her thumbs. "I'm truly sorry that I scared you and hurt you. I thought . . ." How could she possibly explain what she had thought? "I'm sorry. Here, let me see that cut."

It was only a superficial scratch. Sue looked at the bloodstain on the yellow scrap of cloth and shook her head. How could she have made such a foolish mistake? Poor Sev still was shaking as she hugged him to her once more. There still was that other question, but she'd put it to him later. She almost laughed as she realized how ridiculous the question would sound.

"Can you speak a foreign language, Sev?"

Halfway there, Nick had convinced himself that such an extravagant present at this particular moment was the worst thing he could have done. If she had any suspicions, this would tend to make her more suspicious. If nothing else, it had already heightened his guilt. An expensive toy to help cover his wayward tracks. But it was too late now.

He pulled the shiny, new, lemon-yellow Mercedes roadster alongside the classic Mercedes convertible and turned off the ignition. The woods were so quiet surrounding the cottage that he knew they both heard him drive up. So he sat in the see-how-much-I-love-you-and-I-haven't-been-cheating-on-you present and waited for them to run out to welcome him.

Nick opened the door when he saw Sev, laughing and jumping with joy, round the corner of the cottage. Nick got out of the car and stood up just in time to catch his son as he leaped into his arms.

"Daddy, Daddy!" Sev squealed with delight. "I knew you were coming today!"

"Hey, how's my boy?" Nick said, truly delighted that Sev looked and felt so healthy. "Gimme a big hug, Severino. Ummmmm. You're strong as an ox, boy," Nick said, and laughed.

"Wait'll you see me kick my ball, Daddy."

"You're getting all your muscles back, Sev. Make a muscle for me." Nick felt his still-thin bicep but was amazed at the improvement. "Well, all right! Ummmmm, I love you, baby."

"Did you bring my Atari, Daddy?" Sev said, wriggling to be let down.

"Of course I did," Nick said, lowering him to the ground and ruffling his hair. "You're my baby. Uncle Buck sent along a couple of things too."

Nick felt a lump in his throat as he watched Sue step off the porch. She stopped in the light of the porch lamp and they stared at each other. The soft light was perfect and she looked better than he ever remembered. Her hair looked lighter, pale blond glowing in the yellow light, a healthy color to her face, and her legs looked long and sensuous in the dark, tight-fitting jeans. A white cardigan was thrown over her shoulders, and the soft curve of her breasts, her nipples, were clearly visible under the thin white T-shirt. Her stance and the lighting created a most romantic image, sensual and desirable. Nick expected to feel a sensual arousal, but he didn't. Guilt.

"Is that your sister, kid?" Nick joked to Sev, hoping to relieve the tension in his shoulders.

"That's my *Mom!*" Sev laughed, hitting Nick's leg with his fist.

"That's the girl I married?"

"For better, for worse," Sue said with a smile.

"Nawwww, she never looked that hot. Come 'ere and gimme a kiss. That's the only way I'll know for sure."

Nick watched her approach, slowly and sexily. She was wearing heels, that's why her legs looked so long and sensuous. He could tell by the way she moved that she was ready for him. Nick swallowed hard as she neared him. It was the first time he remembered in a long time wondering if he'd be able to get it up. He had to relax. And then they were kissing and she felt warm and sexy and smelled wonderful.

"What's this?" Sue said into his ear, looking at the new car.

"It's for you, Nancy Drew. Your own little yellow roadster. You like it?"

"Nick, you didn't," she said excitedly, loving the sleek machine. "You did, didn't you? Oh, it's wonderful!"

Sue finally decided, during dinner, that it was her fault, that she had become permanently paranoid. She had tried so hard, for so long, to come up with logical explanations for Sev's behavior that now she assumed she must be mentally creating the uneasiness she sensed between Nick and herself. It was nothing visible in Nick's demeanor, just an uncomfortable something she felt at the back of her neck. It was clearly obvious how happy he was to be with Sev, and, she supposed, with her as well. It was all in her own head. And it was all the fault of those

123

inept contractors. Not only did the toilet cause the temperature of the water in the shower to vary, sometimes scalding you, sometimes freezing you, but also the goddamned thing flushed loudly enough to be overheard on the telephone! It was the contractor's fault that she felt unsure of her husband's loyalty!

And why was she being such a complete ninny? Why couldn't she just say, "Nick, when I heard the toilet flush that night, I wondered why you and Teddy were working in our bedroom?" and Nick would say, "He was falling asleep on me so I put him in a cold shower to wake him up and I was changing into my robe," and that would be that? It probably was all that simple, and she was eating her heart out, burning with jealousy because she couldn't imagine that any man, including her husband, would be capable of keeping his hands off Tara Dobbs's beauteous body. Mandy had been absolutely right. She should have called Teddy, on any pretense, and she could have cleverly wormed it out of him. But that seemed so cheap and tawdry. She had to be direct and honest. There was no relationship without total honesty, and the longer she put off facing up to it the more strain she would place on their marriage. If they had gotten through the heartbreaking ordeal with Sev, they certainly could handle a silly bit of jealousy. But then, Sev's problems were not quite behind them. They still had a lot to deal with.

"So what do you two do all day, except lie in the sun, I mean?" Nick said, brushing Sue's cheek with his hand. "I feel like a ghost compared to you bronzed devils."

"Yeah, Daddy," Sev laughed, "you look white."

"New Yorkers are supposed to look white," Nick said, slapping him lovingly. "It's the proud badge of the Manhattanite. You two look like Los Angeles flakes."

"I take it you weren't altogether thrilled with the Coast," Sue said, and smiled, getting up to get the dessert. "And I was so looking forward to becoming bicoastal."

"Your Mom looks very sexy, kid," Nick grinned.

"Noooo," Sev whined, kicking the legs of his chair. "We gotta play Atari before you play horsey."

For the first time that evening, both Sue and Nick felt comfortable with their laughter. Nick playfully shoved Sev's head.

"You don't miss a trick, do you, cowboy?"

Nick rested on his side in the double bed, his head propped up in his hand, gently smoothing his hand over her naked hip. He

124

sighed deeply and shook his head slightly as she recounted the near-drowning incident.

"We should have given him swimming lessons," Nick said in a quiet voice. "They start babies out now at six weeks old."

"That's in California," Sue said, lighting a cigarette. "You don't throw kids into cold New York pools. People would think you were crazy. And anyway, we didn't . . . and he almost drowned."

"It almost seems like the little guy has a magnet . . . just sucking up the bad luck, doesn't it?" Nick said, cupping his hand around her warm breast.

"God, I know," she said, blowing smoke over Nick's shoulder. "Maybe it's us. Have we done something to be punished for?" Now, why did I say that? she asked herself as she felt his hand lift off her breast. Then she felt a rush of anger. But why should she feel she had to screen her conversation? It was absurd. Debilitating!

"And what's the rest?" Nick asked, wondering if she really meant for him to answer that question. "The talk about . . . concentration camps?"

Sue lay back on the pillow with her left hand behind her head and began telling him about Sev's references to Dachau, about the armband incident, the guttural sounds he was making in the conversation with his "friends," intending to finish with a reminder about his most timely knowledge of Billy's death. She was shocked when Nick dropped his head on her shoulder, laughing.

"You think it's funny?" she asked, pushing his forehead up so she could look at his face.

Nick couldn't stop laughing. "You gotta admit, it is funny . . . that part of it, anyway. Can you imagine me saying, 'Doc, you've got to do something. I'm worried sick about my son. He's saying'"—Nick dropped his head and broke up again—"'he's saying . . . wiener schnitzel!'" Nick rolled onto his back, his belly jerking with laughter.

Aside from his laughter being contagious, it *was* funny when you put it in that context. Sue tried to laugh quietly so as not to give him *too* much satisfaction. But she couldn't. It did sound too ludicrous for words. The whole bed began to bounce with their laughter.

And just when their laughter was beginning to subside, she said it again, "Wiener schnitzel," and they both went into gales

125

of laughter again. Why hadn't she seen the humor in it before? Because in the back of her mind she knew there still was an ominous ring to it when coupled with the rest of it.

Even as he laughed, Nick still felt a sense of disaster. He had not once felt close to an erection, and by this time Sue must have noticed it too. It wasn't that he didn't want to be excited, he wanted *desperately* to be excited. And that was going to be the problem. He was trying too hard, had *her* on his mind, and the unfortunate combination was apt to leave him impotently flaccid. He might be able to hang his problem on his worry about Sev, but not if he continued laughing like a hyena. He just had to relax, that's all. He wanted to make love to Sue. He had to.

Their laughter stopped abruptly when they heard Sev's scream. It was a bloodcurdling scream and Sue felt goose bumps pop up on her forearms as she jumped from the bed and ran toward Sev's room, Nick right behind her.

Sev had jammed his body into the corner of the wall and his feet still were pushing against the mattress as he tried to move farther away. Moonlight from the window made his face glow with an eerie pallor, and terror gleamed from his eyes. When Sue bolted through the door, his eyes widened further and the scream that came from his throat was ear-piercing.

"Noooooooooooooooooo!" he begged. "Pleeeasseeee, nooooooo!"

"Sev, it's me!" Sue screamed to make herself heard. "It's me, Sev! Mommy!"

Nick jumped on the bed on his knees and pulled Sev away from the wall, holding him tightly against his naked chest. He rocked the terrified boy back and forth, grimacing when Sev screamed again. Nick felt the hot tears from Sev's eyes running across his chest as he held him closer.

"It's all right, Sev," he said soothingly. "It's all right. Nothing can hurt you. I won't let anything hurt you. Where is the pain?" he asked, feeling an emptiness growing in the pit of his own stomach.

"Does it hurt in the same place as before, Sev?" Sue asked, sure that the cancer had begun again. Her chin began to quiver as she thought she would not be able to go through it all again.

Nick was having the same thoughts. He knew it was too good to be true. The cancer had merely been arrested and now it was on the rampage again. Sev would suffer wretchedly again, and

126

they along with him. "Where does it hurt, Sev?" He almost cried as his son's body convulsed with sobs.

Sev began to shake his head. "It . . . doesn't hurt . . . it's *them* . . . I don't want it . . . anymore. . . ." He buried his face in Nick's chest and sobbed.

"It doesn't hurt?" Nick asked, glancing at Sue. Sev rolled his head back and forth against him, indicating "no."

Sue sniffed and folded her arms across her naked breasts. "Are you sure, Sev?" she asked, remembering how much he loathed the radiation treatments. Perhaps he was lying to avoid being subjected to those awful rooms at Sloan-Kettering. "If it does hurt, you have to tell us." And maybe he was thinking about poor Billy, wasting away, then dying.

"Noooo!" Sev cried. "It's those pictures I see. I don't want them to make me watch anymore!"

"He had a nightmare," Sue said to Nick, hoping he would reassure her it was that and nothing more.

"Is that it, Sev?" Nick asked, feeling slightly relieved himself. "Was it a nightmare?"

Sev shook his head again. "They don't . . . usually make me watch it . . . when I'm asleep. I don't want it anymore!"

"Dreams can't hurt you, Sev," Nick said, smoothing the back of his head. "They just scare you for a minute, that's all. And, sometimes, if you tell someone about the dreams, that puts an end to them. They won't come again." Nick took him by the arms and held him away from him so he could look at his face. "You do believe me, don't you, Sev? I'm your daddy and I love you . . . and you can trust me," he said softly, looking at Sue and meaning it as much for her as he did for Sev. "Tell me about the dream now before you forget it, and you'll probably never have it again."

Sue picked up a pillow and held it against her to cover her nakedness. Nick sat back on his heels, facing Sev as the words gushed from his mouth.

"It always starts . . . they are these children playing and running on a hill . . . and grass . . . and they are best friends. All of them like each other." He sniffed and wiped his nose with his arm. "They *love* each other. They talk and"—his face reflected puzzlement—"sometimes they talk funny and I don't know what they are saying . . . but sometimes I do." The sniffing had all but stopped and now he stared out the window, mesmerized as he recalled the familiar sequences. "And then they get bigger and they like each other, all of them, just the same. They go to school and they play music like Mom, only not with the orchestra. Then the grandmother . . . only she's not a grandmother . . . just seems good like one . . . gives him this nice instrument and he likes it but the other one doesn't because he doesn't have so good a one, but they still like each other." Sev's face took on a worried look and he began to rock back and forth, nervously. "And then . . . bad things start happening in that place where they live and . . . some people are very afraid and they start hiding from . . . they are afraid that they'll die. If they don't hide from them, they are afraid . . ." His voice began to rise and the terror was coming back into his eyes. Sev's mouth squared and the tears welled in his eyes again. "Then there is these stars and . . . and his cross is all . . . all broken on the ends or something . . . and . . . and . . ." He began to sob again. "I don't know what else. That's all I can remember. Will it stop now, Daddy? Will it not come back now that I told you, Daddy?" Sev threw himself against Nick's belly and wept.

An hour later, with Sev sound asleep again, Nick held Sue in his arms. This was the perfect opportunity for him to come clean, to admit his foolish mistake and beg her to forgive her. But he couldn't do it. Something told him that telling her was the wrong thing to do, that she might not be able to accept it. So, instead, he made up his mind to end the affair with Tara Dobbs and hope that Sue never found out about it. Now that he was here with them, realizing that they were the only things that meant anything to him ultimately, he found it even more difficult to believe he had betrayed them, so foolhardy to let his lust endanger the happiness they had found together.

"Do you think that's where he got it, then?" Sue asked quietly, moving her arm in the small of his back.

"It has to be. He watched a lot of TV. He saw some movie about the war, the Holocaust, and it left such an impression on him that he's beginning to dream about it. That's got to be it. But I think you'd better come back in with me and let Sev get a thorough checkup . . . just in case, you know."

"I know," Sue said. "I'm almost afraid to take him back in, Nick. If it's coming back . . . I just can't stand it. I think I'd rather not know."

Nick held her tighter. "It's not coming back. He had a nightmare, that's all." He kissed her softly on the lips. "Feel like playing horsey?"

"It's the last thing on my mind right now," Sue said, and laughed softly. "And from what I've seen so far, it's the last thing on your mind, too."

So she was aware of it. "I was hoping you wouldn't notice. I hate to face up to it, but I must be getting old. I guess my days of being constantly horny are over."

"My ass," she said, slapping him on the back.

"Your ass is more beautiful than ever."

"That's not what I meant."

"It's what I meant."

"You're sweet," Sue said, pulling back a bit as the perspiration became a bit sticky between them. "Now explain how he snatched the news of Billy's death out of thin air."

Pedarius watched from the front porch as the two-car caravan pulled down the driveway, the boy waving at him from the open white convertible and the woman waving from the smaller yellow car behind it.

So they'd be gone a week or ten days. Good. By that time he'd have worked out all the details. Involving Hines was a masterstroke. All the suspicion would be laid on him.

The boy stood up in the seat to wave one last time. Pedarius smiled broadly and held his hand high, waving his hand only slightly, in the dignified manner of royalty.

"I'll be ready for you," he said quietly, "you detestable little son-of-a-bitch."

IX

Nick had assured the three of them that there were infinitely better restaurants for the money they were about to lay out, but Mandy had not yet visited the place and she wanted to see the hotel which claimed to have "all the style and panache of a Cole Porter lyric." Sue was all for it, and Buck didn't care where they went.

Le Trianon at the gloriously restored Helmsley Palace smelled of riches. It was all candlelight, dark paneling, impressive paintings, a spacious setting of serious and tasteful posh. Exquisite potted orchids, and tasteful flower arrangements in silver at every table gave the room a serene elegance. The four of them looked right at home, decked out as they were in formal attire.

They had been to the opening of a new musical written by a friend of Buck's and had avoided the remainder of a disastrous evening by ducking out of the theater at intermission. Mandy's concern of "but what will he think?" was met with Buck's "fuck 'em if he can't take a joke." There followed a list of non-committal things to say to someone who has just "created" something ghastly and who is too close to it to realize its awfulness.

"It's very, very interesting."

"I just can't believe you did it!"

"My God, I'm speechless!"

"I just can't tell you how I feel about it. I didn't want it to end."

"And then," Mandy said, leaning in and coming dangerously close to dipping her black gown in the mustard sauce, "you hug him warmly, kiss him wetly on the cheek and get out as fast as you can."

Everyone laughed except Buck, who smiled slightly. "Your tits are coming out, my dear."

"They're supposed to come out, *my* dear," Mandy said without missing a beat. "That's what Valentino had in mind, my dear. And besides," she added, lifting her wineglass, "men are supposed to like it when tits pop out unexpectedly."

"On their old ladies?" Buck said, enjoying the playful put-down.

"You've got a point there, Bucko," Mandy said with a smile. "He's got a point there, you know, familiarity and all that stuff considered." She drained the wine and waved the empty glass at the sommelier behind her. "Four thousand dollars for this rag and still I'm his old lady."

"Four thousand dollars?" Buck said, pretending outrage. "We should be eating the dress."

"There's plenty under it in case you're still hungry when you finish," Mandy said, pleased he'd left himself wide open for her retort.

"Touché," Buck said, flushing a bit as he laughed.

"You two are too much," Sue said, thrilled to be in their company, out on the town and with Nick. "I can't tell you how much I've missed you both, not to mention you," she said, patting Nick's hand. She was feeling a little tipsy, they all were getting a bit drunk and it felt great. She needed to relax, to unwind. Tomorrow she had to take Sev for his examination but tonight was for fun.

Nick and Buck tried to talk business but finally gave up when Sue and Mandy began hissing them. After two more bottles of wine, the four of them were laughing at everything. Mandy had been talking a blue streak all evening, being with the three people she cared most about and felt most comfortable with, and now she was telling about her seven days on St. Croix two weeks ago, alone, without Buck.

". . . but it was wonderfully quiet and just what I needed. The hotel is very small and isolated from everything, and . . . I want champagne with my praline soufflé," she said to Buck, who was giving his order to the captain. "Uh . . . oh, there are only twelve rooms in the hotel and it's all white and informal, you know. It's two stories and . . . uh, I was on the ground floor. There were six rooms across, you know, and they all share a . . . uh . . . a common veranda. Well . . ." Mandy stopped and looked at each of them as they burst into laughter. "What? What is it?"

Sue grabbed her wineglass as she almost tipped it over. She had been sure Mandy had cleverly set them up for it, but now she wasn't so sure. "They all shared a *common veranda?*"

"Yeah, what's so funny about that?" Mandy said, still not getting the pun.

The three of them laughed even harder. Nick lifted his hands like a conductor. "All together, now . . ."

"A *common veranda!*" Nick and Sue said in unison.

Suddenly Mandy's eyes lit up and a smile spread across her face. "Oh, my God. Carmen Miranda!" Then she laughed. "Can you stand it? My best line in two years and I'm too drunk to hear it."

"Your delivery is getting a lot better," Buck said with a smile. "She told me that two weeks ago and made me promise not to use it."

"You bastard," Mandy said, feeling a rush of nausea from all the wine and cocktails.

"Do you think they buried her with all those hats?" Buck asked. "Common Veranda, I mean?"

"Couldn't, old man," Nick said, affecting an Oxford accent. "Health hazard. Fruit flies, you know?"

Later still, Buck began to talk more freely about himself than he ever had as far as Sue could remember. And what he said was reassuring.

". . . and the rheumatic fever kept me in bed for what seemed to me at the time, forever. As a result, I became more introspective, more independent . . . creating my own little world and somehow feeling capable of handling the problems that popped up in it. You have to do that when you're so isolated, and that's more than likely what's happened with Sev. I wouldn't be at all surprised if he's not aware that he defeated that cancer shit himself and now, even though he may not be consciously aware of it, feels capable of doing almost anything for himself. That's why he's talking to himself. He's working things out in his own little world. Don't worry about him so much. I have an idea you've got a very self-confident, independent little cuss on your hands."

Sue smiled, warmly and affectionately, as she pulled Buck's head to her and kissed him on the cheek. "I love you, Buck. Thanks."

"We're going to be late," Sue said as they came out the front door onto West Sixty-ninth Street.

133

It was a glorious day and Sue was delighted that Sev didn't seem to be upset about going back for a checkup at Sloan-Kettering. Perhaps Buck was more right than he knew. Maybe Sev did know that there was nothing wrong with him now and so there was no cause to dread a visit to the treatment center.

Sue quickly suppressed her desire to take the new lemon-colored roadster out of the garage, because at the time it made a lot more sense to take a cab. Just then she spotted "Mr. Shakespeare" strolling down the sidewalk toward them, using his cane more as a prop than for support. She tied her silk scarf onto the strap of her bag as she awaited his approach.

"Good morning, Mr. Saunders," she said, smiling cheerfully. "How well you look."

"Ah, Mrs. Arcomano," he said resonantly, "what a pleasant surprise. I've missed you. You look radiant, my dear, and with good cause. Our boy is looking his old self again. I'm so pleased."

"Yes, he is, isn't he," Sue said beaming. "And we have you to thank, at least in part. The house worked out beautifully. It's secluded, peaceful, the air is divine and the woods are now in full glorious color. Where did you find out about it?"

The ancient actor looked puzzled. "I'm sorry, my dear," he said, twisting his head a bit and smiling. "Now, what is this again?"

"The cottage you recommended to me," Sue reminded him. "It worked out wonderfully well. It's a perfect place for Sev." His expression told her he still wasn't following her. "The cottage in Stonington, Connecticut? The one you told Anna . . . or Sev about? They . . . or rather, Sev, told me you gave him the number to call and . . ."

"Stonington, Connecticut?" he pondered, placing his forefinger to his lips. "No, I don't believe I know the place. Perhaps someone else may have told the boy about it. I don't think I've ever played Connecticut."

The honking horn made Sue turn and look for Sev. Her heart bumped slightly when she didn't see him on the sidewalk. Her eyes went immediately to the honking car and then she saw him waving to her from the open door of the Checker cab.

"Hurry up, Mom!" he shouted.

Another car pulled up behind the cab, which was blocking the street, and the driver immediately added the sound of his horn to the other driver's irate warning.

134

"Oh, God," Sue said, moving away from the actor, "I have to run. I'll talk to you later, Mr. Saunders. And thanks anyway . . . for whatever . . . being a wonderful person."

"Why did you do that, Sev?" she asked, climbing into the cab and closing the door. She gave the driver the address and then turned back to Sev.

"You said we were late," he said, lowering the window glass a bit.

"Well, not that late," she said, sitting back and sighing deeply. "You didn't even say hello to Mr. Shakes . . . Mr. Saunders."

"It's okay, Mom," Sev said, looking out the window. "I know not to call him Mr. Shakespeare."

Sue smiled at his precocious awareness. "He didn't seem to know what I was talking about when I thanked him for telling us about the place in Connecticut. You did tell me that he was the one who told you about it, right?"

Tap your finger to your head, Severin. Sev looked up at Sue and tapped his forefinger against his temple.

"What is that?" Sue said, reading the gesture correctly. "You mean he's senile?"

Nod your head yes, Severin. Sev nodded.

"How do you know about senility?" Sue asked, suspecting that the old actor might indeed be slightly forgetful. "Do you know for a fact that he gets things confused?"

"Oh, *Mom*," Sev said, getting onto the seat on his knees and looking out the rear window. "I talk to him a lot." *He sometimes forgets my name.* "He sometimes . . ." Sev stopped and shook his head no. He didn't like to lie, not even if *they* told him to.

Sev was a minor celebrity at Sloan-Kettering. All the experts wanted to have a look at the boy who had recovered so miraculously. Sue was afraid that so much attention might upset Sev even further, and while she didn't intend to interfere if his doctor said otherwise, she asked that he conduct whatever tests he felt necessary, as privately and as quickly as possible. The doctor agreed.

On the third and final day of the examinations, Jimmy Higgins went in with them so he could keep Sev company while Sue talked to the doctor in private. Sue was very happy to see the working musician again, and Jimmy Higgins was just happy.

"I promise you, I've never felt this way before," he said through a near-constant grin. "I'm nowhere near as promiscuous as you heteros would have us fags be, and, quite frankly, I'd all but given up on finding someone I really cared about. You know, more than just sex. But here it's happened and I don't know what to do about it. I do know, however, that I can't think of anything else. I'm walking around like some silly schoolgirl, my head in the clouds, forgetting any responsibilities I might have. Heaven!"

Sue laughed, feeling genuinely pleased he had found love. "Then what do you mean, you don't know what to do about it? Go with it. Love is the only thing that means anything, Jimmy. Wallow in it. Have fun." Sue kept watching the glass doors, feeling it was about time for Sev to come running out into the reception room.

"It's a little hard," Jimmy laughed, "and that's neither descriptive nor a pun, but it's a little hard to wallow in it when he's in San Francisco and I'm here."

"Oh, you poor baby," Sue said, taking his hand in hers. "I just assumed he lived here. How awful for you. Well, you obviously can't go there. Can't you talk him into coming East?"

Jimmy sighed and shook his head. "He's stuck on San Francisco. It's the *only* city in the world, he says. Plus he's just opened a small restaurant, with a partner . . . his ex-lover, actually. Just what San Francisco needs, right? Another restaurant."

"And just what you need too, right?" Sue added. "An ex-lover around."

"You're wonderful, Sue," Jimmy said, pulling her close to kiss her. "I miss you so much. You always seem to know exactly what I'm feeling. I really do love you, you know?"

"I know. I feel the same way about you, and I hope you're not setting yourself up to get hurt. I know how awful it is to be separated from someone you're mad about."

"Oh, come on," Jimmy teased, "Connecticut is hardly . . ."

"I'm not talking about Nick, silly," Sue half lied. "I'm talking about a boy I was crazy about in school. He moved away and I was sure I would just waste away, pining for him the way I did. That's when I gave up the violin, as a matter of fact. He was in my music class and we both played the violin. I swore that I would never play the violin again until he came back to me," Sue said and laughed but still remembered the pain. "But

136

I did stick by my oath. I took up the cello instead, half hoping that I'd put on some weight from moving it about. But anyway . . . God, that story was so dull, I've forgotten the point I was trying to make."

"That you understood my dilemma, my torment," Jimmy said, and laughed.

"Oh, yes, I do understand. But don't take that to mean you should do anything foolish like . . ."

"I shouldn't quit the Philharmonic and move out to . . ."

"Bite your tongue!"

Twenty minutes later, Sue was sitting in the doctor's office, hearing exactly what she wanted to hear. They could find nothing wrong with Sev.

"I have no explanation . . . there is no explanation," the doctor told her quietly, "so we won't dwell on that aspect of it. I'm sure that will make you quite happy, that we make no more fuss about the boy's . . . recovery. I can't think of any reason why he shouldn't start school in the fall."

Sue beamed as she took out a pack of Tareytons. "Do you mind?" she asked, holding up the cigarette.

"I think you should mind," the doctor said with a slight smile, adding, "but no, I don't mind."

"I know," Sue said, digging for the lighter, "but this is not the best time for me to try to kick the habit. It's a crutch I'm beginning to depend on more and more recently." And the smoke did feel good, did feel calming. "So what about the other . . . weirdness . . . his propensity for scaring me half to death with . . ."

"I wouldn't worry so much," the doctor said, idly trying to make some order out of the disarray on the desk before him. "I can't tell you why, exactly, but it seems that persons who have been very close to death sometimes undergo personality changes . . . drastic changes in some cases . . . uh . . . from introvert to extrovert, for example. That sort of thing. And undoubtedly, your son, because he was in bed for so long with nothing to do physically, developed his mental processes more quickly than would other five-year-olds who are constantly on the run and concerning themselves with more ordinary things. His retentive abilities are obviously beyond those we expect of a young boy, which would explain the somewhat startling things he comes up with. He may have picked up this knowledge from television, from bits of conversation between you and your husband, friends, when you were not even aware he was listening. Strange meanderings for a five-year-old, I'll grant you, not typical nightmare material for . . ." The doctor's hands stopped shuffling the papers and he looked at Sue with a slight smile. "Enough of this 'fine example' charade," he said, pulling open the top drawer of his desk. "My not smoking is obviously wasted on you so I think I'll join you. But not a word about it, please. The staff here thinks I gave it up two years ago. I'll blame all the smoke in here on you, if you don't mind."

Sue laughed. "No, I don't mind taking the rap, but you're quite wrong about not influencing me. Now that I know you've got the habit, I'll probably never give it up."

"How can you add to my guilt so happily," the doctor said, and laughed, drawing deeply on the French cigarette. "Don't you know the suicide rate is heaviest among doctors and psychiatrists? But you're right. It is a very civil, pleasant way to pass the time, isn't it? As a matter of fact, I'm not sure I trust people who don't smoke and don't drink. They're usually colossal bores, don't you think?"

Sue thought about it briefly as she laughed. "I think you may be right, Doctor. Too self-righteous and critical, usually. Good point, especially about nondrinkers, I think. Very picky, complainers, and you're right . . . no fun."

The doctor was serious again. "There is one further thing, Mrs. Arcomano. I am fascinated about the boy's rather precise perception regarding the death of . . . uh . . ."

"Billy."

". . . the death of his friend Billy. That leads me to speculate that he may have developed . . ." The doctor stopped speaking and pushed the button on the intercom box. "Is Dr. Brubaker here, Marge?"

"Yes, he is, Doctor," the voice came back, "and he's all set up."

"Ask him to come in, please." The doctor adjusted the glasses on his nose and folded his hands in front of him. "To digress for just a moment, I mentioned to you that I thought the boy's lack of concern over the drowning incident could probably be attributed to a loss of fear about death and dying. I'm sure that Severin knows how near he came to dying and he may also be aware that he probably saved himself, for the most part. This may have given him a sense of . . . well, a fearlessness, almost a sense of immortality, as it were. And by freeing himself of the

138

mortal fear of his life suddenly ending, he just may have re-moved some mental block, triggered some mental ability that we all more than likely have. What I'm trying to say, and going about it quite clumsily, is that your son may have developed an ability for extrasensory perception. It's only a thought I have, a feeling . . . nothing more, but I . . ." The doctor stopped again and stood up behind his desk as the door opened.

Sue snuffed out her cigarette and turned to watch the small, bearded man move with short, quick steps across the small of-fice, his hand extended toward his colleague. The small man was neatly dressed in medium brown, and the suede shoes ex-actly matched the color of his suit. He flashed a quick, cour-teous smile at Sue just before clasping the other doctor's hand.

"Abe, how well you look," the doctor said, shaking his hand.

"And you, my friend," the smaller man said in a rather high voice. "Are we ready to be disappointed again?"

The doctor laughed. "Abe, I'd like you to meet Mrs. Arcomano, the boy's mother. Mrs. Arcomano, may I present Dr. Abe Brubaker, parapsychologist *extraordinaire*."

"How do you do," Sue said, suddenly realizing that these two professional men thought that Sev might have powers of ESP. It had occurred to her as well, but the fact that two authorities considered it a possibility sent a small chill up her spine. She felt her buttocks tense involuntarily, then experienced a slight shiver throughout her entire body. Now she wished she had brought Nick along. He had volunteered to take the morning off if she thought it necessary or helpful. Perhaps he could have made some sense of the list of credits Dr. Brubaker was reeling off. Sue was too busy thinking of the consequences of Sev hav-ing the abilities of extrasensory perception really to listen to what the expert on parapsychology was saying. She believed it was possible to possess those mental capabilities but she wasn't sure she could believe that her son was capable of it. She was completely at sixes and sevens, whatever that meant, and now Dr. Brubaker was saying something about numbers.

". . . so I'll try him on my secret 'Warsaw Hilton' test and be done with it. I know you'd prefer we not overwhelm the lad with attention, so I won't take up too much of your time . . . and his."

Sue became aware that both men were smiling at her, ob-viously waiting for some response. She shifted rather uncom-fortably in the leather chair and cleared her throat. "Uh . . . what is it? The . . . Warsaw Hilton test? What is that?"

Dr. Brubaker smiled and waved a short finger at her. "If I told you that, Mrs. Arcomano, it wouldn't be my secret anymore, would it?"

"No, I guess . . ."

"It's my own test," he continued in his shrill voice, "and it will tell me exactly what I need to know. I'll warm him up a bit and then get right to it. Perhaps you would like to grab a bite of lunch and I promise not to keep your boy more than seventy-five to ninety minutes."

Stop with the numbers already, Sue thought, skipping over the seventy-five and deciphering the ninety as an hour and a half. She was glad they couldn't see the mess inside her head. Then again, she thought, glancing up at Dr. Brubaker, perhaps *he* could.

Sev thought it was very funny *they* told him everything the little doctor was thinking or reading but that they didn't want him to let the doctor know that he knew. Each time the doctor would look away, Sev would grin and try desperately to keep from laughing. It was a good joke they were pulling on him.

"Now, Severin," Dr. Brubaker said, picking up the large white cards, "let's try this and then I'll let you go, okay?" Dr. Brubaker smiled, trying to relax the boy, as he watched him nod his head. "I will concentrate on what is written on each of these cards and I would like you to tell me if you can picture in your own mind the printing I am looking at and thinking about. Just relax now and tell me anything that comes to mind during the next few minutes. If nothing comes to mind, that's okay too. Ready?"

They had already told him the numbers printed on each of the three cards, but he was not to let on to the doctor. *1812, 1917 and 1941.* "What do they mean?" Sev asked them. *They are dates of the beginnings of wars, but they also have a funny meaning to the doctor.*

But even when *they* explained it, Sev didn't see why it was funny.

Driving through the heavy midtown traffic, Sue kept glancing at Sev in the rearview mirror as he traded playful slaps with Jimmy Higgins. They had found nothing wrong with him at Sloan-Kettering, and Dr. Brubaker had been very disappointed by Sev's performance.

"A very charming lad," the parapsychologist had told Sue, "but an unlikely candidate, I'm afraid, as a clairvoyant. I'm

140

sure the boy thought me a bit crazed when I suggested he might pick up on my thoughts. I think you have a very bright son, Mrs. Arcomano, and very normal."

Sue was both relieved and disappointed. She wanted him to be normal but bright, but she also wanted explanations. She was still concerned about Sev talking about and dreaming of such horrible events, but she decided not to worry so much, if she could manage it. Now she could concentrate on worrying about Nick.

Jimmy got out in front of his apartment building on Seventy-eighth Street and stood looking at Sue and Sev in the elegant, open car. "It's perfect for you," he said with a smile. "Nick knew what he was doing. It gives you class."

"Thanks a lot," Sue said, and laughed, keenly aware of the affection he held for her.

"Hey, Jimmy," Sev said, leaning over the bucket seat on the passenger side, "do you know what 1812 . . . and 1917 and 1941 mean togeth . . . uh, have in common?" He giggled in anticipation of stumping his friend.

"You can't stump me, wise guy," Jimmy laughed, cuffing him lightly on the ear. "Those are . . . uh . . . those are all years of wars. How do you like that?"

"No, no," Sev laughed. "I mean besides that?"

Jimmy realized he had spoiled Sev's joke, so he decided to set it up for him again. "Oh, I see, it's something else, huh? I don't know then. What do 1812, 1917 and 1941 have in common?"

"They are . . ." Sev paused as he forgot that word again. *Adjacent*. "Oh, yeah. They are ad . . . jacent suites at the Warsaw Hilton!"

Sue's mouth dropped open. She glanced at Jimmy Higgins's surprised face, then they both broke into laughter. Sev laughed when they did.

"You're teaching him Polish jokes?" Jimmy Higgins said, not really believing that he had picked it from Sue. "I'm surprised at you."

"Don't look at me," Sue said, looking back at Sev. "Where did . . ." Then it hit her. Dr. Brubaker's "Warsaw Hilton" test. But he wouldn't tell her anything about it because it was his secret. Why would he have told Sev then? He said Sev hadn't picked up on anything. Perhaps that's why he told Sev, because the test was a bust. But what a strange thing to tell a small boy.

Dr. Brubaker was stunned when she got him on the phone

141

later in the afternoon. "But I *didn't* tell him, don't you understand? Those are the numbers printed on the cards, they are the numbers I hoped he'd be able to pick up on but he didn't . . . at least I thought he didn't. All I got from him was a blank stare. This is incredible."

Now Sue was getting nervous again. "But couldn't he have seen the cards? Could someone have mentioned the dates, the numbers to him . . . somehow?"

"I think not. No, I'm sure not," Dr. Brubaker said, his voice rising even higher than before. "But for the sake of argument, let's assume he did see the cards. So he knew the numbers. How then did he know of the rather foolish joke I made up myself, tying the numbers together? That's why I call it my 'Warsaw Hilton' test. And nobody, except a few intimate friends, knows why I've given that name to it. I'm more than a little embarrassed that you now know I've used an ethnic slur to label what I consider to be a most scientific test of parapsychological aptitude. Trust me, Mrs. Arcomano," Dr. Brubaker said excitedly, "the boy picked this up from me this afternoon . . . and not verbally!"

Sue listened as the man practically demanded another session with Sev. Dr. Brubaker now was positive the boy was playing games with him, hiding his "gift" for some reason. The doctor begged for another chance to try to convince the boy to be comfortable with his amazing mental capabilities.

"Not . . . not just now," Sue stammered, now totally and utterly confused about everything. "Maybe later, but just now I think he needs . . . I want him *well*, Dr. Brubaker. I know I shouldn't feel this way, but it scares me to think he might be able to . . . to do that sort of thing. It's just not a good time, believe me. He needs quiet and . . . look, I'm not thinking too clearly at the moment, as you can plainly hear." Sue cradled the phone against her shoulder and lit another cigarette. "I promise you I'll call you back when I've thought this thing through . . . maybe in a month or so. . . ."

"Please, Mrs. Arcomano," Dr. Brubaker pleaded, "this boy may be more exceptional than we think. Promise me you'll be in touch with me. And *believe* me, it's nothing to worry about."

Easy for you to say, Sue thought, as she slowly hung up the phone without saying good-bye.

X

As they left the Museum of Modern Art, Sue remembered the
stretched-out bikini bottom that had washed down around her
knees during her ordeal with Sev in the water. It wasn't too hot
out and they still had plenty to talk about as they walked.

"Why don't we walk up to Bergdorf Goodman," Sue said,
slipping her hand around Mandy's arm. "I need to pick up a
new swimsuit. The one I have keeps falling off me."

"Hummm," Mandy said, and smiled. "Maybe I'll take the
old one. I could use some attention. And speaking of that, are
things any better . . . in the bedroom, I mean, between you and
Nick?"

"I've all but forgotten about it," Sue said, "what with worrying about Sev so much." And the truth was she didn't dwell on
it constantly, the way she had during the first few days. By now
she had assumed that Nick's temporary disinterest in sex was a
result of the constant concern and pressure of Sev's well-being
and unusual behavior. "And Nick is feeling the same strain,
plus the added pressures of Arcodan. But to give you a more direct answer, our bedroom has been used mainly for sleeping
during the past few days. But we'll get back to normal . . . once
we get back to normal."

"And they say Stengelese is dead," Mandy said with a laugh.
"The game is never over till it's over, huh?"

"I think you're quoting Yogi Berra, but I won't bet on it.
Anyway, you know what I mean," Sue said, looking back, then
pulling Mandy across the narrow street in midblock. "Oh, did I
tell you Jimmy Higgins is madly in love? A long-distance love
affair. The other guy is in San Francisco."

"Everybody's in love but me," Mandy complained lightly as
she stopped to eye a Chinese screen in a shop window. "Too

drab," she commented as they moved on. "What would you think about my leaving Buck?"

Sue stopped suddenly and stared at her. "Oh, God, no," Sue said, truly stunned. "Mandy . . ."

"I mean, what would you think about my *telling* Buck I was leaving him? Do you think I might get his attention? Would he care, do you think?"

"You ninny!" Sue said, sighing in relief. "You know how much Buck needs you. You . . ."

"Being needed is not enough anymore," Mandy said, slipping the sunglasses off the top of her head and down to the bridge of her nose. "I have needs of my own and I think I'm being a fool to settle for something that feels comfortable—*feels* comfortable, I said, and please make a note of that—because most of the time it's not really comfortable at all."

"Poor Mandy," Sue said as they rounded the corner to Fifth Avenue. She hoped her friend would drop the subject and lighten up again. Selfish though it was, Sue really didn't want to consider Mandy's problems just then. She felt all but buried by her own worries.

"Poor little rich girl," Mandy said with a sigh. "I wonder if it's possible to have it all? Perhaps security and passion are not compatible. Did you ever think of that? Maybe you've got to go for one or the other, but not both?"

Sue suddenly got the uncomfortable feeling that Mandy was not talking about herself but rather about Nick and her. Any other month of any other year of their marriage, Sue would have said, "But what about us, my dear?" At the moment, that comment didn't seem too appropriate. She *was* competing with Arcodan for Nick's attention. And she wasn't at all sure that the agency was her only competition.

"You've missed your cue again, Sue," Mandy said. "You were supposed to say, 'But we both have it all, Amanda, now shut up.'" And I would say, 'But of course you're right,' and that would be that. But now . . ."

"What are you running on about?" Sue asked, feeling a headache starting at the base of her skull.

"I am, I know," Mandy said, sensing Sue's rising irritability. "I'm trying to decide just how honest friends should be with one another, you know? Just how much we should . . . tell each other."

Sue stopped abruptly at the corner of Fifty-seventh and Fifth and turned to face her friend. She looked Mandy directly in the eye and prepared herself for whatever it was to be. "Everything," she said, inviting Mandy to spill whatever secret she wanted.

Mandy was taken aback by her directness, and she still wasn't sure if she should, or even if she wanted to tell Sue about her call to Teddy Baer at Arcodan. Now she really had put herself on the spot. She shifted uncomfortably and looked across the street toward Bergdorf Goodman. "Well . . . uh . . . I think you'll find a better selection of bikinis at Bloomingdale's," she blurted out.

Sue stared at her for a moment, then began nodding her head in disbelief. "Well, I can see how you'd have misgivings about steering me away from Bergdorf Goodman to Bloomingdale's but . . ."

"And since we're so close, we could stroll up to the Russian Tea Room for some blintzes before . . ."

"Before we stroll back down to Bloomie's for a bikini?" Sue said through a funny smile. "You're very weird, you know? Are you always affected like this by a visit to the museum? I feel like I'm trapped in a counterfeit Dali lithograph."

In a quiet corner of the Russian Tea Room, Nick fiddled anxiously with his knife as the waiter poured more coffee for the two of them. He had told her it was all over, that they couldn't see each other again, but the fact remained that he *wanted* to see her again. He glanced briefly at Tara Dobbs's reddened eyes and wondered if she knew how he felt, knew how weak he was, knew that he probably could be made to reconsider his decision. With Tara Dobbs he almost hated Sue and Sev being part of his life. And with his family he wondered why he thought *she* could possibly bring him any more happiness. Suddenly he felt selfishly egotistical, something he had never felt about himself before. Perhaps the power from his success was going to his head, changing him, and not for the better. Was Tara Dobbs merely a tool with which he tried to extricate himself from the responsibility of dealing with the strange and frightening changes in his son's behavior? Hadn't he downplayed Sev's freakiness to Sue because he didn't feel capable of facing the possibility that his son might be seriously, terribly neurotic? More than ashamed, Nick suddenly was aware that he felt unnervingly fragile.

"I'm not blaming you, Nick," Tara Dobbs said softly, "not
145

for anything. I hope you understand that. I knew exactly what I was getting into . . . and I thought it worth the risk." She attempted a small laugh. "And I want you to know, you're the first man I've cried over in a long time."

"Don't cry over me," Nick whispered, placing his hand on hers. "You deserve much better than me. You can have anyone you want."

"That's very funny," she said, "considering the reason for this little tête-à-tête."

Nick blushed. "You know what I mean."

She smiled. "I know . . . and what you meant is rather funny too. You were an exception, but as a rule men I'm attracted to see fit to creep away rather than make a direct approach. The undesirables, on the other hand, are all over me like flies. They interpret a quick glance as the most lascivious invitation, and their horniness is impervious to the most cruelly direct insults. But if I see someone I really want to meet, it seems I have to roll my eyes and practically lick my lips before they find the courage to come up to me. It's maddening."

"You are an intimidatingly beautiful woman," Nick smiled. "They're afraid of rejection."

"Isn't it better to try and be rejected than stand across the room for days looking all moon-eyed and wishful?"

"I'm the wrong one to ask."

Tara Dobbs stared at his wonderful face, her lower lip protruding in a pout. "Yeah," she said wistfully. "Why couldn't you have stayed across the room and minded your own goddamn business?" The tears welled in her eyes again. "I don't like this, Nick. I don't like this at all."

"I know, baby, I know."

"I still find it peculiar," Mandy said as she briefly examined a cerise one-piece bathing suit dangling from a plastic hanger, "that a world-renowned parapsychologist would use a Polish joke to designate a scientific test. You know we're past the days, thanks mainly to Mike Wallace, I suspect, where we accept a doctor as a god, just because he is one . . . a doctor, I mean. Perhaps your Brubaker is a charlatan."

"Anything is possible," Sue said flatly, eager to find a suit and get out of the crowded store, "but I have reason to believe that what he says about Sev is true. It's the closest I can come to an explanation for his . . . behavior." She had almost said "his weirdness" again. She had to stop using that word to describe Sev. The word itself made her tense up.

"How about this one?" Mandy asked, holding up a yellow bikini with small pink and blue flowers scattered across the bra and on one side of the bottom. "I think it's you."

"I love it," Sue said, taking the hanger from her. "Where did you find . . . *Mandy*, I told you I don't fit into that size anymore. And you wanted to go for blintzes. Indeed. But it is perfect if we can find one that fits."

Mandy stood outside the louvered door as Sue slipped into the small yellow suit. "Is there a train I could take up? I'm not all that thrilled about driving up there by myself," she said.

"I'm not sure, but there must be. It might not come to Stonington but I could meet you wherever they see fit to dump you," Sue said, stepping into the yellow briefs. "Or you could drive back up with Sev and me on Sunday."

"That would be the thing to do, of course," Mandy said, "but I couldn't possibly leave before the following weekend. I'll check about the train." She was envious as Sue stepped out of the small booth to examine herself in the mirror. The suit looked perfect on her, and the beginnings of a tan made her firm figure look stunning. "My God, look at you. You look about eighteen. Why would you possibly worry about a couple of lousy blintzes? The suit is perfect. It even fits your tan lines, and it's so *small*. I have to carry mine in a two-suiter. Whale bones don't fold, you know."

"Yeah, it looks pretty good, I guess," Sue said, turning to get a back view in the mirror.

"Pretty good, my ass," Mandy said, reaching in her bag for a cigarette. "Get that silly thing off and let's get out of here. I need a drink."

Sue was almost dressed when she smelled the smoke. She turned and Mandy was peering over the louvered door at her, taking another drag from the brown cigarette. "I don't think you're supposed to smoke in here . . . but let me have a drag before you put it out." As Mandy passed her the cigarette, Sue noticed the rather strange expression on her friend's face. "What?" she asked as she passed the Sherman back.

"I called Teddy," Amanda Buchanan said in a monotone, finally saying the words she had decided Sue should hear, "and he's never been to your house."

147

* * *

Anna Polanski didn't like what was happening to him. He was becoming sassy and, at times, almost obnoxious in his exhibitionism. He had been such a nice boy, so disciplined, so polite and easy to control. Now there was a defiance about him, an independence usually associated with teenagers. That was when they began to suspect that they knew much more about everything than did the authority figures about them and they began to test the "rules." But Sev still was her baby. It was too soon for him to try to break away. She half-suspected that perhaps Sue had been too lenient with the boy up there in Connecticut, let him get away with too much just because he had been so frightfully ill. She supposed they all had pampered him too much but, on the other hand, the poor thing had been through the absolute worst. And all those weeks away from her probably had given him the idea that he was divorced from her authority. But she loved him dearly, enough to straighten him out, slowly but surely.

She shook her head as she heard him turn the volume up on the TV even louder. Just to annoy her, she knew. He still was pouting because she had refused to let him have any more cookies that close to dinner. But she had to be firm. That was the only way she ever would regain his respect and the surest way to rid him of his newly acquired arrogance. She also would have a talk with Sue, suggesting a more strict disciplining of the child.

"It never fails," Anna said to herself, brushing her hands together over the board. "Get your hands in flour and the phone is bound to ring." She wiped her hands on her apron as she headed for the wall phone near the breakfast nook.

Sev sneaked through the doorway behind her, went quickly to the counter, opened a bottom door to use as a step and reached up to grab a handful of cookies from the plate pushed back to the wall.

"Hello?" Anna said into the phone, spotting Sev at the same time. She covered the receiver and raised her voice to the boy, "Sev! I told you no!" She sighed heavily as he smiled his defiance at her, then she returned her attention to the caller. "No, she's not here now. Who's calling, please?"

"Brubaker!" Sev said in a coarse whisper as he darted past her into the dining room.

Anna's mouth dropped open as the caller repeated the name

in her ear a split second later. And that was another thing, she remembered, in addition to his becoming a show-off. He seemed to be anticipating things lately, as if he had some secret knowledge before something happened. This was not her Sev.

"Yes," she said into the receiver, "Yes, I'll tell her Dr. Brubaker. She has your number?"

Sev climbed up on the window seat and stuffed two of the cookies into his mouth at once. *They* were mad at him, but he was mad at *them*, too, for making him watch that dream again. Anna would be mad at him as well.

You can't tell them, Severin. They don't understand.

"I will if I want to," Sev said in a whisper. "You scared me again."

They don't understand, Severin. You'll be in trouble with them. It's our secret.

"I like to see their faces when I know. It's fun."

You musn't tell them.

"I will too! You make me watch *that!*"

You must know, Severin.

"No!" Sev shouted out loud. "I'll do what I want to do!" Sev turned and saw Anna standing in the doorway, dabbing at the corner of her eye with her apron.

"We'll see about that when your mother gets home, young man," she said quietly. "I can't believe you'd do this to me, Sev. I thought you were my boy."

Sev did love her and now he felt badly that he had made her cry. He jumped down from his perch and ran past her, dropping the remaining cookie on the floor in front of her. He ran up the stairs to his room and closed the door behind him.

He turned down the volume on the television and sat on the floor in front of it, not really seeing the flickering picture. It was wrong to be mean to Anna. But *they* made mistakes too. *They* told him they were going back to Connecticut in the morning, but he knew they weren't going back until Sunday. So everything *they* said was not right.

It was a few minutes after five when Anna handed the small case containing two fresh shirts for Nick to the uniformed chauffeur. She walked out onto the sidewalk and looked both ways as the man climbed back into the long, black Cadillac and pulled away from the curb. Sue was late, Anna thought, but then Sue needed some time to herself, away from Sev. And it made Anna feel good that Sue trusted her enough not to call every half hour to see that everything was all right. Anna was proud that she was trustworthy and efficient. She was alone in the world, except for the Arcomanos and a couple of friends, but she felt good about herself because she knew she was a good person, caring and thoughtful of others. And because she cared, she knew Sue would be upset about Nick's sudden trip to Boston. He said he would be back on Saturday, but she'd be upset nevertheless. And rightly so, Anna thought. Nick didn't spend enough time with them lately and that was a fact, though she would never say it to either of them. It was none of her business. However, if she had ever had a husband, she thought she would rather have been poor than have his business keep him away from her that much. And away from the children she had always assumed she would have someday. That was her biggest disappointment, not having children of her own. But then she did have Sev. It was only a phase he was going through. He'd be her baby again once she had him back full-time in the fall. He was a good boy. He just needed a firmer hand at this point.

"And some food," she reminded herself, going back inside the town house. Of course, he wouldn't really be hungry after wolfing down all those cookies. She'd have to start hiding them from him. She stopped suddenly and shivered, looking up the stairs toward the just-audible sound of the television. If she *could* hide them from him.

It was six-thirty when Sue dropped off Mandy on Central Park West. Both of them were a little loaded from the afternoon drinking session, Mandy more than Sue.

"Please assure me that I did the right thing?" Mandy said, holding Sue's left hand in hers. "Telling you, I mean."

Sue smiled, though she really didn't feel like it. "You did the right thing, Mandy. You're a good friend. It's time I faced up to the possibi . . . probability of it. It'll be simpler to deal with it now."

"I feel worse than you do, I'm sure," Mandy said, opening the taxi door. "Just . . . just do it the right way, you know. Don't give him any ultimatums, Sue. Work it out easily."

"Well, I wouldn't count on that," Sue almost snorted. "But don't you worry about it. You did the right thing. I'll call you tomorrow."

No ultimatums my ass, Sue thought as the driver turned in on Sixty-ninth Street. That's exactly what she'd give him after he gave her some lame-brained excuse for lying to her. She still couldn't believe that Nick had actually lied to her, point-blank. She was beside herself with outrage as the cab approached the town house. Perhaps this wasn't the best moment to face him, she thought, and besides, he probably wouldn't be home yet. She thought about Sev, then decided it was Nick's turn to worry about their son. Let him come home to him for a change. And if he didn't, Anna was there and more reliable than either of them.

"Take me back down Fifty-seventh Street," she said to the driver as he began to slow in front of their house. She'd let them worry about her for a change. She really didn't feel like a movie but it would kill two hours and give Nick time to wonder what had happened to her. And she would be calmer by then, hopefully.

Sue really didn't stop to think what *Annie Hall* was about specifically, only that it was hilarious. But once she was inside the darkened theater and the adultery, the lying, the falling in love then out of love played out before her, she cried softly throughout the entire film.

A young man two seats away from her was laughing hysterically during the first part of the film. Then when he became aware that she was crying, he grew quiet, began to cough, then finally moved away. Then, ten rows in front of her, she heard his laughter booming out again. *That*, she knew, was funny, and she laughed briefly in spite of her morose mood.

She walked back home up Central Park West, all the while trying to come up with some explanation why Nick would have told her that Teddy Baer was with him that night. She even decided at one point that perhaps Nick was curious what it would be like to sleep with another man, that he and Teddy had done it and that was why Teddy told Mandy he had never been to their house. Strangely, and she laughed to herself again, she thought she would have been able to handle that. But only because it was ludicrously impossible, and knowing Teddy Baer, even if it had happened, she would not have considered him a threat. On the other hand, while she knew she was attractive, maybe even beautiful, Tara Dobbs made her feel like a frump. And that she couldn't handle.

Please, Nick, she thought as she put her key in the door, please have some excuse other than Tara Dobbs. Sue knew as soon as she stepped into the foyer that he wasn't home. It was too quiet in the house. Though it was nine o'clock and past Sev's bedtime, she knew that Nick still would be playing with him if he was home. Her sigh was both of frustration and relief.

She heard the TV in Anna's room as she peeked in at Sev. He was asleep, so she knew Nick would not be in their bedroom, but she went down to check anyway. She flicked on the light, sighed, then threw the Bloomingdale's bag in the middle of the huge bed. She went immediately into the bathroom to put some eyedrops in her eyes before checking with Anna as to the day's happenings.

Staring at her reflection in the mirror, Sue realized it was best that Nick was not home just then. Mandy was right. She should be very calm about the whole thing. Maybe there was a logical explanation that had escaped her. She prayed there would be one.

Just then Anna knocked at the door. "Are you all right?"

Sue splashed some cold water on her face. "Come in, Anna. I'm sorry I'm so late. Did you have any trouble with Sev?" She walked out of the bathroom patting her face with a towel.

"Oh, you look so tired," Anna said, folding her arms about her waist. "I'll warm your dinner for you. It's all ready."

"I've been a very bad girl, Anna," Sue said, and smiled. "I should have called to let you know how late I'd be but . . . I felt like being irresponsible. What can I tell you? But I'm not really hungry. I'll get a glass of milk or something." Sue went over and hugged Anna Polanski. "I'm sorry if you went to a lot of trouble about dinner. I got a little smashed, I'm afraid. Oh, but the entire day wasn't wasted," she said, retrieving the bag from the bed. "I did find this cute little thing at Bloomingdale's." Sue pulled the yellow suit out of the bag and it was barely a handful. "My God, I thought there was more to it than this," she said with a laugh. "I may be run in by the shore patrol."

Anna laughed and shook her head. "I think you had Nick in mind when you bought that."

If only you knew, Sue thought. "He did cross my mind a couple of times today. Has he bothered to call yet?"

Anna hated to pass on the message. "He said he was sorry he missed you, but . . . he sent a man for an overnight case and two fresh shirts. He had to fly to Boston on the six forty-five flight and he'll be back on Saturday. But he'll call. . . ."

"Goddamn him!" Sue exploded. "Goddamn him!" In a fury she threw the bikini against the mirror and watched as the bra

152

slipped down behind the long, heavy chest of drawers. Sue fell across the bed and started to cry.

Anna was stunned that she was so upset. Anna started to say something, then thought better of it. They must have had a fight. That had to be the reason Sue hadn't called home when she knew she would be out so late. Anna thought she had better stay out of it. She went over to the bureau to see if she could reach the bathing-suit piece that had slipped behind it. No, it had fallen all the way to the floor behind and she knew she couldn't budge that piece of furniture. She had tried before.

"Don't bother with that," Sue said, sniffing and wiping at her eyes. "I'll get it tomorrow. I'm sorry, Anna. I just need to cry for a while. Everything is just piling up and . . . it's all right. Go to bed. I need to feel sorry for myself for a while."

"I understand," Anna said, going to the door. "Just let me know if you get hungry later. Good night."

Sue almost hoped he wouldn't call because she didn't know what she would say to him. About eleven-thirty, with nothing else to do, she took a wire hanger from the closet and bent it out straight to try to get her bikini top from behind the chest.

She stretched out on the carpet and poked the hanger behind the chest until she felt it hook onto something. God only knows what's back there, she thought as she slowly pulled the wad toward her. That's probably where her gold hoop earring disappeared.

She got up to her knees and pulled the wire hanger all the way out. The new yellow top had collected some cobwebs and also a piece of white paper, folded in half. Sue shook the webs off the bra and tossed it onto the bed, then picked up the folded paper.

Sue read the note quickly, then once more, slowly. Then she propped the note on the carpet against the chest and leaned back against the bed, staring at the bold, slanting handwriting, closer to an architect's printing than to script.

Even her writing was perfect.

> I wanted to wake you but I couldn't.
> You're even more beautiful when you sleep.
> These early calls will be the death
> of me. See you tonight.
>
> Love,
> T

153

XI

Sue finally fell asleep about four-thirty, and was awakened an hour and a half later, when the buzzer went off on the digital clock. She took the car out of the garage and loaded their things into it while Sev and Anna had breakfast. They said their good-byes to Anna and were on the road by seven-thirty.

Sev was being uncharacteristically quiet and Sue was grate-ful for it. She didn't feel like chattering away with him, trying to come up with answers for his usual stream of unanswerable questions. She was even more relieved when, an hour later, he fell asleep in the bucket seat beside her. Then she felt almost as alone as she needed to be.

She was especially shocked, stunned by Nick's callousness in bringing Tara Dobbs to their home, sleeping with her in their bed. It made it so much worse somehow, much more hurtful. That he would be so reckless made her wonder if perhaps it was not the first time he had been unfaithful to her. He was, after all, incredibly handsome, with a natural, sensuous quality to his every move. Why had she been so naïve? Women must have thrown themselves at him, made themselves so available that he could not help but be tempted. Because she had felt so satisfied, so content, she assumed that Nick must feel the same way. She suddenly felt a total fool, so gullibly Pollyannaish, so betrayed. But now she knew, and he didn't know that she knew. She couldn't decide what to do about it. So she cried some more.

Sue stopped at the supermarket in Stonington for supplies. It was the last thing she felt like doing, but she had no choice. She would get it over with as quickly as possible and get back to the cottage. The lack of sleep finally was catching up to her, and Sev suddenly was very animated and feisty.

"Let me have a dime, Mom," Sev said, standing in front of the cart and pushing it back on her.

"Sev, stop it," Sue said, adjusting the dark glasses on her nose. "What do you want? I'll get it and pay for it at the checkout."

"No," he whined, "it's for the machine up there. I want to try to get that little airplane. "Please?"

Sue sighed and dug a dime out of her coin purse. "You know you never get what you want out of those machines, Sev. And you're not doing it again, okay? Only one dime. And don't go outside."

Sev ran back down the aisle toward the front of the store. Once he was out of her sight, he cut across the store and went directly to the exit door, out onto the sidewalk and to an empty phone booth. He grabbed one of the wooden milk crates stacked by the booth and dragged it inside. He carefully climbed on top of the crate, lifted the phone from the cradle and punched the number on the buttons.

"Hello?"

Sev smiled as he recognized the old man's voice. "We're back," he said into the receiver.

Pedarius was taken aback for an instant, then relieved that the game was under way once more. "How nice, my friend. I look forward to seeing you."

"Can I play in your yard?" Sev asked eagerly, anticipating the jungle games he could play.

"I'll be very disappointed if you don't," Pedarius said quietly.

Sue was startled to glimpse Sev standing in the phone booth outside the huge plate-glass window. She left the cart and rushed outside, furious he had so willfully disobeyed her. Sev hung up the phone just as she pushed the booth door open.

"I thought I told you not to leave the store," she said, lifting him down off the crate. "What are doing in here?"

"I wanted to see if Daddy was home," Sev said sullenly as he watched her lift the crate out of the glass enclosure.

"Don't tell me that, Sev," Sue said irritably. "You don't know how to use a pay phone. Why do you seem so intent on disobeying me lately? Why?"

"I miss my daddy," Sev said with a pout. "And I didn't really call him. I was just playing like I did."

"Did you put your dime in there?" Sue asked, reaching toward the coin return. Before her fingers touched the small tray, she heard a coin drop into it. She stopped and looked back at Sev, wondering why the coin would have waited so long to drop.

156

"Did you do that?" she asked, actually believing he had.

"What?"

She studied his face for a second, then retrieved the coin from the phone. "Nothing," she said as she took him by the hand and went back inside the store. She could hardly wait to get back to the cottage, stretch out on the bed and close her eyes.

After a lunch of soup and sandwiches, Sev climbed onto his bed and pretended to fall asleep. He lay very quietly for thirty minutes or so until he was sure she was asleep. Then he quietly sneaked out of his room, opened the screen door very carefully so she wouldn't hear its creak, then ran down the path toward the hole in the garden wall.

Pedarius sat in the gazebo picking at the remains of the shrimp salad Hines had prepared. The salad actually was quite acceptable, but the maestro had his mind on the boy. Pedarius was beginning to grow impatient. He had been certain the boy would have shown up by now. Perhaps the woman had forbidden him to come over this afternoon. But he wanted them both over, and if things were as he thought, she would not be able to prevent the boy from sneaking away and crawling through the crumbling wall.

Pedarius covered the salad with his napkin and pushed it away. He poured himself another glass of white wine and twisted in the white chair to look toward the back of the garden. Where was he? Pedarius was very anxious to get on with his plan.

As Sev crawled through the small opening in the wall, he noticed at once that it felt different inside. The air felt humid, but warm and sticky rather than cold and clammy. This was more like he felt a jungle should feel. Now if only there were animal and bird sounds he could play Tarzan. He stepped up onto the low brick wall around the pool and began slowly to circle the water, as if on a tightrope.

Be careful, Severin. The water is very deep.

Sev stopped and looked down into the dark green water. He shook his head. "Nuh-huh," he said. "I can see the bottom."

Those are vines. The water is deep beyond them.

"Nuh-huh," Sev disagreed, not really sure but still testing *them*. But then *they* had been right after all about them coming back to Connecticut today rather than Sunday. The water didn't look deep. And besides, *they* had told him once not to be afraid of water. *They* had taken him into it with *them* in that dream and that's why he had wet the bed. That was *their* fault.

157

Sev crawled about in the thick growth, criss-crossing the garden, trying to get close to a squirrel, which finally scampered up the tall elm tree. Then, through the bushes, he saw the old man sitting in the vine-covered gazebo. It'll be a good joke, Sev thought, sneaking up and scaring him.

Pedarius heard the rustling in the bushes behind him and knew that the boy was coming at last. Pedarius's heart began to pound with excitement and anticipation, tinged with fear of the unexpected, the unknown. What would the boy do? What could he do? He had to be following a plan as well. *Their* plan. But what could he do? What could such a small boy possibly do to harm him?

Pedarius clinched, then unclinched his hand. He felt strong and supple. He slid down in the chair and tried to relax. He knew what he had to do. The scenario was laid out and workable. He was as prepared as he could possibly be. He must not panic. He would follow the orchestration as written, step by step.

Sev quietly sneaked to the back of the gazebo, smiling to himself as he prepared to surprise the old man. Sev didn't know what they meant, the words *they* told him to say, but the words sounded good as he ran them over in his mind. He stumbled over a rock and stood very still for a moment, hoping the old man hadn't heard him. Then he crept very close to the domelike gazebo, put his lips close to the thick ivy and took a deep breath.

"*Guten Tag*," Sev said in his scariest voice, thrashing his hands about in the clinging, green growth.

The wineglass snapped in Pedarius's hand as his entire body jerked involuntarily. The bowl of the glass rolled off the table and smashed on the flagstones, the spilled wine running off into his lap. He'd thought he was prepared for anything, and in an instant he had been made nervous as a cat. Perhaps *they* only meant to torment him further. The boy surely could not do him bodily harm. He pushed the broken stem toward the center of the round table and took the napkin to dab at the wetness on his trousers. He cleared his throat and forced a rather shaky smile.

"*Guten Tag, mein Freund*," Pedarius said nervously. "*Wie geht's*?" How would he respond to that?

Fine.

Sev shifted uncomfortably, realizing he had made the old man spill the wine. "Fine," he said, trying to determine if the man was angry at him. "I'm sorry I scared you. I was only playing."

And playing it very well, Pedarius had to admit, including the passable German accent. "It was not your fault," Pedarius said, struggling to calm his nerves. "Have you had lunch?"

"Yeah, we did," Sev said, feeling more comfortable now that the man didn't seem to be angry with him. "My mom is taking a nap. Do you take naps too?"

"I surely do," Pedarius said, wadding the damp napkin and dropping it into the salad bowl. "And I enjoy them immensely now. But I remember I used to hate them when I was your age. I always was afraid I was missing out on something when I had to go inside for an afternoon rest. But that was a long time ago."

"I know," Sev said, watching a small spider dangle on a silken thread from the top of the gazebo.

I'll bet you do, Pedarius thought. "Where did you learn . . . learn to speak the German language?"

"From Anna," Sev said, reaching for the broken stem of the wineglass.

"And who is Anna?"

"She takes care of us," Sev said, examining the piece of glass. "That's sharp now."

But not sharp enough to plunge into my heart, you little bastard. Pedarius took it from him and placed it in the bowl, under the napkin. "And too dangerous to play with, my friend. Someone could get hurt."

Sev grimaced. "Oooh, we don't want that to happen, do we?" he said with childlike innocence.

Not just yet, Pedarius thought, not without witnesses. "Does your mother know you're over in the garden?"

"She . . . where else would I be?"

Pedarius laughed at the clever evasion. "Perhaps we should call her so she doesn't worry?"

Sev frowned. "Not yet, please? She might make me come home. She doesn't feel good."

"Then you're doing her a favor by letting her rest peacefully, is that it?"

"Yeah," Sev agreed quickly. "She needs her nap."

"Well, then, we'll wait for a little while before we disturb her. And I think you're probably right. She'll know where you are. I did extend an open invitation to you, didn't I, to play in the garden?"

Sev smiled in relief. "Yeah. What have you got to play with?"

"Let me think," Pedarius said, having thought about it two weeks before. "I do have a collection of antique toys. Would you like to see them?"

"Yeah, let's do that," Sev said happily.

"Do you know what antique means?"

"Not electronic?"

Pedarius laughed again. "Precisely. They are very old and quite interesting. I think you'll be fascinated by the ingenuity of the craftsmen before the discovery of the electronic chip. Come, my friend. Let me show you my toys."

The phone jarred Sue out of a rather fitful sleep and for a moment threw her into that dreamy space where she really didn't know where she was. She jumped again on the second ring, then lifted the phone off the hook. It was Mandy, not Nick.

"I feel like such a shit," Mandy said apologetically. "I knew I shouldn't have told you that crap. That's why you left so abruptly, isn't it? Me and my big mouth. How do you feel?"

"Lousy, if you want the truth," Sue said tiredly.

"Oh, God, I knew it. And it was absolutely none of my business, that's the really rotten part. And you know something else? Something worse even? I thought about it all last night. I really think, Sue . . . I really do, that I maybe told you so I'd have someone to commiserate with. So you'd feel as lousy about your marriage as I feel about mine. Is that sick or what? Oh, of course, the main reason was because I love you but the other was a big part of it, I know. I think I'm going to see a shrink, Sue. I'm desperately unhappy lately and it's more than just feeling sorry for myself. I'm not coping well. Sue, I'm so sorry about that ridiculous call to . . . and then telling you about it. Can you ever forgive me?"

Sue felt as if her head were being squeezed in a vise. She just wanted to sleep and sleep and sleep. "You did the right thing, Mandy. I needed to know."

"I hope that's the truth, Sue," Mandy said quietly. "And what do you think about the other, about me seeing a shrink?"

"If you think you need to see one, then you probably do, Mandy. He'll assure you that your problems are no different from five million other women and then you'll feel quite a part of the crowd again."

Mandy paused for a second. "Are you being facetious?"

Sue sighed deeply, more than ready to get off the phone. "I don't know what I'm being. I need some sleep."

"I'd like to come up on Wednesday, if that's all right with you. The closest I can get by train is to Mystic. The man said it's only five or ten miles from Stonington, and I'll get in at six-thirty P.M. I'd take a cab but I don't know if I . . ."

"Six-thirty on Wednesday, Mystic. I'll be there to meet you. We'll talk then."

After Sue hung up, she listened to see if she could hear Sev stirring in his room. The house was quiet, so she rolled over on her side and closed her eyes again. The phone rang again, almost immediately. This would be Nick.

"Why did you go back early?" Jimmy Higgins asked in a bright, cheery voice. "I called the house to take you out to lunch."

"I'm sorry I didn't call you, Jimmy," Sue said softly, closing her eyes and massaging the bridge of her nose with her thumb and index finger. "We just decided to come back early. But thanks for thinking of me. I'll take a raincheck on lunch."

"We'll make it Fisherman's Wharf," he said with a laugh.

"Anyplace you like," Sue said without thinking.

"Didn't you hear me?"

She had to think about it. Fisherman's Wharf. San Francisco. He was going to do it. "No, Jimmy . . ."

"Yes!" he said ecstatically. "I'm going to do it. To hell with the Philharmonic. You were right, my darling. Love is the only thing that means anything and I'm not going to sit there in that folding chair in Avery Fisher Hall and let it pass me by. I've made up my mind, Sue. I'm going to do it!"

Love doesn't mean shit! Sue wanted to say, but instead she began to cry. "Don't do it, Jimmy. You've worked so hard and . . . think about it, Jimmy. Please think about it." How could he possibly make such a foolish mistake?

"I have thought about it and thought about it some more. It's what I want, Sue. You did the same thing, so how can you possibly try to talk me out of it? And look at you and Sev and Nick. I'll tell you the truth, Sue. I think you are probably the only truly happy person I know."

Sue felt a real rush of tears coming on. "I have to talk to you later, Jimmy. I'm . . . I have a headache and . . ."

"Is Sev all right?" Jimmy asked with concern.

"Yes, he's . . . I'm just tired, that's all. I'll call you later and . . . and we'll talk. I'm sorry. You sound very up and happy and . . . I'll talk to you later, Jimmy."

Sue buried her face in the pillow and sobbed. What else could possibly happen? Murphy's Law was prevailing. Everything that could possibly go wrong was going wrong.

Pedarius sat in the large chair in his bedroom watching the boy play with the valuable collection of old iron toys. Soldiers, trains, cars and several banks which deposited coins with cleverly designed mechanisms.

"Put the coin in his hand," Pedarius instructed like a kindly old grandfather. "Now press his other arm . . . that's right."

Sev laughed as the iron monkey plopped the quarter into his mouth, then held his hand back out for the next one. He didn't understand how the various toys moved without batteries inside them. The old man told him he could select two of the painted soldiers for his own, so Sev picked his two favorites and carried them to the ottoman in front of the maestro's chair.

"I'll take these two unless they are your best favorites," Sev said, making the soldiers "walk" across the upholstered stool.

"They are my favorites and I'm very pleased that you like them too. They are yours."

Pedarius watched as the boy took the soldiers around the room, letting them walk across the tables, along the paneled wall and finally over to the sliding panel of the dumbwaiter, which was slighly ajar.

"What's this?" Sev asked, sliding open the square door a bit more.

Pedarius took a deep breath. "Why, that's Alice's entrance to Wonderland," he said. "I thought all children knew about that wondrous place. Don't you know her story?" Pedarius held his breath as the boy set the soldiers on the platform inside the door. "Would you like me to tell you about Alice's discovery of Wonderland and her adventures there?"

Sev turned back to look at him, then a smile slowly spread across his face. "Yeah," he said, retrieving the soldiers and running back across the room to the ottoman. "Tell it."

Pedarius smiled. He would have to make the story even more enticing than Carroll had. He would describe a place so enchanting that no boy could resist searching for it. And it would lie waiting for him, only a short trip away, down the small lift.

* * *

It was three o'clock when Sue awakened and the house was still quiet. She knew before she looked in his room that Sev would not be there. He never would have slept that long in the afternoon. Sure enough, the room was empty.

She went back to her room, slipped on her shoes and lit a cigarette, then went outside. She immediately headed for the clearing in the back of the cottage but again had the feeling that Sev was not there either. He would be over at the big house.

Sue has halfway to the stone wall when she heard the faint ringing. She stopped and listened. It was her phone, all right, but she knew that by the time she got back the caller would have given up. This time it would have to be Nick. She winced slightly as the migraine grabbed the left side of her head. It was all his fault and she hoped he was worried to death. Sue suddenly felt all alone, with no one to seek comfort from. And if that weren't enough, she felt a total wreck physically. If only she could be alone in the cottage for a while, lock herself from sight, without the responsibility of Sev.

Sue didn't stop to think how awful she had to look until she had knocked on the door and stood waiting for someone to appear. She ran her fingers through her hair and could tell by the feel of it that it would appear a bit disheveled. And with the tip of her finger she could feel the puffy bags under her eyes.

Raymond Hines opened the door and did not recognize her at once. "Yes, ma'am?"

"Hi," Sue said, realizing by the man's blank stare that he didn't know who she was. "I'm from the cottage and . . . is my son over here playing?"

Hines's eyes lit up and he smiled thinly. "Ah, yes. I didn't know you for a minute there. Yes, the boy's here with Mr. Pedarius. I'm sorry I didn't know you. Come in, Miz . . ."

"Arcomano," Sue said, stepping past him and smoothing her hair again. "I hope he hasn't been . . ."

"Mom!" Sev said as he ran down the stairs into the living room. "Look what he gave me. Two soldiers. And he's got banks that take money out of your hand and eat it."

Sue looked up the staircase and saw the maestro coming down behind Sev. Pedarius looked very fit and seemed genuinely glad to see her. She smiled at him and relaxed a bit, comfortable that she felt welcome.

163

"They're beautiful," Sue said, fussing for a second with Sev's hair before looking back to their host. "I hope he hasn't been bothering you . . . maestro."

Hines looked back and smiled before disappearing through the doorway to the kitchen. He was glad to know it wasn't just he. She didn't know what to call the old man either.

"We've been getting on very well," Pedarius said, taking her hand. "You should be very proud of this young lad. He's very advanced for his years." Pedarius frowned slightly, still holding her hand in his.

"What?" Sue asked, sensing what he was about to say.

"You look tired, my dear," he said. "You see, that's what the big cities do to people. Too much pressure, too frantic a pace. There's nothing like the country for peace and serenity."

Sue shifted a bit awkwardly, ready for him to release her hand. "I didn't realize how awful I must look until I was knocking on your door. I woke up and . . ."

"No, no," Pedarius said gallantly, "I didn't mean that. You just look a bit tired, that's all." And then it occurred to him that perhaps the boy had gotten a poor medical report. "It's not, uh . . . you didn't . . ." he nodded toward Sev.

"I'm all well," Sev said happily. "I can go back to school after summer is over."

Sue nodded to the musician. "It's true. They told me he's one hundred percent. He's healthier than I am at the moment, as a matter of fact."

Pedarius smiled. "That's wonderful news. I'm very pleased for you." He turned and took Sue by the arm. "Now let's get you fixed up. You need a good pot of tea and perhaps something a bit stronger as well." He watched Sev run ahead of them into the sunny living room. "I'm very glad you're back," he said to Sue. "I feel very comfortable with you and I'm in desperate need of conversation. I'll have Hines take care of us while we solve all our problems, then perhaps the problems of the world. Who knows?"

Sue settled in the soft club chair by the marble table and watched Pedarius stride erectly across the huge room and through the door Hines had exited by. Pedarius was very grand and theatrical but his affection toward Sev and her seemed genuine. And he had to be very lonely up here after all those years in the public eye. He said he needed to talk to someone, and certainly she did. Perhaps as an outsider, not really knowing either of them, he could offer solid, objective advice. At the same time, it did seem a bit tawdry to burden the old man with her marital problems. It would depend on how the conversation developed.

She took her compact and lipstick from her handbag, wishing that the bottle of Excedrin were stashed in there as well. This definitely was the worst headache she could remember. Maybe the tea would help. Sev kneeled in front of the marble table, holding a small, painted soldier in each hand. "Sev, I want you to promise me that you will not leave the house again without telling me, okay?"

"I didn't want to wake you up, Mom," he said earnestly. "And you'd know where I was."

"I don't want you to do it again," Sue said, wiping the corners of her mouth with her middle finger. "It's okay to wake me up, Sev. Promise?"

"Yeah," he said quietly. "Do you think I could ask him for some lemonade?"

"I'm sure he'll have something for you, Sev. He's a nice man and he likes you. What were you two doing?"

Pedarius observed her closely during the tea and sensed that something was troubling her a great deal. He was aware, too, that she probably was considering confiding in him, perhaps asking his advice about whatever it was. If he could get her into a rather personal conversation, it would be a perfect opportunity to have the boy play elsewhere. He felt sure he knew what the boy would do. The mere thought of it made his palms glisten with perspiration. He casually rested his hands on his legs so his trousers would absorb the moisture. At that very moment he felt the first tingle of pain in his knuckles. He glanced quickly at his hands and saw that the swelling in his joints had begun already. He must not waste more time. It was up to him to make the conversation more personal, to draw her out. He prayed the pain would not come too quickly. That could spoil everything.

Pedarius leaned closer toward Sue, making it obvious he didn't want Sev to overhear. "I'm faced with a bit of a problem here and I thought perhaps you could advise me," he said, quietly confidential. "It's Hines. He's been with me for several years and while I've never really been all that satisfied with him, I have made do, you understand. He's not terribly bright, but that's not the worst of it, I'm afraid. Things have begun to disappear lately and I feel sure the man is taking them. I pay

165

him well enough, but . . . I think that when I was ill for so long he saw an opportunity to make some extra money for himself, thinking I was too ill to notice that some of the silver was missing . . . or that I wouldn't care somehow. Well, I don't really trust the man any longer and I don't want him around. I was wondering if you knew of an agency in New York which could provide me with a live-in, perhaps a couple, to take care of the place? It's such a nuisance, really, to think of breaking new people in, but I'm afraid it has come to that. I just can't have the man about much longer."

Ten minutes later, Pedarius had cleverly edged Sue closer to her own problems. He could tell she was ready to confide in him. This time, when he leaned in to her, he touched her hand gently. "Something terrible is bothering you, my dear. Won't you please confide in me? Perhaps together we'll discover that it's not really as bothersome as you think. I'd truly like to help you if I can."

Sue was genuinely touched by his warmth and sincerity. She wanted to talk to him but the mere thought of telling of Nick's infidelity caused her eyes to well up with tears. And besides, she couldn't talk in front of Sev. She was afraid if she said anything at that very moment that the tears would rush out and she might cry for hours. So instead of speaking, she nodded toward Sev.

Pedarius understood the gesture immediately because it was just the opportunity he had waited for. He flashed a kindly wink at Sue, then turned toward Sev. "If you'd like, Severin, you may take your soldiers upstairs for a farewell reunion with their friends, the troops together for one last time, you know?" He could tell the boy thought it a fine idea. "Perhaps the lot of you can find Alice, do you think?"

"Yeah!" Sev said happily, gathering the two soldiers in one hand. "We're going to play with your friends," he said to them, heading for the stairs.

"Is it . . ." Sue started to ask.

"It's all right," Pedarius assured her quietly. "There's nothing he can harm. Make yourself at home," Pedarius said to him, "and if you find Alice, you may invite her down for tea."

Sev stopped on the first step, turned back and ran across the room toward Pedarius. He leaned across the back of the sofa and whispered into the old man's ear, *"We know what you did!"*

Every tendon and vein in the old man's neck stood out as his

166

head whipped around to stare at the boy, his face registering shock and disbelief. The boy stood there calmly, staring back at him, a thin smile on his lips.

It happened so quickly, Sue could not imagine what had passed between them. "Sev?" she said, not really knowing what attitude to take. "What did you . . . what did he say to you?" she asked of the old man.

Pedarius forced himself to regain his composure. With one final look into the boy's eyes, he turned slowly back to Sue, rubbing at his earlobe. "It's nothing, my dear," he said, forcing a rather foolish grin. "Static electricity, you know. He gave my ear quite a good shock." He managed a brief laugh as he turned back to Severin. "That's quite a good trick, my friend. Now off with you."

Sev laughed, believing he had actually given the man's ear a small jolt, then turned and ran up the stairs toward the paneled bedroom.

"I'm sorry," Sue laughed. "He's a real mess, isn't he?"

"He's a very clever lad and he delights me without end."

"What was that about Alice?"

Pedarius chuckled. "I told him the story *Alice in Wonderland* this afternoon and he was fascinated. And don't worry about him. There's no way out of the room except down these stairs and there's nothing of value to worry about." Pedarius leaned toward the table and pulled the tray with brandy and two small snifters toward him. "Now let's forget about the boy for a while and find out what is making you so very unhappy. What has stopped the music for you, and I mean that both figuratively and literally?"

Pedarius noticed that the pain had increased in his hand as he tried to grip the brandy decanter. The swelling also was moving into the joints of his fingers, and the steady ache was now at his knees and ankles. He would have to endure for a few more hours. He glanced at the woman's eyes as she began to speak. Now she was involved in her own problems, but she was sure to notice his hands sooner or later. He wondered if they'd hear the sound when the boy fell. He *would* climb into the contraption, he *would!* He had to.

It was not exactly dark, but the light was subdued when Sev entered the master bedroom. The man had closed the wooden shutters before he came downstairs. The darkly paneled walls and the slits of light through the shutters to the floor made for a

167

very dramatic effect. He tiptoed over to the ottoman and sat down, holding the soldiers on his knees and staring at the small, square panel at the opposite end of the room. The story was vividly in his mind and he *knew*, it was too perfect not to be, that this was the entrance to Alice's wondrous place. The thought of it frightened him a little, but his curiosity was peaked. And his mom was right downstairs in case he needed help coming back. But he wouldn't need help. All he'd have to do is wish himself back.

Don't, Severin. He's trying to harm you.

Severin didn't answer but merely shook his head. The old man wouldn't try to hurt him, especially not with his mom down there with him. The old man liked him and he liked his mom too. *They* wanted him to do too much. He had already scared the poor old man for *them*. Now he wanted *them* to leave him alone, let him have some fun for himself. He wouldn't watch if *they* tried to show him the pictures.

He left the soldiers on the ottoman and got up very slowly. He took a deep breath and started to move toward the opening behind the sliding panel. He held his hands out to the sides for balance and carefully put one foot in front of the other, in a straight line, inching across the cool parquet floor.

You are not to enter there, Severin! We forbid you!

"No," Severin said quietly, moving closer to the opening. "He likes me. You don't like him, but he likes me. I'm tired of playing with you. You scare me. He's not the one who scares me all the time. You do."

No, Severin. Listen. You will fall. He knows you will fall!

"She tumbled down," Sev said mutinously. "That's the way you get there. But it doesn't hurt. That's the way you get there!"

Don't, Severin! You'll be hurt. We don't lie to you.

"You do too!" Sev said angrily, though he really couldn't remember if *they* had or not. He slid back the door and looked inside. It was just as the old man had said. He placed his hand on the wooden platform and pushed down. It felt solid, as he knew it would. *They* just didn't want him to know how nice it was down there. *They* probably knew already and didn't want him to have the fun that *they* did.

You are forbidden!

The strange crash in his head startled him for a second, then he put his toe against the paneling and pulled himself up and into the opening. He started as the platform seemed to settle an

168

inch or two, then it felt solid and secure, so he pulled himself all the way in.

He sat there for a long moment, scarcely breathing as he waited for something to happen. It smelled a bit musty inside and he could feel a slight draft coming up from beneath, around the sides of the platform. When was it going to happen?

Sev finally decided that the door had to be closed before he would tumble into the enchanted land. He hoped it wouldn't be too dark as he reached forward and pulled the door shut in front of him.

It was dark, very dark, and he had to reassure himself that there was nothing to be afraid of. Everybody had always told him that, that there was nothing to be afraid of in the dark. Everything still was just as it was around him, only he couldn't see it now. But nothing had changed. He relaxed a bit, then remembered that he had to wish. He closed his eyes and wished he could go to the land where he could make himself as big as he wanted to be. It almost worked. He felt a slight movement of the platform. He would have to wish harder, but it was hard to concentrate with *them* screaming in his head. He gritted his teeth and clenched his fist tight.

"I want to go," he said to himself. "I want to go, I want to go."

Finally, in desperation, he began to bounce on the platform, hoping to get started. The platform moved two more inches. He held his breath expectantly, then bounced again, harder this time.

His breath was taken away as the small platform suddenly plummeted through the small shaft, scraping against the walls on one side, then the other. *They* were right. He was falling! He had expected to drift down, over and over through the air. Just as he opened his mouth to scream, the small car struck the bottom of the shaft and he felt all the wind go out of his body. His head snapped back against the side of the enclosure and Sev felt himself going limp. As his eyes fluttered closed, he saw a cloud of dust whoosh up past him and then he was only vaguely aware that some of the dirt settled on his tongue. And then even *they* were gone.

In the kitchen, Hines cringed as he heard the dumbwaiter fall again. He quickly moved over to the opening in the wall and closed the small door all the way. Dust was coming out of the opening and would settle on the freshly mopped floor. He stood quite still for a moment, expecting to hear the old man shout at him, "What now, Hines?" But he didn't yell. Perhaps he hadn't heard the noise, what with the woman talking to him in there. But one thing was perfectly clear. He would either fix that lift himself tomorrow or bring someone in to fix it. It would be one less thing to worry about. But now he had to clean up that broken glass in the gazebo, and he knew as soon as he got out there that the old man would want him inside.

Sue felt even worse that she had told Pedarius about her situation at home. She felt silly even as she realized during the telling that there was only one thing to be done. She and Nick would have to talk about what had happened, civilly, and only then would she be aware of the extent of the damage done to their relationship. She knew that she still loved Nick and wanted to be with him, provided, of course, that his fling with Tara Dobbs was no more than an affair of the flesh, a brief infatuation which hopefully had played itself out already. But he hadn't even bothered to call her yet, and that impounded the hurt that kept the tears flowing. And the pain at the base of her skull was now so intense that she almost winced each time she moved her head.

"But you're an intelligent woman," Pedarius said softly, "and I can see in your eyes that you know the answers. Of course, it helps to talk to someone about hurtful situations, but the solutions must almost always come from one's self. That you must talk this out with your husband is all too obvious. If both of you were to pretend that the other didn't know, if you left it as a never-to-be-mentioned subject, it would only serve to destroy whatever feelings you hold for one another. Love is a constant, true love, and should survive disappointments, misunderstandings and, yes, even the uncontrollable, lust. It is, in my opinion, impossible to remain faithful to one person for a lifetime, an idea that only fools cling to. But love . . ." A rush of physical pain combined with the genuine remorse he felt at the moment, the irony that he could still *feel* loving and being loved, caused a gasp to escape his lips and his eyes to cloud with tears. That he had been capable of such horrors, that they continued at the very moment, should have hardened his emotions to unfeeling. But then that was his punishment, wasn't it? To suffer endlessly for so small a prize. That was fact. Now was the wrong time to give in to self-pity. He soon would have time to think clearly again, to grasp at the leash of his own fate. The pain was becoming unbearable. He wondered if he'd be able to stand at all. And then he was aware that the woman was staring at him. "I'm sorry," he said, sniffing and wiping at his eyes. "That's why I never married, I'm afraid. I never felt capable of . . . the necessary commitment." He leaned back slowly, careful to conceal the pain he felt. "But you have made that commitment and I know you think it worth saving."

"I knew what I had to do," Sue said, "even as I was boring you with the whole thing. But I do appreciate your confirming it for me. You're a very nice man and I thank you for being a friend to me . . . us," she added, suddenly remembering Sev upstairs. "I'd best drag him down from there and get us home." She started to get out of the chair, then sank back into the softness. "I have to impose on you further, maestro. I have the most excruciating headache, way beyond simple aspirin, I think. Do you, by any chance, have anything stronger? I'll try anything."

"I have just the thing for you," Pedarius said, glancing through the window toward the gazebo. Hines was not there now. Hopefully he had returned to the kitchen. He didn't think he could make it up the stairs himself, at least not without hobbling. "Hines!" he shouted crisply. He heard the clatter of a pan and knew the man would come into the room momentarily.

"Yes, Mr. Pedarius," Hines said from the doorway.

"Would you please bring the small bottle of capsules, the one with the green cap, from the table by my bed?" He turned back to Sue. "Two of these and all pain will be gone within an hour, trust me. I suffer from a swelling of the joints, an arthritic stiffness from time to time, and I know how effective pain killers are. This is just what you need."

"Excuse me," Sue called to Hines as he climbed the stairs. "Would you tell my son to come down now? We have to be going."

Hines paused briefly, nodded, then continued his climb. The old man's hands were swollen again. He'd be in a foul mood and would want him gone as soon as the woman and the boy had left. And that was fine with him. He didn't want to know what the old man did to rid himself of the swelling. He was just glad he didn't have to administer those shots anymore.

"My God," Sue said as she noticed the musician's swollen hands for the first time, "I didn't notice before. How awful for you. Was this the reason you . . . Were you suffering with this while you were performing?"

"It was not inconsequential to my decision to retire, but as I said, it's not always so bad. It comes and . . ."

"Here you are, Mr. Pedarius," Hines said, setting the vial on the marble table. "The boy is not upstairs. Should I look for him in the garden?"

"Not upstairs?" Sue asked, looking toward the stairs to try to imagine if he could have sneaked down past them. She supposed it was possible, but not likely. "Let me check," she said, getting out of the chair. "Sometimes he likes to hide and he's very good at it. I promise you, we'll be out of your way in a moment or two." Please, Sev, she thought, none of your mischief now.

Ten minutes later, Sue was frantic. She and Hines had completely searched the house, and Sev was nowhere to be found. Pedarius had gone into the garden, calling to the boy but only for the benefit of the young woman. He knew where the boy's body was, and that knowledge made the pain more endurable. By tomorrow night, for better or for worse, he would be in Paris.

Sue went out into the garden to assist the old man in his search for Sev, and Hines went out the front door to check the front of the house. As soon as he stepped out onto the front portico, Hines remembered the sound he had heard earlier. His heart stopped for a moment as he considered the consequences. It had to be what had happened. The boy was lying at the bottom of the dumbwaiter shaft and it would be blamed on him. His first inclination was to run away and never come back to the big house. Then he realized that they might think he had pushed the boy down the shaft. What else would they think if he simply disappeared? That was no good. He would have to go back and find the boy. It wasn't really his fault. He was planning to repair the thing tomorrow. Then he remembered the old man telling him to forget about it for the moment, the day he wanted him to go into town for the medicine. That was the excuse he needed.

Hines turned and ran back into the house and directly to the kitchen. He was panting as he opened the door in the wall and leaned forward to look down the shaft. There he was, all right, and he wasn't moving. There would be hell to pay for this. The small body looked twisted and quite dead.

"Hey!" Hines whispered coarsely through the shaft. "Can you hear me, boy?"

When there was no movement at the bottom of the shaft, Hines pulled himself back through the hole, wrapped his arms
172

about his waist and rocked back and forth from one foot to the other. He had to get them in there and right away. It was not his fault!

"In here!" he started to yell, feeling rooted to the spot. "In here!" he shouted louder. Then he was running through the living room toward the door to the garden. "In here! He's in here! Help me! The boy's down there! The boy's down there!"

XII

The big scorpion crawled up the boy's naked arm, its barbed stinger curved in an arc over its back, always in ready position, always ready to strike. His damp, moldy domain had been disturbed and he was angry, searching for the bold intruder. While he didn't seek trouble, he would defend himself to the death if challenged, even sting himself to death in the frenzy of panic. He edged his body under the boy's shirt sleeve but his progress was halted when his curved tail hooked onto the light material. Instead of straightening his tail to allow his progress under the shirt, he backed out and pulled himself up onto the shirt and moved up the cotton material toward the boy's neck.

Sev was aware of *their* voices in his head before he regained consciousness. *They* were warning him not to move, not to open his eyes, to lie perfectly still, to keep his breathing quiet and steady. He had to believe *them* now, to trust *them* implicitly. *They* were his friends, not the old man. Everything *they* said was true, he knew that now. The old man was trying to hurt him.

Then he came to and heard the frantic voices outside the shaft and felt some little things crawling on him. Something was crawling in his hair and another was crawling slowly up his neck toward his chin. But he was listening to *them*. He didn't move a muscle and dared not open his eyes. He had to trust *them* to protect him, at least until his mom got him out of there. He imagined at first that cockroaches were crawling on him but then he realized that they felt much larger, scarier. Now the one was coming up his chin toward his mouth. If it walked on his lips he was afraid it would tickle so much he might have to move to try to blow it away. He felt the sweat begin to seep through his pores.

175

Don't move, Severin. They will not harm you if you stay quite still and calm. You will be safe soon.

Sev felt his left eyelid twitch as the one in his hair crawled off onto his forehead. Then he felt it stop, probably aware of the movement of his lid. He wanted to cry, to sit up and knock them away but he knew he couldn't. So he lay there, waiting to hear his mom's voice above him. Then there were more little legs crawling up his naked leg. It might crawl under his shorts. He couldn't lie still much longer, no matter what they said.

"Oh, no! My God!" he heard his mother say above him. Her voice echoed in the shaft and scared him more. "Sev! Can you hear me, Sev?" He dared not move.

"He's dead!" Sue screamed, pulling her head back out of the opening. "He's dead, I know it. Oh, please, do something! Get him out of there!" She grabbed onto Hines's arm and her nails dug into his flesh. She suddenly felt a rush of nausea and the vomit came out of her mouth before she could reach the sink. The pain in her head was almost unbearable as she choked and heaved her stomach empty.

Pedarius stood in the doorway to the kitchen, watching coldly as Hines took a flashlight and a push-type broom from the utility closet. He wanted to shout at the idiot, to tell him to leave the little bastard down there, but of course he couldn't. But it really didn't matter now. He was dead. Pedarius almost laughed when he realized how well his plan had worked, the precision with which the "accident" had occurred. But he also felt like sobbing with relief. Then he realized that he had to play the game through, to help the woman, to show his grief over her loss.

Pedarius moved toward Sue, grabbing a towel from the rack. He turned on the faucet and wet the end of the towel, pressing it against her forehead.

"One of you hold this flashlight here," Hines said loudly, peering down the open shaft.

"Help him," Sue said to Pedarius, taking the towel from him. "Help *him*, I'm all right!" Sue sobbed as a dry heave convulsed her body.

Pedarius moved to the other man's side and took the silver flashlight from him, slowly closing his swollen fingers around it. Had the woman not been there, he would have clubbed the stupid man senseless then and there and been done with it. Instead, he leaned against the wall and held the light on the narrow shaft.

176

Hines grasped the broom handle by the end and lowered it into the tunnel, hoping to pick up the slack cable on the end of it. He hooked the cable, began drawing the broom back out, then dropped the thin wire again. He took a deep breath, then began the maneuver once more.

"Hurry, please, hurry," Sue said, moving over behind Hines. She held the damp towel over her mouth and tried to muffle her sobs with it.

On the fourth attempt, Hines hooked the cable and then he had it in his hands. He dropped the broom behind him and leaned into the shaft, grabbing the cable with both hands. It would have been easier to handle the small wire with gloves, but he couldn't waste any more time. Slowly, he dead-lifted the platform and the boy's body closer to the opening in the kitchen wall.

Sue realized that the old man would not be much help with his gnarled hands, so she took the flashlight from him and moved him out of the way without so much as an apology. Her heart was pounding as the handyman brought her son closer to the opening. And then they both saw him at the same time.

"Be careful, ma'am," he grunted, nearly exhausted by the strenuous pull, "those things are on his skin. They'll sting him . . . if . . . we're not careful . . . if they haven't already."

Sue grimaced through her tears, and her breath came in sharply as she saw the hideous-looking creatures crawling on Sev's pale face. There was not a sign of life in his body at first glance, but then she thought she noticed an almost imperceptible rising of his belly. One of the scorpions was on his upper lip and seemed ready to venture into his nostril. Another was just under his chin, crawling down his neck. Her first impulse was to grab Sev and pull him into the room, but she knew the scorpions would dig their stingers into him. Then she saw the one moving under the thin cotton shorts.

"There's one under his clothes," she said in an hysterical whisper to Hines.

"Get it first," Hines grunted, sure that the cable would slip through his sweaty hands at any moment. "Then you can flick the others off."

Sue careful lifted the elastic wasteband of the shorts away from Sev's belly and then she definitely felt that he was breathing softly. "He's alive," she said through her clenched teeth, watching the evil-looking arachnid slowly crawl toward the opening she had provided.

Perspiration now was running down Hines's forehead as his arms began to tremble under the strain. "Now just flick him quick with your fingernail . . . then . . . them others."

Sue held her middle finger with her thumb and moved it close to the yellowish scorpion, then with one quick motion flicked it off Sev's belly. It flew against the brick wall and dropped down past the platform. Quickly, she rid him of the one on his neck, then focused her attention to the one, the largest of the three, which had actually started to enter his nose. Out of the corner of her eye she saw Sev's eyelid twitch slightly, probably caused by the tickling sensation at the bottom of his nose. With one sure motion, the last scorpion flew against the brick wall, but this one bounded back and landed on the platform and started for Sev again, moving very quickly, his tail vibrating angrily.

"Pull him out of there!" Hines shouted. "Hurry! I can't hold it no more!"

Sue ducked her head into the opening, grabbed Sev under the arms and lifted him toward her. When he was free and safely in her arms, she turned quickly and carried him to the butcher block table behind them. She gently lowered him to the table and stretched him out on his back as she heard Hines let the platform drop back to the bottom of the shaft. As soon as his head touched the table, Sev opened his eyes and blinked rapidly against the bright light above him. He stared up at his mother's frightened expression.

"Are they all off of me?" he asked as his body trembled in relief.

The sound of the boy's voice startled all three of them, but it stopped Pedarius in his tracks. He couldn't believe his ears. The monstrous child was not only alive, he also seemed well. He stopped behind the woman and peered over her shoulder.

Sue took Sev's face in her hands and kissed him wetly on the mouth. Then she pulled back and looked at him, still unwilling to believe that he was conscious and talking. She ran her hands over his body, not knowing what she expected to feel. Then she began nodding her head, almost feverishly. "They're all . . . they're all off of you. Do you hurt, Sev? Where do you hurt, baby?"

"He looks okay," Hines said from the end of the table, praying that the boy was all right. "He looks okay, don't he?" he said to the old man. Hines was rocking back and forth again, nervously awaiting their accusations, some sort of chastisement.

178

"I don't hurt, Mom," Sev said, rubbing at the itching sensation under his nose. "They won't hurt you if you stay very, very still." He nodded his head to make sure they understood that he knew what he was talking about. "It's right. They won't. One crawled right over my eye."

Sue reached down and hugged him to her as the tears started again. "Are you sure you don't hurt? Please tell me if you hurt somewhere, Sev."

"They didn't hurt me cause I was very still," Sev repeated.

"The fall, I mean. Don't you hurt from . . . anywhere, Sev?"

"Nope," he said with a smile, "I don't. Not anywhere."

Sue turned and looked for confirmation from Hines. Was it possible that he wasn't hurt at all? Hines shrugged his shoulders and managed a small grin. Even so, Sue thought, as she returned her attention to Sev, he should see a doctor. How could he possibly have stayed so still with those *things* crawling on his face? "How did you know that, Sev?" she asked in amazement. "How did you know they wouldn't bite you . . . sting you if you stayed quiet?"

Sev turned his head slightly and stared directly into the frightened eyes of Pedarius. "Ask him," he said quietly. "He knows."

Pedarius's hand flew to his mouth as the boy challenged him openly. His body swayed slightly as the other two turned to look at him. He opened his mouth and breathed through it. What was he to say? That the boy had unseen accomplices guiding his every movement? And then he remembered that he was being threatened by the words of a child. He was not thinking clearly. He must not panic. Pedarius opened his mouth but no words came forth.

"Did you tell him about scorpions?" Sue asked, too addled really to realize that the entire conversation was pointless.

"No, I . . ." Pedarius finally blurted out. "I don't know what I may have said that led the boy to . . . no, we didn't talk about . . . I don't know." Pedarius felt that he might collapse at any second. "I'm sorry, I . . . Hines, help me. I must sit down."

Hines grabbed a straight chair from the end of the table and pushed it under the old man as he sagged downward. "I think the boy's all right," Hines said to Sue. "If he can stand up there ain't no bones broke or nothing. Can you stand up, boy?"

Sev started to get up but Sue held him down with a hand to his chest. "I'm okay, Mom," he whined, pushing her hand away. "I was just scared for a minute, that's all. Can I please get up now?"

The three of them had quite different thoughts as they watched the boy move about in the kitchen, demonstrating for them how unaffected he was by the whole ordeal. He did appear to be all right, Sue thought, but she remembered vividly the consequences of not following up on his teacher's report that he had been complaining of stomach aches.

"Shouldn't I have a doctor examine him at least?" Sue asked to neither of them in particular.

"*Mom*," Sev whined.

"Sev, go lie down on the sofa for a few minutes and then we'll go home, okay? Please?"

He'd better do it, Sev thought, or else she would have him back at Sloan-Kettering. He flashed her a mild expression of disgust as he stomped out of the kitchen.

Sue dropped into one of the chairs around the table and rubbed at her aching temples. "Shouldn't I take him to the doctor . . . although I haven't the foggiest idea . . ."

"I can't tell you how dreadfully sorry I am," Pedarius said, determined to have them out of his house within ten minutes. "I should have remembered that damned lift being up there." He flashed a scalding look at Hines for Sue's benefit. "Hines, would you bring the capsules from the tea table," he ordered gruffly. As soon as the man disappeared through the door, Pedarius whispered to Sue, "He assured me that the lift had been repaired last week. That's what I was telling you about him. I just can't trust him anymore. You poor dear," he said, placing his hand on hers, " I hope you can forgive me for being so careless. If it will make you feel better, I'll call a doctor in town and ask him to come out for a look at the boy. Perhaps that would be best."

"Oh, thank you," Sue said gratefully. "I do think he's all right, but I would feel so much better if . . ."

"I'll take care of it." He turned and took the vial from Hines. "Now a glass of water, if you please." Pedarius shook out two of the capsules in Sue's hand, almost grimacing at the pain in his own hands. He didn't try to replace the small rubber cap. He motioned with his head for Hines to give the water to the woman. "Now swallow them down. That's right. I assure you that these will take care of your headache at least. Now you go back to the cottage and get some rest. I'll take care of the telephone call. It may take him a couple of hours, but please try not to worry."

"Thank you so much," Sue said. "Thank you both. And it's nobody's fault, please believe that. He just . . . gets himself into trouble, that's all. I . . ."

"Would you like Hines to help you back to . . ."

"No, no," Sue said, getting up from the table, "we'll be . . . we've caused you quite enough trouble for one afternoon." She managed a small laugh, though she really didn't feel it. "Well, you can't say it's dull being around Sev and me."

If only you knew, Pedarius thought. "No, not dull," he smiled. "Not dull at all."

She had to know, Nick thought as he shoved his shaving gear into the leather kit. Somehow she had found out. That's why she had left so abruptly, no messages, nothing. And Mandy was being strangely polite and uncommunicative. She knew too. After all, who else was Sue likely to confide in? So now he'd have to face up to it.

"Nice timing, asshole," he said to himself in the mirror. As if Sue hadn't been through enough as it was, worrying herself ragged with Sev for months on end, now she had to contend with a cheating husband. On the other hand, they were both intelligent people, they loved each other and if they were both sensible they could work this out and put it behind them.

He put the leather kit into the larger bag and flopped across the bed. He dialed the number again and rolled onto his back, telling himself that she'd pick up this time on the third ring. When she didn't, he gave up hoping, but let it ring ten more times nonetheless. How could she have found out? How? And where could she be? He knew that she couldn't possibly let the phone ring without picking up if she was at the cottage.

He hung up the phone and covered his eyes with his forearm. What to do? Perhaps she was on her way back to the city at that very moment. He decided to have a sandwich and try her again in half an hour. If he couldn't reach her by then he'd get the car from the garage and drive up.

He hoped Anna was not in the kitchen. She was acting strangely toward him too.

As soon as they got back to the cottage, Sue insisted that Sev go to his bedroom and rest until she threw together something

181

for dinner. Her head was pounding, she was tired and emotionally spent and wanted to feed Sev and lie down until the doctor got there. Watching him walk alongside her on the way back from the big house, she had decided that he was all right but also felt that he should be checked out by a physician. And she had another thought as well.

Remembering it, she sagged suddenly against the cabinet and almost dropped the can of soup. The dizziness probably was a signal that her own body was past exhaustion and near breaking. But it had occurred to her as they walked back that perhaps Sev had suffered brain damage when he was ravaged by the cancers and so near death. That certainly would explain his strange behavior. And maybe it wasn't severe enough to have been picked up by the doctors, just enough to render him incapable of making normal judgments as to his own safety, his own mortality. Shouldn't he have known better than to crawl into the lift? Shouldn't the potential danger have been evident, especially to an exceptionally bright young boy? Then again, perhaps the special knowledge the experts at Sloan-Kettering said he possibly possessed after having ridded himself of malignant growths made him feel infallible, quite capable of plotting his own destiny, fearless to the point of endangering himself constantly. And when he removed the pressure from that part of his brain concerned with the instincts of survival, perhaps it allowed for the development of his capacity for extrasensory perception.

Sue suddenly realized that the dizziness wasn't passing, that she was feeling drowsy to the point of dropping in her tracks. She set the soup can on the counter and steadied herself with both hands against the edge. The capsules. She was obviously having a reaction to the medicine he had given her. The pain in her head had subsided a bit, thankfully, but now she began to wonder if she could make it to the bedroom without falling.

She filled a glass with water, took a sip, then almost dropped it into the sink. Carefully she moved along the counter toward the door, too drowsy to be frightened but still concerned about falling. How prophetic that they had been talking about *Alice in Wonderland* that afternoon. Nothing seemed normal anymore. She floated above ordinary happenings, real life, in a space where everything went wrong every five minutes. She suddenly flashed on the bottle of capsules in the maestro's hand and wondered if the label didn't read, "Eat Me." She stopped and shook

182

her head. At the moment, she had to concentrate on getting to her own little bed. Sleep. She wanted to sleep. Needed to.

And then she was standing by her bed. She smiled as her eyes began to close and she could feel the sleep so close, so warm and comforting. Sue sagged onto the bed as the phone rang.

It was an effort but she managed to pick up the receiver and place it against her ear before she fell back across the mattress. She smiled as she heard his voice.

"Sue, where have you been?" Nick said, relieved that he had finally reached her. "I've been trying to reach you for hours."

"Where . . . have I . . . been?" she slurred, then smiled tiredly as she realized she didn't know the answer. "I don't know. Where have you . . . been?"

Nick felt a rush of anxiety as he realized that something was wrong with her. It was unlike her to be drunk but under the circumstances anything was possible. "Are you all right? Where's Sev?"

"I'm . . . sleepy . . . baby." Wasn't she supposed to be mad at him? He probably wasn't coming home to dinner again. Well, tonight she really didn't care. She needed to sleep. But there was something she had to tell him. What was it?

"Sue, listen to me. What's the matter? Have you been drinking?"

Sue nodded her head slowly. "I almost . . . dropped the glass in . . . in the sink." She could barely keep her eyes open. She had to tell him something.

"Where is Sev?" Nick demanded. "Let me talk to him, Sue."

Then she remembered. "You have to . . . let the doctor in. I . . . have to . . . sleep now." The phone rolled out of her hand and against the pillow as she peacefully gave in to the medicine. Immediately Sue Arcomano was dreaming that she heard her husband's voice calling to her. But she couldn't tell where it was coming from.

Raymond Hines cut the length of cord from the spool, looped it neatly, then picked up his tool box and headed back into the house. It was already dark and he should have been home an hour ago. It was just like that old fool to let that dumbwaiter go unrepaired for months, then insist that he close it up after his working hours were over. And putting nails in that nice paneling was a crime, but if that's what he wanted, that's what he'd get. Hines was relieved that the old man hadn't blamed him for the boy falling down there, but Hines suspected he was letting him know it was his fault by making him nail it shut now. He could have been on his second beer down at the tavern by now. And what he was going to do with that cord he hadn't the foggiest. He would just do what the old man told him to, that's all. Just do it and get out of there.

Pedarius sat in the big chair in his bedroom, waiting for Hines to come back up. Pedarius's hands were aching badly now but he would have to forget the pain for a few more minutes. He shook his head angrily as he stared at the small panel in the wall. Why couldn't the boy have been killed? It would have been so much simpler. It had been a perfect setup with his mother there as a witness. But it hadn't worked. It was impossible to believe what he was going through.

He wondered briefly how many others there were who knew what he knew. He couldn't be the only one. How many others had committed acts so vile that they were punished as he had been? How many knew that nothing was outside the realm of possibility? That inexplicable forces were present, that they could wreak havoc beyond comprehension, beyond all accumulated knowledge. That reality knows no boundaries. That mankind's knowledge of the infinite possibilities of himself and his world is hopelessly shallow.

And while thinking these thoughts, Pedarius could not help but consider the possibility that he was mad beyond rescue. That he had somehow inflicted the pain upon himself, that he had only imagined the curse, that his mind and not the instrument brought a temporary relief. After all, had he not admitted that all things were possible? Why then should he believe anything other than his own depraved insanity? It was possible that he had tortured himself all these years. Had he only imagined that he was being challenged by *their* surrogate? Had he driven himself so close to the brink of self-destruction that he had made *their* threat come true, but only in his own addled mind?

Then he remembered the boy's eyes, his words. Pedarius's confusion, his doubts were strangling. Now he was faced with another mental puzzle. Was an insane man aware of his madness?

Hines stood in the middle of the room, shifting nervously as he waited for the old man to answer. Then Hines realized that he probably hadn't even heard his question. He cleared his throat and asked again, "What do you want me to do with this rope?"

184

Pedarius was startled to see him standing there. It took him a couple of seconds to shift gears, to get back to the present. He took a deep breath and pulled himself out of the chair. "Just put it there on the chest," he said as he steeled his nerves for the task at hand. He had to force some strength into his hands and arms. "Nail that door shut before we're faced with another near-disaster."

"It's pretty near going to ruin your paneling over there," Hines said, pointing at the far wall. "I think I might be able to fix that thing myself tomorrow and then . . ."

"Just do as I tell you," Pedarius said quietly, "and be done with it. Don't concern yourself with defacing the wood."

Rich people didn't care about anything, Hines thought as he carried his tool box to the wall. They could always buy something new. He knelt over the box, opened it and searched in the top section for the right-sized nails. A nail big enough to penetrate the paneling and catch the door would more than likely cause the wood to split. But that was the old man's problem now. He had warned him. Out of the corner of his eye he saw the old man walk up behind him. Now he was going to stand there and look over his shoulder. He was sure to make a mess of it with the old fool watching. Hines picked up a few medium-sized nails and the smaller hammer and prayed that the wood didn't split all the way to the ceiling.

He felt the old man bend over and glanced down to see what he was reaching for in his tool box. When he saw him pick up the large claw hammer, he prepared to tell him that he was using the smaller hammer so he wouldn't make a mess of it. Then he guessed that the old fool was going to try to help him. He'd best just stay quiet and let him do what he wanted.

Hines's body stiffened as the hammer crashed into the back of his skull. His eyes flew open wide and the smaller hammer fell out of his hand and bounced off his knee. The second blow sent his head forward, and his face smashed against the paneled wall. He was immediately in shock and so didn't feel any intense pain as he pushed himself away from the wall and looked up toward the old man. He saw the hammer coming down at him and saw, rather than felt, the head of the instrument bury itself in the middle of his forehead. He did not see the sudden gush of blood, however, because he was dead by the time he hit the floor.

Pedarius reeled back from the awful sight. He had not intended to hit the man hard enough to cause serious bleeding. The blood fairly gushed from the round indentation in the man's face and ran across his wildly staring eyes. It was obvious from his crumpled position that he was quite dead.

Pedarius was at once both horrified and pleased with himself. He quickly ran into the bathroom, grabbed a towel and returned to wrap the man's head in it. Without wasting a second, he grabbed Hines under the arms and slowly dragged him over to the bed. The pain in his entire body was intense but he knew he had to ignore it for the next hour or so and do what had to be done. He lifted the lifeless body onto the bed and bent down to remove the man's shoes.

It was disgusting, repulsive, touching the dead flesh and even more repulsive looking at the man's naked body when he finally had stripped him of all his clothes. He had intended dressing the dead man in a pair of his own pajamas, but then he decided that it would be a waste of time. The cloth would be burned away anyway. He tossed the pajamas on the end of the bed, pushed the body into a normal sleeping position and pulled the thick comforter over him.

Pedarius desperately needed to rest but there was no time. He had much to do yet. First he would take the cord down to the back of the garden and get that done. That would not be too strenuous and he could manage to get his breath. Then he would load some of the silver and a couple of paintings into Hines's pickup, bring the cans of gasoline back into the house with him and he would be ready for the boy. Pedarius had watched the woman swallow the capsules. She would be quite incapacitated by now.

Pedarius glanced at his swollen hands and was repulsed by their ugliness. But he also gave himself credit for working against the intense pain he was suffering. He felt a fresh charge of adrenaline and knew he was up to the challenge of the next hours. He would defy them and win. He might decide later—in Paris, perhaps—that he had had enough of life. But that would be his choice, not theirs.

XIII

He felt a tingle of energy in his fingertips as he wrapped his hand around the neck of the Stradivarius, like a minute electrical charge from the taut strings. It was as if the instrument were alive and knew of the miraculous powers it possessed. That the artfully crafted creation had a soul of its own was not so far removed from Pedarius's belief. If its miraculous vibrations could soothe his painfully twisted joints back to supple, why then not a soul intertwined in its formerly living pieces?

A fresh, warm breeze stirred his hair as he stepped out the door into the garden. There was an unmistakable smell of rain on the breeze, distinctly different from the smells off the sound, though there were no clouds in the dark blue sky. Again he felt the tingling from the violin as he made his way past the gazebo.

A bolt of bright, white lightning, literally out of the blue, flashed across the sky, causing him to stop in his tracks and look skyward as a whirl of warm wind whipped at his clothes. The gentle twister caused the Stradivarius to lift and jerk in his hand. At that moment he knew he was not insane. *They* were with him, all about him, ready.

"Oh, David, David, David," he said quietly into the air as genuine tears of remorse warmed his eyes. "My poor Anya."

He raised the instrument to his neck, brought the bow to the strings and as the first haunting notes floated through the air, the remembrances flashed vividly in his mind.

Though he couldn't wake her, Sev still clung to his mother and felt protected by her warmth. The awful pictures had started and he could hear the music, faintly, floating across the night from the garden. *They* promised him it would be for the last time. Somehow he sensed it was true.

But he'd have to go soon.

After months of loneliness, after feeling that he'd never again find a real friend in the new town, Hans Gruebber was ecstatic. His mother and father smiled as they listened at the dinner table, happy that their son was happy.

"And he really likes me, Father, as much as I like him. We are almost exactly the same age and we like all the same things, know the same games. His name is David Stubenmyer and he has a sister named Anya, but she is too little to be with us, really. But I have a friend, Father, I have a friend!"

The happy, carefree days of childhood bound them as close as brothers, and that bond united the two families firmly and trustingly, warmly and lovingly. Long, seemingly endless days in the fiercely fragrant forests surrounding the summer cabins which the two families retreated to in August of every year, near the Austrian border. The fresh mountain air revitalized all of them, even the young, sickly Anya. The three of them explored and played themselves to exhaustion each day, then awakened the following morning fresh and ready for new and unexpected adventures.

"You boys must not forget Anya," Frau Stubenmyer would remind them as they headed for the rolling, green hills. "She loves you both so much and depends on you. You are her brother, David, but you, Hans Gruebber, I think she loves you as much. Be kind to her, the both of you."

The evening meals just after sunset were almost festive, gay, sparkling laughter and good-humored joking made them seem like parties or celebrations. And then stories around the crackling fire as the children felt sleep creeping up on them. Warmth. Belonging. Trust. Love.

Back home in Munich, the boys entered their teens, still inseparable, closer perhaps than brothers, sharing the same interests, attending the same school, the same class, then after school the same music teacher, Frau Mueller.

"You two are my prized students," she would say to them, "each of you superbly gifted. You, David, have a natural talent for music, it comes from your heart, but you must not neglect work, work, work for your technique. And you, Hans, are a superb technician but you must learn to *feel* the music, know in your heart what the composer has given you. But you must, both of you, work, work, work!"

188

Later still, another happily relaxed evening with both families around the huge, oval dinner table. Anya's eyes lovingly covered Hans's every movement as he mimicked Frau Mueller's gestures, "Work, work, work!"

"Well, my young lad," Herr Stubenmyer said to Hans, "it's no work for you to put away the wiener schnitzel. What does he do with it, do you think?" Good-natured laughter abounds.

"I can eat as much," David said, puffing out his chest.

"I'll take that bet," Hans retorted, laughing with the rest.

"I think we can't make that much," Frau Gruebber said, and laughed.

And then like the political atmosphere in Germany, the table talk grew more serious. The fire at the Reichstag followed by the confirmation of the new Chancellor. The Nazi Party had prevailed. The attempt by the Communist Party to take over the nation had been crushed. Had this Hitler taken too much power for himself? The Weimar constitution abandoned and the establishment of a Third Reich, which would last for a thousand years.

"A thousand years," the boys would say to one another and try to imagine.

What was happening to political opposition, to civil liberties? Were they not one and the same? And more puzzling to the young Hans, the open hatred that was drifting up as if from the gutters, foul and putrid-smelling. Anti-Semitism? How was it possible that this feeling existed? He knew firsthand and it was unfathomable. Those closest to him and his family were Jews. They were of Germany, every bit as much as he, unequaled in their loyalty, as loving and caring as human beings could be. But the hateful feelings were inescapable, permeating, spreading and causing fear and mistrust where there should have been none.

And then the magnificent Stradivarius set them apart, Hans and David, but the breach had seemed momentary, nothing permanent. It was jealousy. Hans knew that and was aware that it was childish to feel that way, but it seemed to fester within him like an irritating boil he couldn't get at. Why had Frau Mueller given the priceless instrument to David Stubenmyer and not to him? Hadn't she told them, time and time again, that they were equally talented? He knew he had worked much harder, practiced for longer hours than David had, and he had more drive, more ambition than his friend had. He deserved the instrument.

189

He felt deeply that it should have been his. Hadn't it gone to David simply because he was a Jew? Hadn't the Jewess bestowed the ultimate gift on the basis of a shared Hebrew faith rather than as a reward, a celebration of talent? Didn't Frau Mueller's flagrant discounting of talent indicate an anti-Aryan prejudice?

The instrument was unmatched in its craftsmanship, and its rich, resonant tones enhanced the talents of anyone who touched its rich patina. Hans Gruebber was quite aware of the growing resentment he felt at David Stubenmyer possessing the instrument, but was not consciously aware that the aching envy was gradually manifesting itself as an understanding and an acceptance of the near-boiling hatred stirred by the Nazis. He saw less and less of the Stubenmyers, but wasn't it mainly their fault? Weren't they keeping more to themselves? His father and mother practically never mentioned their close friends anymore, and when they did, it was done in whispers, it seemed.

The arrests, the roundups were now public knowledge, but Hans Gruebber was not prepared for the news that his father had for him one evening.

"It's true," Herr Gruebber assured him. "The Stubenmyers are to be arrested the day after tomorrow. I saw the list today with my own eyes. They are to be sent away; where, I do not know. I have thought and thought, Hans, believe me, my son, and there is nothing to be done."

Sev didn't want to go out into the dark during this bad part, but *they* told him it was time. Just as he stepped off the porch of the cottage, a loud clap of thunder roared across the sky, causing him to cry out in surprise. It matched perfectly the sounds in the horrifying tale he was "watching" again and made it seem even more real, more frightening. But he knew it was getting closer to the end, and although that was the really bad part, it would be over soon.

He could see better where he was going when the lightning flashed, so he ran faster toward the wall. He could tell from the sound of the music that the old man was near the back of the garden. Waiting for him?

"Quickly," Hans whispered urgently as the four of them climbed into the car. *"We can't waste any time. It's all arranged."*

190

"Hans, how can I ever repay you, my dear friend?" David Stubenmyer said, placing his hand on his shoulder. "You are very brave to risk your life to help us. We are forever in your debt."

From the backseat, Hans felt Anya's hand on his neck. "I love you, Hans Gruebber, and we all thank you."

Later, as the car wound around the mountain road, Hans broke the silence of the past fifteen minutes. "I'm sorry that you couldn't bring more with you but I'm sure you understand. And you, David, I know how you must hate to part with the Stradivarius but it was the only way my father could strike a deal with these greedy bastards. They only agreed to sneak you across the border when they learned the value of the violin. I hope you understand."

"At the moment, I can only think that you love us enough to risk your own safety for my family. There is no greater treasure in life than a friend such as you."

The fear generated by the five people in the black car speeding through the night created a tension that could almost be smelled and touched. The silence in the car made the terror more stifling, and the sight of approaching headlights caused hearts to pound and breathing to stop.

Later, there were sighs of relief, though the worst was still ahead of them, as the car came to a halt in a clump of trees just off the road.

Hans Gruebber could not control the shakiness in his voice as he prepared himself for the near-impossible. "We have to walk the rest of the way," he whispered, wiping the perspiration from his brow with his finger. "They are waiting for us at the cabin in the woods, and they will take you the rest of the way to the border. We must not talk after we leave the car, so I will say goodbye to you now."

The tears flowed freely as kisses and hugs were exchanged in the black sedan. A fine mist fell on the windshield, and distant claps of thunder echoed through the mountains. Then the five figures emerged from the car and moved off through the forest.

Had they heard the hysterical moans and grunts coming from Hans Gruebber's tight throat, they might have suspected they would be safer if he returned the luger to his pocket. In his nervous condition, his finger could easily have pressed involuntarily against the trigger, injuring one of them or himself. But he walked ahead of them, carrying the gun stiffly in his right hand, seemingly ready to defend them all in case of discovery.

191

Frau Stubenmyer was the first in the single file behind their leader, and so was the first to fall, fatally shot through the forehead, when Hans Gruebber turned suddenly and squeezed the trigger. Herr Stubenmyer was shot through the chest as he bent toward his fallen wife, then through the back as he lurched forward.

Whining cries of anguish, like those of a wounded animal, came from Hans Gruebber's throat as he stood staring at the horrified expression on Anya's face. She held her face in her hands and slowly shook her head back and forth in total disbelief.

He had to close his eyes to squeeze the trigger again, then again. When he opened his eyes, Anya was sprawled on her back in the path, and David was rushing toward him holding the violin case like a weapon. Before he could get off another round, he was struck in the face with the case and he reeled backward, dropping the gun in the grass.

He quickly scrambled to his knees and desperately felt for the gun in the wet growth beside the path. Just as his fingers felt the warm metal, he saw David Stubenmyer disappear through the trees, off to the left of the barely visible trail.

Hans Gruebber could hear his prey moving noisily through the dark forest ahead of him and knew that he must catch him and complete the grisly work he had started or he could never again take a peaceful breath. David Stubenmyer would not rest until he avenged the slaughter of his family. But beyond that fear, his obsession of having and holding the Stradivarius as his own was almost realized. He had done the unspeakable and there was no turning back now. He realized the insanity of the moment but was helpless to control it.

The thrashing sounds in front of him stopped suddenly. He ran a few yards more toward the last sounds he had heard, then stopped. It was deathly quiet in the forest except for the dripping of water through the leaves. In the distance, the rolling roar of thunder.

And then he was truly stunned. Hans Gruebber stood transfixed as the music began, the familiar composition he knew so well, the notes he wished he had written himself. David Stubenmyer was playing his own composition, the one that had so impressed Frau Mueller that she had decided he was the one who should have the instrument left her by her grandfather. That was the reason for her giving the violin to David Stubenmyer,

Hans Gruebber finally realized. That magnificent composition, and it was that, magnificent. "Rapideus," he had called it. The work was both simple and bafflingly complex, the work of a genius, and hauntingly beautiful. And here, in his moment of supreme terror, the music wafted through the night, surrounding his senses. But why had he halted his escape to uncase the violin? That in itself panicked Hans Gruebber even more. Slowly, holding the luger in front of him, he made his way toward the source of the music.

And then he saw why his friend had stopped. David Stubenmyer was standing in a small clearing, his back to a rocky embankment which surrounded him on three sides and from which there was no escape. His feet were planted wide apart as his arm brought the bow across the strings, then back, producing the most wondrous sounds in the natural stone amphitheater. His eyes blazed defiantly at the sadistic monster who had murdered his family. There was no doubt in his mind that he was taking his last breaths.

"At the moment you die, Hans Gruebber, you will hear the music you are hearing now . . . and you will know that it is we who kill you! You know the notes well and the notes are me! What I say is true and I speak before God! "Rapideus" will bring you untold agony, it will haunt your every waking moment until I come for you! Now, you accursed demon, now!!!!"

Hans Gruebber closed his eyes and squeezed the trigger until the explosions became quiet clicks. When he opened his eyes, David Stubenmyer's lifeless eyes still glared at him as his body lay slumped at the bottom of the rocky wall. He still clutched the violin and the bow in his hands.

As Hans Gruebber took the prize for the nightmarish bloodbath from the death grip, the middle finger of his dead friend's hand plucked a last note on the first string of the violin. And then it was his, in its leather case and under his arm. As he left the clearing without looking back, Hans Gruebber wished desperately that it was three days ago and that the maniacal plan had not yet entered his mind. That he had done this awful thing was, even three minutes later, inconceivable.

Sev crouched by the hole in the wall, terrified, until the shots stopped ringing in his ears. He prayed that *they* were telling him the truth, that he had gone through the horrible thing for the last time. He shivered a bit, though the winds which were beginning to pick up were very warm and balmy. Then he took a deep breath and crawled through the wall into the garden.

The trees swayed in the erratic breeze, and the leaves of the lush plants were in constant motion, their rustling murmur completing the darkly portentous effect, a perfect setting for the unexpected. Sev desperately wanted to turn back, to run home to the safety of his mom. But she was asleep. She really wasn't protecting him as she should. And *their* constant reassurances that he was safe were insufficient. He was terrified, so much so that he crawled slowly toward the round pool; he didn't trust himself to get to his feet. It was too dark and scary. He might fall. Once he got to the pool he would know where he was. Then he could find his way.

Pedarius saw the boy crawl through the crumbled opening in the wall. Pedarius took one step back toward the trunk of the tree and stood quite still, holding the violin and bow in one hand and reaching back with the other hand to steady himself against the rough bark. The ache in his fingers was somewhat relieved but he could tell as he felt the end of the cord that his hands were not as free of the arthritic crippling as they should have been. That knowledge only heightened his mounting hysteria. He should have been completely free of any pain, his joints should have been as smoothly mobile as a young man's after suffering the agony of that damned composition. It was always so. It was both his punishment and his relief. Why had it suddenly failed him? Perhaps because he had known in the back of his mind that the confrontation was at hand. Perhaps his concentration had been affected. He moved his legs ever so slightly. There was stiffness there as well. But this was a matter to contemplate later. He returned his complete attention to the boy, who was crawling slowly toward the pool like some mythical creature, half human, half animal. His eyes were strange. There! When he turned his head slightly, his eyes seemed to glow like the flat surfaces of a cat's.

Pedarius reminded himself that *they* probably could do anything. He must not be shaken by anything this small creature seemed to do. It would all be an illusion. He wanted to cry out in rage, in pain, in terror, but he dared not. He stood very erect, frozen, waiting.

Sev crawled to the edge of the pool and raised himself to his knees, his hands resting on the low brick wall around the water. He felt a presence near him but he couldn't see anything because of the constant movement of the big leaves. He looked down at the mirrorlike surface of the dark water and saw a pale reflection of the clear sky above. And just then a flash of lightning cracked across the sky, bathing the rustling garden in a light brighter than sunlight, creating an effect of blacks and whites rather than colors.

In the reflection of the pool, Sev saw the man, standing tall and erect, his eyes wide with terror, directly across the water from him. His head jerked upward, his lips curled back in an angry snarl and he was horrified by the rumbling, growling shriek that came from his throat. He was further startled when the old man screamed in supreme terror in response to the beastly, flesh-ripping warning that had passed his own lips. Sev scrambled to his feet, hysterical with fear, screaming at the top of his lungs.

"Nooooooooo!" Pedarius screamed toward the treetops. His entire body wobbled on his weakened knees. He was ready to die, he wanted to die, his heart was threatening to shut down, pounding unevenly in his chest.

No, Severinnnnn. No! Stay down!

Sev didn't hear them as he scrambled up onto the low wall surrounding the well. His knees locked and he stretched his hands toward the evil old man, his fingers seeming to claw their way through the air toward him. "Give it to me!" he screamed hysterically, stretching toward the violin. *They* wanted him to have the violin and then it would all be over. "Give it to me!!!!!"

Get back, Sev. Now!!

"Nooooooo!" Pedarius screamed as he pulled on the cord tied around the tree behind him. He felt the cord pull out of his hand and he slumped back against the rough bark.

The limb which had been held back by the light cord whipped around through the air and caught Severin in the back of the head, flipping him up in the air and headfirst into the dark, green water.

Pedarius screamed again as the limb continued to switch through the air above the well. His hands clawed at the bark of the trunk behind him as his eyes watched the water churn up over the low brick surrounding wall. He half expected to see the boy bob back to the surface immediately. Instead, as the water smoothed again, he watched a series of bubbles pop to the surface and burst. His breath came in sharply, then again, and then a cackle of hysterical relief bent him almost double. He

195

panted for breath as he moved closer to the water to peer down into it. The water churned again and more bubbles rose to the surface, but in the darkness the old man could see nothing more.

But he screamed again and jumped back when the small hand broke through the surface and clawed the air, desperately searching for something to grab onto. The frantically groping hand was directly in the center of the well, well away from the sidewalls.

Again, the bright white of the lightning illuminated the boy's predicament. The long bolt seemed to hold in the sky as Pedarius peered down into the terrified eyes.

The boy was struggling furiously just under the surface of the water, held suspended by the thick green vines, which wrapped themselves about his shoulders, around his neck and across his forehead. The eyes were wide with panic, pleading for air, glowing in the flash of lightning. His hand, out of the water to his wrist, crisscrossed the surface as his fingertips seemed to try to breathe with their clutching motion.

"Haaa!" Pedarius screamed down at him, bending at the waist and holding the violin up in the air behind him. "Haaaaa!"

Then it was dark again and the small hand continued to grasp at nothing. Pedarius stumbled backward a few steps, took a few deep breaths, then with bitter tears streaming down his face started to move toward the house. His legs ached; in fact, his whole body ached. Had he won? Was this what his glorious victory was to be? Wouldn't *they* merely choose another surrogate to effect *their* revenge? Perhaps *they* already had. Could he not be waiting already, in Paris?

He stopped at the gazebo and leaned against it, listening. The boy probably was drowned by now but it had been foolish of him to believe that he would be rid of *them* so easily. *They* had been guiding his destiny all the time, from the very moment he had murdered *them*.

Of course it was *they* who sent him to that awful place. *They* were the cause of his becoming an unequaled master of violin almost overnight. It was part of *their* plan, part of the curse he had scoffed at. He should have known. It was foolish of him to believe that the Stradivarius alone had elevated his skills so quickly to genius. That his artistry was exceptional should have been obvious to all who heard him play. Why then was he not summoned to Berlin to perform for the personal pleasure of the

Führer himself? For the elite, for those capable of appreciating genius?

Of course, *they* had arranged that he be summoned to that death camp, to Dachau, to perform for the perverse officers who so calmly went about their lives amid the grisly horrors. It was part of the torture, a constant reminder of what he had done, a humiliation, a debilitating humiliation which David Stubenmyer had arranged for him.

And *they* guided his escape to England. How easily the invading forces had accepted that he was one, David Stubenmyer, a Jewish inmate who had been forced to perform for the German officers at Dachau. As proof of his identity he had the birth certificate of David Stubenmyer and the original composition, "Rapideus," in his violin case. And with very few questions, he had in his possession the papers required for travel to London.

Had he known how much control *they* had over him, he would not have been so brazenly daring when he chose the name for himself. Pedarius, an audaciously arrogant anagram of "Rapideus," was chosen in total disdain for the already disregarded curse.

In a matter of months, he was acclaimed the greatest violin virtuoso since Paganini. Pedarius fame spread like wildfire, his artistry worshiped by the music world, his celebrity sought by society. All part of *their* plan.

With one last glance toward the back of the garden, Pedarius left the gazebo and headed toward the house. He knew without looking that the swelling had begun in his hands again. There was a time when he was free of it for months on end. He sighed tiredly as he went through the open door into the house.

In Rome he had realized that the curse was indeed real. Three days before an important concert, he had been horrified to feel the stiffness in his joints. He had summoned a doctor at once but his medicine had no effect. The pain grew worse. In horror, he closed himself in his hotel room, refusing to see anyone. He had sat for two days in the darkness, unable to believe how grotesquely gnarled his wonderous hands had become. Then suddenly, on the third day, he knew what had to be done. How he knew he could only guess, but he knew.

The pain was by then so great that he had to force his hands to grip the bow. As soon as he struck the first notes of "Rapideus," a vivid account of his relationship with David Stubenmyer began to play out before him. He relived every moment of it as if it had happened the day before, experiencing the same terror and horror of the murders as if for the first time. By the time he finished, he was emotionally exhausted, as repulsed and nauseated as if he had emptied the luger only seconds before. When the tears of anguish had subsided, he realized that his hands were no longer twisted, that there was no pain at all. And at that moment he knew. The curse was real. *They were* still with him. As unbelievable as it seemed, it was true. *They* would not leave him; the prophecy would be with him, threatening, until he took his last breath.

How, then, could he possibly have doubted the warning *they* shot at him when the woman had interrupted his concert with the first six notes of "Rapideus"? Because it was too terrifying to accept. And he had actually touched the boy while he was still inside her body. That was probably the moment *they* took over his body, when he became *their* instrument. Why had he doubted that *they* were capable of such a thing, when he already knew of *their* unearthly powers?

Pedarius was near exhaustion as he bent down to pick up the metal can of gasoline. He almost wished he had let the boy do whatever he was supposed to have done. Why was he making such an effort merely to go on breathing? Was it the fear that there was even greater suffering after death?

The vines held Sev quite securely in the chill of the smothering water. That he was so close to the surface, to oxygen, made him struggle even more. Each time he moved he felt more strength go out of his body, felt more like taking in a huge gasp of water to relieve the ache in his chest. *They* told him he would be safe. But he was not safe. He was drowning!

Stop, Severinnnnnnnnn! Stop struggling! Be still. STOPPPPP!

Their screams stunned him for a moment and he relaxed in the grip of the water vines. At once he felt better, more secure. Then he realized that he didn't need to take a breath as badly as he thought. He was in *their* hands once more, and if he did everything *they* told him he would be all right. He had to believe that.

That's right, Severinnnnnn. Now move your hand all the way to the side and take hold of the vine around your arm. That's right. Now pull yourself up to the wall. Easy. Don't break it.

Sev pulled gently and felt himself move sideways through the water. The vines still wrapped around him but they were flexible enough to allow lateral movement. Now *they* wanted him to slip his left arm out of the tangled vine and take hold of the larger vine with both hands. It worked! With one more tug he felt both his hands touch the wall of the well. He felt another rush of mild panic. He had to have some air!

Now put your foot against the brick there. That's right, Severinnnnn. Now push!

Sev pushed with his toe and felt himself move upward. He felt the top of his head break the surface and he twisted his face upward but could not get his mouth or nose out of the water. He had to! Now! He had to breathe!

Reach up with both hands, Severinnnnn. You can reach the top of the wall now. Pull yourself up, Severinnnnn!

Sev began to cough as he felt his hands latch onto the low brick wall. With the last of his strength he pulled and his head broke through the surface of the water.

The first mighty gasp was half air and half water that he had held in his mouth. He coughed and gagged the water out and then got his first good breath of oxygen. His lungs heaved air in and out as he pulled himself farther up. He draped himself over the low wall, his belly resting on the single row of bricks. The vines still clung to him, around his chest and across his head, giving him the appearance of a half-human nymph risen from the deep.

He had had enough. He didn't want to do this anymore. Once he had his breath, Severin Arcomano began to cry softly. He wanted to go back to the cottage. Why hadn't she come for him by now? He was cold and frightened and he wanted no more of it. Then he thought he felt something nibbling on his leg in the water and with a squeal of terror he kicked his legs up and over the wall and rolled into the dirt, drawing his legs up to his chin in a fetal position. He wouldn't move until she came for him. They couldn't make him do any more. He sobbed, rolling his wet hair back and forth in the mud.

You don't have to do any more, Severinnnnnnnnn. I will do it for you now. I am David and you are me. We are one. Relax, Severinnnnnn. Sleep.

Even as he closed his eyes, he dreamed he was getting to his feet, then moving quietly through the forest.

As Pedarius poured the fuel over the furniture and rugs in the living room, he wondered if he'd be able to drive the old pickup. He had to, that's all. He had to. But only for a short distance. He would crash the vehicle against a tree or a bridge, take the cash and the violin and disappear into the night. The authorities would find the crashed vehicle with the stolen silver and paintings inside it and assume that Hines had killed his employer and burned his body in the house to cover his tracks. The great Pedarius would be dead as far as the world knew, and the police would be searching for the fugitive Raymond Hines, who, of course, never would be found.

The pain in his body was growing more severe as he put the near-empty gasoline can close to the front door, picked up the other can and carried it up the stairs. He moved quite slowly, wondering if he'd be able to get away from the pickup once he had crashed it.

He almost vomited as he splashed gasoline over the dead body in the huge bed. He had to be burned beyond identification. Of course, if they went so far as to examine his dental work they would know it was Raymond Hines. But Pedarius counted on the local authorities assuming it was the master of the house who had died in his own bed. However it turned out, it really didn't matter at this point. He had his passport, cash and the Stradivarius. He wanted nothing more, other than peace of mind, which would never be his.

Once the bedroom was saturated with the explosive liquid, Pedarius lit the two antique kerosene lamps on the long dresser, then took one last look about the room. Then he turned to the mirror and examined his appearance. He ran his hand through the thick white hair. All the blond strands had disappeared. He flashed on the scene in London, many years ago, as he had stood in front of the mirror seeing himself for the first time with his hair a cold, jet black instead of his natural blond. He had decided at once that it was right. For the great Pedarius, it was right. He was, after all, no longer Hans Gruebber, but the wondrously gifted master of the violin, Pedarius! He had been happy that night, filled with the fantasies of the acclaim which would be his. The world was at his feet. He would have everything.

And this was the final result of all those dreams. A crippled old man who had committed unspeakable horrors, undeserving of air itself. This was the great Pedarius.

He backed slowly toward the door, hesitated for a moment,

then threw one of the lamps against the floor near the bed. With one mighty whoosh, the flames jumped up and the entire bed, Raymond Hines's funeral pyre, was ablaze with an orange ferocity. Pedarius quickly closed the door behind him so that the flames would not spread downstairs too rapidly.

At the top of the stairs, he stopped suddenly and whirled back. The keys to the pickup! He'd left them on the chest of drawers. With a cry of helplessness, he set the other lamp on the cornerpost of the railing and ran back toward the bedroom. How could he have made such a foolish mistake?

For the last sixty miles, Nick Arcomano had wondered how there could be so much thunder and lightning without a single cloud in the sky. Perhaps electrical storms didn't need clouds, but it didn't seem right somehow. Strange.

But at least it had given him something to think about other than Sue and what he was going to say to her, and Sev and Tara Dobbs. What a mess. And everything had gone so well for so long. It was his fault, however, completely, and it was up to him to make it right again.

There were no lights in the cottage when he pulled up, but the yellow Mercedes was parked outside, which probably meant they were both asleep. The wind whipped at his jacket as he got out of his car and then he smelled the oncoming rain. He looked up toward the sky and saw that a few clouds finally had formed. Then he saw the orange glow through the trees. He moved up toward the porch and had a better view of it.

"Jesus Christ," he said aloud.

There was no mistake about it. The big house was on fire. It must just have started or he would have noticed it on his way in. He jumped up on the porch and bolted through the doorway.

"Sue! Sue, it's me, Nick!" he called as he moved quickly through the dark living room toward her bedroom. He flicked on the light and saw her sprawled across the bed, still completely dressed. And still she hadn't moved.

She was a light sleeper. Something was wrong. Nick bent over her and shook her. "Sue, wake up!" he called to her. "Wake up, Sue. What's the matter?"

Sue groaned and her head snapped up, then rolled back on the pillow. Her hand moved up to her head but still she didn't open her eyes.

At least she's coming around, he thought as he quickly ran

out of the room to check on Sev. Lightning lit the room as he came to the door and he knew Sev was not in his bed before he turned on the light. After he flicked the switch, he stood there for a second just staring at the empty bed. Then he panicked.

Sue was blinking and up on one elbow when he bounded back into her room. He sat on the bed, took her by the shoulders and shook her.

"Where's Sev?" he demanded roughly. He could tell she hadn't yet focused on him. "What's the matter with you Sue? Where's Sev?"

"Sev . . ." she said groggily, running her fingers through her hair. "He's . . . Nick?"

Nick shook her again, vigorously. "Sue, listen to me. Sev is not in his room. The big house up there is on fire, do you understand? Is he up there?"

Sue stared at him. What had happened? What fire? Where? Did he say that Sev was up there? Up where? Why couldn't she shake this drowsiness? "Where is Sev?" she questioned him.

Nick slapped her, hard across the cheek. "Pull it together, Sue. Listen to me. The big house is on fire. Do you hear me? Is Sev over there? Can Sev be up there at the big house?"

Finally it sunk in. The big house was burning and Sev was not here with them. Of course he would be there. She started to get up immediately, then almost collapsed again. She shook her head. "Yes . . . yes . . . he must be. Oh, my God, Nick. I don't know . . . I couldn't stay awake. Help me. We've got to get . . . him out of there. Help me, Nick. Hurry!"

The flames were visible now, Nick noticed as he pulled her out onto the porch. She was crying hysterically as he half dragged her down the path toward the wall.

"There's a place in the . . . back there . . . where he goes through," Sue said panting. "It'll be faster." She suddenly lost her balance and fell in the middle of the path. "Sev!" she screamed at the top of her lungs as Nick pulled her back to her feet. "Sev!!!!"

With the keys to the pickup in his hand, Pedarius stumbled out of the bedroom, choking and half blinded by the smoke. At the top of the stairs he picked up the kerosene lamp and carefully started down the steps, fearful that he would trip and ignite the stairs in front of him. And then he saw him.

"You bastard!" the old man screamed, stopping in his tracks.

The boy walked in from the garden, his arms outstretched, the vines wrapped around him and trailing eerily behind him. His face was caked with the red earth and his hair was wet and matted. His appearance was that of a small man who had clawed his way out of a grave and who floated into the room on the warm winds. His eyes flashed as he moved calmly toward the huge stone fireplace. He stepped up on the hearth, then slowly turned back to face the horrified old man on the stairs. He slowly stretched his arms toward him, his fingers clutching, reaching, and his voice boomed across the room.

"Give it to me!" the voice said from Severin's lips. "Give it to me, Hans Gruebber!"

In one quick motion, the terrified old man raised the lamp over his head and hurled it across the room. The flames seemed to leap up from the floor furiously, miraculously forming a semi-circle around the wild-looking child, trapping him against the stone wall.

Pedarius was aghast at how perfectly the wall of flames surrounded his tormentor. He could not possibly get at him through that broiling heat. He screamed as he started to move forward down the stairs. Then his knee gave out and he tumbled down to the bottom and almost into the flames. He kicked his way backward, away from the intense heat, toward the small valise and the violin case. The old man forced himself to his feet and grabbed at the two cases.

"GIVE IT TO ME!" the voice echoed above the crackle of the flames.

Pedarius stumbled again as he tried to move toward the freedom of the front door, and the violin spilled out of the leather case. Groans of sheer terror came from his throat as he tried to gather it up again. He could barely move his legs. They were frozen with pain. But he had to. He was so close. He grabbed the bow and the instrument and somehow managed to get back to his feet.

Just then, the gasoline can near the door exploded and spewed burning fuel across the front wall of the house. They were both going to be incinerated. Pedarius screamed again as he looked frantically about him for a way to escape. But his legs seemed frozen at the knees. The pain!

"GIVE IT TO ME!!!!" the voice boomed above the flames.

With a cry of desperation, Pedarius raised the violin and bow above his head and threw it in the direction of David Stubenmyer's voice. "Take it, then!" he screamed. "Take it and be damned!"

The Stradivarius and the bow arced gracefully through the air, above the flames and directly into the small boy's outstretched hands. Severin Arcomano calmly lifted the violin to his neck, poised the bow expertly above the strings, then began to play the composition as it was meant to be played. The music filled the big room as if amplified as the flames grew hotter, gutting the room between them.

Suddenly the wind whipped down through the fireplace, pushing the wall of flames toward the front of the room and away from the eerily small, vine-covered virtuoso.

The music that had brought him relief for so many years now caused the old man's joints to freeze in place. The skin of his hands split as the joints gnarled and twisted to double their normal size. Tears poured from his eyes as the pain became too much to bear. Then he felt the back of his jacket burst into flame and he felt the hair on his head ignite into a torch.

"Forgive me, David!" he screamed in agony as he felt the life in his body burn away. "Please let me go! Pleaseeeeeeeeee!"

As he ran past the gazebo, Nick saw the figure in front of the fireplace, dressed in some strange costume, calmly playing the violin in the midst of the huge blaze. The reflections on the window pane made it difficult to make out who it was but he could only assume that it was the old man and that he was stark, raving mad. What could he have done to Sev?

"Sev!!!" he called as loudly as he could.

The flames were coming out the door into the garden, and the heat grew more intense. The only way in would be through that window near the fireplace. Sev might already be dead, burned in another part of the house.

Sue came running behind him, panting, frantic with fear. She screamed when she saw him there and pushed Nick forward. "Get him, Nick! Get him out of there, Nick!" she screamed hysterically. She didn't know how he was managing the violin, but it was definitely Sev and he still was alive. Why didn't he try to run? "Get him, Nick. It's Sev, there!"

It was Sev! Nick suddenly realized. How was it possible? What had they done to him? He quickly grabbed a lawn chair and moved up to the window. He should try to attract Sev's attention before he broke the glass. The suction would draw the flames back toward him.

"Sev!" he shouted. "Over here, Sev! Move to the window."
He shook his head in amazement as his son calmly played the
violin like a master. The water that dripped from his hair and
his clothes probably was all that was keeping him alive. Had his
clothes been dry they would have burst into flame. As Nick
raised the chair over his head, the boy finished playing. He
stood calmly for a moment, looking into the flames, then raised
the priceless instrument and tossed it into the fire.

Sev jumped back as the chair crashed through the glass. His
hands flew in front of his face as he felt the intensity of the heat
for the first time. What was he doing here? He backed up
against the fireplace wall and screamed as he felt the heat from
it against his back.

"Sev! Quickly, Sev, over here!" Nick shouted, ready to climb
into the inferno.

Sev whirled around and saw his father reaching through the
window. Sev ran toward him, the vines trailing out behind him.
"Daddy, Daddy, get me out! Get me out!"

*You are a brave boy, Severinnnnn. You will know the fulfill-
ment of truth, trust and love. And with love, we set you free.
You are freeeeee, Severinnnnnnnn. Freeeeeeeeeeeeee.*

And then he was safely in Nick's arms, and the three of them
ran toward the real safety of the overgrown garden as the rain
finally began to fall.

"Readers of weak constitution should beware!"

Publishers Weekly

The Novels of
MICHAEL McDOWELL

THE ELEMENTALS
Avon Original   78360/$2.95

For two fine southern families, the lonely beach resort of Beldame could be very bad for their health, because something is waiting for them. A horror that can shape hideous nightmares out of the wind and sand. Something they don't dare think about. But it's thinking about them, and all the ways to satisfy its terrible hunger.

"Michael McDowell must now be regarded as the finest writer of paperback originals in America."

Stephen King

GILDED NEEDLES
Avon Original   76398/$2.50

In New York's decadent "Black Triangle" of the 1880's, Lena is the murderous queen of a family of criminals, pitted against the outwardly pious Stallworth family. The "hanging judge" James Stallworth unknowingly decrees his own family's demise when he sentences the first of Lena's family to death. When you cross some people, you may wind up dead, but when you cross Lena, you end up wishing you were...and wishing you were...and wishing...

"Riveting, terrifying, and just absolutely great."

Stephen King,
author of THE SHINING

COLD MOON OVER BABYLON
Avon Original   48660/$2.50

In the typical sleepy Southern town called
Babylon; young Margaret Larkin has been
robbed of her innocence—and her life. Her killer
is rich and powerful, beyond the grasp of the
earthly law. But in the murky depths of the local
river, a shifty, almost human shape slowly takes
form...along with Margaret's horrific revenge.

"Double check the locks on the door."
Publishers Weekly

THE AMULET
Avon Original   40584/$2.50

The splendid pendant is more beautiful than anything the residents of Pine Cone have ever laid
eyes on—but none of its wearers will live long
enough to really appreciate it. For once clasped
on, the Amulet cannot be removed, and its spell
of horror cannot be undone. One by one the
townsfolk are being transformed into brutal mur-
derers, and only one person begins to suspect
the deadly link in the chain of deaths.

AVON Paperbacks

Available wherever paperbacks are sold, or directly from
the publisher. Include 50¢ per copy for postage and
handling; allow 6-8 weeks for delivery. Avon Books,
Mail Order Dept., 224 West 57th St., N.Y., N.Y. 10019.

McDowell 4-82